W9-BZX-306

HELL'S DETECTIVE

ALSO AVAILABLE BY MICHAEL LOGAN

World War Moo

Apocalypse Cow

Wannabes

HELL'S DETECTIVE

A MYSTERY

Michael Logan

CROOKED
LANE

NEW YORK

This is a work of fiction. All of the names, characters, organizations, places, and events portrayed in this novel are either products of the author's imagination or used fictitiously. Any resemblance to real or actual events, locales, or persons, living or dead, is entirely coincidental.

Copyright © 2017 by Michael Logan.

All rights reserved.

Published in the United States by Crooked Lane Books, an imprint of The Quick Brown Fox & Company LLC.

Crooked Lane Books and its logo are trademarks of The Quick Brown Fox & Company LLC.

Library of Congress Catalog-in-Publication data available upon request.

ISBN (hardcover): 978-1-68331-171-3
ISBN (ePub): 978-1-68331-173-7
ISBN (Kindle): 978-1-68331-174-4
ISBN (ePDF): 978-1-68331-175-1

Cover design by Andy Ruggirello.
Book design by Jennifer Canzone.

Printed in the United States.

www.crookedlanebooks.com

Crooked Lane Books
34 West 27th St., 10th Floor
New York, NY 10001

First Edition: June 2017

10 9 8 7 6 5 4 3 2 1

GARY PUBLIC LIBRARY

KENNEDY

For the real Urban Kat

3 9222 03192 8588

GARY PUBLIC LIBRARY

KENNEDY

1

et's get one thing straight from the get-go: if ever anybody deserved to fester in Lost Angeles—that stinking pit masquerading as a city—it was me. Of the myriad sins disfiguring the souls of the damned, mine was one of the worst. I didn't deserve a second chance. But I got one anyway.

The night it all began, I was perched at the bar in Benny's, nursing a Ward Eight cocktail and trying not to listen to the clock ticking down the seconds until the witching hour. The sun's last hurrah illuminated eight booths, three of which were occupied by silent drinkers fidgeting on ripped seats. The clock was the sole decoration on the walls, unless you counted the cracks in the plaster. The place reeked of cheap booze, stale cigarettes, and acrid sweat—mostly radiating from Benny. The closest he came to a wash was when he dribbled whisky down his stubbly chin and wiped it off with his frayed shirt sleeve. There were hundreds of swankier places to drink in the city, but Benny and I went back a long way. Besides, prospective clients knew they could find me here if I wasn't in my home office, and the dearth of other customers made it a private place to talk business.

The bell tinkled, and a kid stumbled in. I could tell he was fresh off the boat. His brown eyes were shot through with angry red veins, his thick black hair stuck up in whirls, and a sweat-soaked plaid shirt clung to his pigeon chest. He looked around the booths, scrabbling for a sympathetic gaze. Everybody kept their heads down. Everybody except me.

"You've got a customer," I said.

Benny turned his lugubrious face, all dangling jowls and worn-out eyes, kind of like a depressed spaniel, to the newcomer. "What the fuck you want? We're closing soon."

"Real charming, Benny," I said. "No wonder nobody drinks here."

"You do."

"Correct. And I'm a nobody."

The kid spotted me watching him and latched on like a drowning man to the hand that would stop him from sinking into the black depths below. He climbed onto the wobbly stool next to mine and ordered himself a double anything. Benny poured him a glass of the rotgut whisky he reserved for idiots with rocks for taste buds. Down the hatch it went. The kid wiped his lips with the back of one shivery hand. For a moment, I thought he was going to vomit the drink back into the glass. It probably would have tasted better the second time around. I couldn't blame him for being a mess. I'd staggered in for the first time and sat on the same stool myself a lifetime ago. I was sure I hadn't looked any better.

"Give him another on me," I said to Benny. "The good stuff. He's going to need it."

"Thanks," the kid said as Benny filled another glass, this time with his best bourbon. "I'm Franklin Johnson."

"Kat Murphy."

In the silence that followed, I could almost hear his brain whirring as he decided where to begin. There were too many questions, and he didn't know there were no answers that would bring him comfort.

"What're you in for?" he said.

"Jesus. Dive right in, why don't you? Don't ask, don't tell—that's the rule."

Nobody with any sense talked about their lives before Lost Angeles. There was no point. Everything we knew was gone, never to return. Any good we might have done in our past lives was irrelevant. Only our sins mattered, and we didn't need any further opportunity to relive those.

"Sorry."

"Everybody's sorry. Mainly sorry they're here."

He gulped his drink and stared through the bar top. I'd been around enough killers, goons, rapists, thieves, con artists, hustlers, and politicians to sense that the kid didn't have a bad bone in his body, which was tough luck for him. Weakness bled into the rancid air of Lost Angeles like blood into the water, and the sharks would be circling soon enough. I didn't need him to tell me what he was in for. I'd have bet my life, if it were still mine to bet, that he'd killed himself. At least we had something in common, although suicide was likely his only sin and definitely the least of mine.

I tried to figure out how he'd done the deed. I'd always had a knack for figuring out people—at least, most of the time. Women's intuition, my male rivals upstairs used to call it, their way of soothing their damaged pride when I one-upped them, as I often did. It made me laugh. Women's intuition just meant not having a swollen dick to hijack rational thought every time cleavage bobbed into view. It meant paying a bit of attention instead of making everything about your enormous ego. It meant having enough empathy to put yourself in somebody else's head instead of being perpetually astonished that not everybody thought the same way as you.

I noted his high cheekbones, the sensitive sweep of his brow, and his delicate fingers and put him down for pills and booze. In his last moments, he'd probably pictured his dead body tragically slumped across the writing desk, as pale and beautiful as a marble sculpture, suicide note to his unrequited love in hand. It took a lot less romanticism than he possessed to press a gun barrel against the roof of your mouth, knowing your last thoughts would end up swirling around a bucket of red soapy water once the cleaner was done sponging the gore off the wall.

He was close to weeping, leaning over his drink as his shoulders heaved. I could never stand to see a man cry, particularly if he was going to ruin a perfectly good glass of bourbon with salty tears.

"First day?" I said.

He nodded, shaking loose a single teardrop from his stubby nose. "I don't think I can handle this."

"You don't have any choice," I said, nudging his drink out of the weepy firing line. "You're in it for the long haul."

"How long have you been here?"

That was another question nobody with half a brain in their head wanted to hear—or know the answer to. "Long enough to have stopped counting. Not so long to have forgotten there're better places to be."

"There must be a way out. You've tried to leave, right?"

Benny caught my eye, and a look of understanding passed between us. Either that or he was trying to encourage me to buy another round of drinks. There was no point telling the kid flight was impossible. He was going to try anyway. Everybody did. In my first week, I stole a beat-up old Buick Special I told myself nobody would miss much—the first time I'd stolen anything other than as evidence, but my scruples no longer seemed so relevant in those early days—and went on a bug-eyed tour of the city. Every side street and main road puked up its traffic onto Route 666, the north–south freeway that cut Lost Angeles in two. I trundled onto the asphalt and headed north, out into the white heat and red sand of the desert. I didn't know what I'd find; I only knew it wouldn't be here, and that was good enough for me. Ten minutes out, the city was small enough to fit in the rearview mirror. The Black Tower shot above the cityscape, a never-ending middle finger bidding me farewell.

The desert that encircled the city, save for the stretch where the Dead Sea lapped at the stony shore, was itself bounded by sheer cliffs, but the road dropped into a crevice through the rock. The walls rose for hundreds of feet so the only thing visible other than the road ahead was a strip of burning sky. When I emerged on the other side, swirling dust filled the plain, backlit by the sun so it looked like a seething wall of flame. Rising above the shroud, and the faint outline of the city squatting inside it, was the Black Tower, this time raising its middle finger in welcome. I spun around, thinking maybe the crevice had taken a sneaky fold and bent me back on myself, but the road was as straight as a lawyer's trouser crease. I put my foot down hard, dug my chipped nails into the hot plastic of the wheel, and roared back through the city to the south. Same crevice. Same plain. Same shithole city. I drove for five hours straight, through Lost Angeles after Lost Angeles. I could have zipped along that road forever and still gotten nowhere, so I stopped at the first bar that looked low-rent enough for somebody with not a cent to her name—Benny's, as it happened—and handed over the car keys in exchange for booze. I drank until I couldn't stand up, never mind drive.

There was no airport in Lost Angeles. No train station. No bus service to zip you off to a rustic town in the shade of green hills where you could cool off and listen to the mellow buzz of bees dipping their snouts into flowers. Sure, you could walk into the desert, heading for the cliffs in the hope of scaling them. All that bought you was aching legs and sweaty pits before, blinded and disoriented by billowing clouds of wind-whipped sand in which half-formed faces teemed, you ended up back where you started. You could build a raft from the city's flotsam and jetsam and attempt to row across the Dead Sea, but unlike its buoyant namesake upstairs, here the water was almost as unsubstantial as air, and you would sink. Flounder around in the depths for a while and guess what: you fetched up back on the beach, retching and trembling. There was no escape.

"Look," I said, "you've got to understand, Lost Angeles is just a name some joker gave this dung heap. It's nothing like the real LA, save for the preponderance of assholes. That collective noun's my own invention, by the way. Feel free to use it."

My sparkling wit didn't perk him up, most likely because I'd answered his question by not answering it. I left him sniffling and went to the ladies' room to splash lukewarm water on my face and waft a paper towel at my neck. That was as close as you came to air conditioning in Benny's. I lingered, hoping the kid would scoot before I had to start giving it to him straight. No such luck. When I came out, sweating again in the crushing heat, the sharks had cruised in. I hadn't seen these three specimens before, but I'd seen their like: mean men with threadbare souls, all twitchy eyes and fixed grins, looking to hand out some punishment before they got theirs. They were still at the foreplay stage: one of them had buried his fingers in the kid's hair and was jerking his head around. Another was flicking him on the cheek. The third was leaning on the bar, brushing dandruff from his shoulder into my cocktail and watching the show.

The other drinkers had developed a deep fascination for the grain of the warped wooden planks that passed for a floor. There was no point trying to help, and they knew it. This was going to be the first in a long line of hard lessons, and the sooner the kid learned, the better it would go for him. Anyway, these clowns were the least of his worries. Soon enough, the sun would slide below the horizon, and the countless hatches on the Black Tower would open to spew out the Torments. Soon enough, the kid would find himself back in his silent apartment, lamenting his loveless life and reaching for the pills. Soon enough, I'd be back in the motel room, staring at the body sprawled bloody at my feet and lifting the still-warm gun barrel to my mouth. No, the worst thing about Lost Angeles wasn't that you were stuck here with the dregs of humanity. It was that you were stuck here with yourself.

So I knew I should stand aside and let the dance play out. But he looked so helpless in the face of their raw brutality. Besides, I still had time to kill, and it wasn't as if there was any other entertainment in Benny's.

"Hey, assholes," I said.

The three of them jerked their thick heads up on equally thick necks.

"You calling me an asshole?" the leaner said.

"I was making a general clarion call. You answered. You're flaking into my drink."

He picked up my glass. It looked tiny in his hammy fists. "Cute umbrella."

"You never know when it's going to rain dandruff on your beverage. I figure it's best to be prepared."

He unfolded himself from the bar. He was a head taller than me, his eyebrows shook hands in the middle, and he was packing at least a C cup of pure muscle. Had this missing link been around in the nineteenth century, Darwin could have saved himself a whole lot of grief by parading him around lecture halls as conclusive proof that man was descended from apes.

"Real funny," he said with a snarl he probably practiced in the mirror. "I hate funny."

7

"With a face like yours, I'd have thought you needed a sense of humor. You know this place has protection, right, Benny?"

"Paid my dues to Flo last week," Benny said. His hairy-knuckled hand was spidering along the counter to where he kept the sawn-off shotgun strapped underneath. He wouldn't use it unless they started smashing the bottles behind the bar.

"Let me count the many fucks I don't give about your protection," the big goon said. "Besides, I'm not going to break anything except this turd's face."

"The kid's with me," I said. "Do anything to him, I'll take it personally."

He looked me up and down—and up again for good measure, in case he'd missed something that justified my tough talk. Upstairs, a lot of men had underestimated me, but with the judicious application of dirty tricks such as ball tweaking, shin scraping, and kidney jabbing, I was pretty handy in a scrap when I had to be. And most men, even the biggest douchebags, had tended to hold back in fisticuffs with a woman—in public, at least. Behind closed doors, when a wife or girlfriend got lippy, the fists swung faster. The rules were different down here. Most people had done something real scummy to end up in Lost Angeles, and there were plenty of deadly ladies running with the gangs. Everyone was a potential threat—save for the obvious cases like Franklin, who wore their fragility like a cracked windshield. If you were smart, you didn't discriminate. This muscle-bound oaf didn't strike me as the smart type, though. That suited me just fine.

At five foot ten, I wasn't a small woman, but I was still his physical inferior. Sure, I had a ropy strength, but my shoulders were narrow, and I had slender hands, which he probably imagined would break on his big, dumb jaw should I try to punch him. His gaze settled on the gun holstered over my black blouse. He had his own piece, but he struck me as a hands-on kind of guy. He was probably wondering if I was fast enough to pull my weapon before he closed the distance between us. His eyes changed, sharpening with intent. He'd made his decision.

I didn't see the knife he'd palmed until he slid it into the kid's eye, as casual as an Italian spearing an olive with a toothpick. The kid managed a short scream before the blade bit into his brain and silenced him. The goon pulled out the knife, sticky with blood and ocular fluid.

"Oops," he said.

He came at me fast, blade at the ready. Not fast enough. He'd miscalculated. It wasn't hand speed that mattered. It was how quickly you decided to act, and if Lost Angeles had taught me one thing, it was to shoot first and worry about the consequences later—which was ironic considering that the one time I'd done that upstairs, it had brought me here. I'd made my decision before Franklin's skull thumped to the bar. The rest was just follow-through. I was far from a crack shot, but at that range it was easy to shoot him between his beady eyes. Nobody's skull is thick enough to stop a bullet, although the moron probably ran it close. He went down so hard, the plastic clock fell off the wall.

I held the piece on his two pals, freezing them as they belatedly reached for their own guns. "Get him out of here."

They grabbed the big lump by the arms and dragged him to the door. "We'll see you around," the one who'd had the kid by the hair said.

"Be sure to buy a lady a drink when you do. But hold the dandruff. Gives me wind."

When they'd gone, I reclaimed my seat, sitting at an angle so I could monitor the door.

"Couldn't you have waited 'til they ordered drinks?" Benny said.

"Saving up for a new clock? Let me make a contribution. Give me another double of the good stuff."

I set the glass by Franklin's outstretched hand, lit a cigarette, and waited. Benny dumped a handful of cocktail napkins into the blood haloing the kid's head and limped off to clean up the bloody mess on the floor. The bar fell quiet again except for the squelch of Benny's piebald mop. No sirens sounded outside the window. Gunshots weren't a rare commodity in Lost Angeles, and it wasn't as if there was any law to do anything about them anyway.

I felt it right on time: a shockwave of reset that made me blink and sent the cigarette smoke spiraling into a frenzied whirlwind. The kid spluttered and sat up, one hand clawing at his eye, the scream back on his lips high and girlish.

"Relax and have a drink," I said.

He pulled his hand away and goggled at his blood-smeared palm. His blue eyes were as watery—and intact—as they'd been a few minutes before. "They killed me."

"Don't worry, death doesn't take here." I took a long draw on my cigarette. "The good news is you can drink, smoke, and eat as much crap as you like. It isn't going to end you. The bad news is you'll wish it would. Welcome to Lost Angeles, Franklin. Welcome to Hell."

2

Franklin ran out of the bar, his wail receding into the distance. I helped myself to his whisky, which as far as I could tell hadn't been contaminated by tears, blood, or dandruff. Normally I restricted myself to two a day. Drinking myself witless hadn't helped a bit, and my wits were my main asset. At the moment, though, I was at a loose end between jobs and figured I might as well. Benny would make me cough up for the abandoned drink anyway and pour it back into the bottle when I wasn't looking.

Franklin's reaction was completely normal. I'd been stabbed, shot, strangled, bludgeoned, electrocuted, drowned, suffocated, run over, and burned alive (a salutary lesson about the perils of smoking drunk in bed) enough times to develop a certain sang-froid about kicking the bucket, but the first few times, I took it hard. It wasn't dying that threw you into a tailspin. The real kicker was coming back from the few minutes of blissful nothingness and remembering where you were.

My first experience of Lost Angeles citizens' stubborn refusal to lie down and die already had come the morning after my jaunt in the Buick. I'd woken up with a head full of nails and battery acid swilling around my guts. The hangover hadn't been the only thing putting the hurt on me. Being blind drunk hadn't spared me the visit to the motel or the sights it contained. The memories still burned in my drink-addled brain like neon lights fizzing bright and lurid through a dense fog. I set out for Benny's to try again.

The powers that be had dumped me into a one-room flop in Desert Heights, a slice of urban squalor clinging to the north-west perimeter of the city like a boil and oozing up against the moat surrounding the Black Tower. That was where all newcomers started out. Nobody told me this was Hell. I didn't have to pass under the drooling heads of Cerberus. I didn't have to pay the ferryman to navigate the River Styx—you could cross the torpid, orange-brown water free of charge every day courtesy of the Route 666 bridge. There wasn't even a welcome brochure. I'd opened my eyes to a squalid room, the shot still ringing in my ears, and known.

Heaven would have had air conditioning, leather sofas, and a panoramic view of the clouds. My pad had barely enough space for a mattress—which looked, felt, and smelled like it had been humped rigid by a hundred filthy hobos—and a floor lamp with burn marks on the shade. The cracked window looked onto the next block, which was so close I could lean out and touch the wall. The dim, ramshackle staircase down from the eighth floor stank of piss and unwashed bodies and echoed with sobs and shrieks seeping out from under hundreds of mildewed doors.

The picture didn't get any rosier outside. My building was one of thousands, each shedding its leprous brickwork into piles of rubble. There were no street names, no numbers on the buildings. You could only recognize where you lived from the individual shapes of the crumbling tenements, which made it nearly impossible to get home after dark. The tower rose brutishly above the district, its smooth black surface gobbling up the sun's morning rays. The streets themselves were steeped in gloom; the slum blocks were pressed so close that light only reached street level when the sun was directly overhead.

The damned were everywhere, bent-backed and shuffling, banging their foreheads bloody against walls, crying out for their mothers, lovers, children, or God to save them. I already knew better than to waste my breath. The despairing horde was small potatoes compared to the sand borne aloft by the desert wind, which gusted and eddied through the maze of alleys. The shifting red canvas coalesced into ephemeral shapes: half-formed creatures with screaming holes for mouths, grainy pits for eyes, and twisted fingers that seemed to pluck at your sleeve. Dust devils, the locals called them. Some people thought they were the collective product of our terrified imaginations. Some considered them another form of punishment. After a while, I developed my own theory as to what they were.

I'd staggered through the alleyways, crunching on broken glass and dodging turds, until I cannoned off a skinny guy who had a scar in the shape of a question mark hugging his right eyebrow and a moustache so wispy that a stiff breeze could have blown it off. He was new, like me, or he wouldn't have been in Desert Heights. I could tell from the sharp, hungry look in his eyes that he wasn't going to be there long.

"What you got in your pockets?" he said.

I put my right hand in my trouser pocket and pretended to rummage. "I think I've got some fluff I could spare. Should help fill out your top lip."

I was hoping my jibe would distract him long enough for me to kick him in the nuts and run. It didn't work. Enterprising ratbag that he was, he'd already found himself a kitchen knife, which he gaily stuck in me without further preamble.

I wouldn't recommend being stabbed in a vital organ. Reducing your brains to gazpacho with a nine-millimeter bullet turns the lights out instantly. Drowning is uncomfortable at first, but toward the end, it's peaceful. Even being splatted by a truck is quick and relatively impersonal—provided the driver hasn't mounted the sidewalk and chased you for a few hundred feet, as happened to me during one particularly messy case. A stabbing is intimate in all the wrong ways. He'd swung the knife in from the side and managed to slide the blade into my heart. The pain was bad, but the scrape of blade on ribs and the throbbing sense of violation were worse. I found myself flat on my back, choking on syrupy blood. My heart took one last heave, and I had long enough to hope I was gone for keeps this time before sweet nothing wrapped me in its arms.

When I perked up, his hands were in my pockets, searching for cash. He was out of luck on that score. The car had bought me booze, nothing more. I'd managed to eat the first few days thanks to the soup kitchens that the Church of the Penitent, the only functioning religion in the city, set up daily on the slum's edge. I must have been the first person he'd killed down here, because he went into momentary lockdown when I sat up. I reacted first and brained him with a handy piece of masonry. I may have hit him more times than strictly necessary, adding my hoarse scream to the din of sinners' voices as I did so. As I trip-walked away, two old women in rags scurried out of nowhere. They picked him clean in seconds and dissolved back into the dust.

I repaired on foot to Benny's, caked in gore, shaking and obsessively fingering the ragged tear in my blouse where the wound should have been. Nobody gave me a second glance or offered to help, which told me a story I didn't want to hear. The stolen car had bought me two weeks of free cocktails, so I set out to drink myself into the oblivion I couldn't achieve any other way. This was to become a pattern in the early months—until I found out no amount of booze could blank out what came at nightfall.

So I wasn't about to judge Franklin for flying off the handle. He'd get used to it eventually, or end up like one of the muttering loons roaming the streets, long skeins of saliva hanging from their chins.

I slipped out a last cigarette as the door flapped open to admit another customer looking to fortify themselves before going out to face the night music.

"Good evening, ma'am," Benny said, his voice dripping smarm. "Welcome to my humble establishment."

I was about to swivel to see who'd turned Benny into barman of the year when a flame ignited by my ear. It flickered at the end of a gold Zippo attached to a slender hand with purple manicured nails. I dipped my smoke into the fire before turning to take in the woman lowering herself onto Franklin's vacated perch. She wore a smart lilac jacket cinched around the waist and a hip-hugging skirt that advertised her curves. She had curly black hair and cheekbones so sharp that a man could kiss her and shave at the same time. Her eyes were almond in color and shape. I could see why Benny had undergone a personality transplant. Her lips were kinked into a smile that offered a potential lover damnation or salvation in equal measure. Despite the conclusions people drew from my penchant for trousers and close-cropped red hair, I didn't swing that way. Even if I did, I already had damnation, and salvation was out of my reach. I wasn't buying what she was selling.

"Good evening, Ms. Murphy," she said. She was a Brit, tones polished to a lickspittle shine, voice high enough to retain its femininity but somehow still deep enough to resonate in the pit of the listener's stomach.

"Do I know you?" I said.

"No, but I know you."

That was the funny thing about reputations. You worked hard to build up a name for yourself, then when you had one, there was no escaping it. Everybody thought they knew you, when all they really knew was the tiny piece of yourself you put on show. Not that I really knew myself either. I'd spent so long being a cardboard cutout of a private detective that I'd forgotten how to be anything else.

"A lot of people know me," I said.

"My name's Laureen," she said, offering up her hand. "A friend told me I'd find you here. He also told me you have an aptitude for solving problems."

I let her hand hover. "Everybody else's but my own. Which friend put you on to me?"

My snub didn't seem to bother her. "Oh, somebody you did a job for a while back. You probably wouldn't remember him."

She could have been right. I'd done a lot of jobs, in the Angeles both Los and Lost, and most of them had slipped into the haze of time—although one job, my last in the real world, I would never forget. Still, I didn't like the way she brushed off my question. Prospective clients liked to name-check the mutual friend who'd recommended me, mistakenly thinking it would earn them a discount. There was something else I didn't like about her, something I couldn't put my finger on. It wasn't how she was dressed, the way she so clearly used her looks to get what she wanted; a smart operator used every tool at her disposal.

No, my disquiet went deeper than that. She hadn't even gotten to the proposition, and I already knew my answer would be no. When you worked enough cases, you developed a nose for when a job was going to be a heap of trouble—the kind of assignment you only took when the rent was long overdue and dumpsters outside restaurants were beginning to look appetizing. I'd been on a run the last few months, so I had a modest stack of cash tucked under the loose tile behind my toilet. I didn't need any more grief in my life.

"Cut to the chase. Can't you see I'm busy?"

"I'd like you to find something for me."

"It's always in the last place you look. I advise you to look there first."

"Let me clarify. I'd like you to retrieve a stolen item."

"Somebody pinched something in Lost Angeles? My flabber is gasted."

"This isn't a run-of-the-mill theft. It's a very significant item."

As she sat there, composed in the face of my hostility, I worked out what was bugging me. One shaft of sunlight still penetrated the bar; in a short while, that too would be gone. The other drinkers were shuffling their feet and drumming the tables, avoiding looking out the window to where the Black Tower loomed above the skyline. Yet she looked like she was ready for a night of dinner and theater, maybe followed by a few cocktails and some giggles with her pals. Something wasn't right.

"There're other investigators out there," I said, my voice strained. "Go ask one of them."

"I've been led to believe none of them are as good as you. I'll pay twice your normal daily rate."

"I don't need the money."

"You're drinking in this pigsty, and you tell me you couldn't use a few more dollars?" She turned to Benny. "No offense meant, you understand."

"None taken," Benny, the lecher that he was, said. "Fancy a toot on the house?"

"I choose to drink here," I said. "Don't you know downmarket's all the rage these days? You just missed the furs-and-diamonds set."

For the first time, her composure wilted. A frown crinkled her forehead, and her clutch purse endured a particularly firm clutching. "Playing hard to get? I can respect that. How does four times sound?"

Now I knew for sure that the job stank. She'd told me how valuable the stolen object was, started high on my fee, and jacked the price up too quickly. Sure, she clearly had money, but I'd dealt with enough wealthy clients to know they were the biggest misers. Whatever Laureen had lost was undoubtedly important, to her at least. She wanted it back bad—way more than I wanted the money.

"Sorry, I've got a previous engagement. Don't you?"

I looked over her shoulder, toward the tower, and raised my eyebrows. I gave it the finger surreptitiously, my version of the sign of the evil eye. In my experience, even the most hardened assholes did something similar, or at least flinched, when you made the smallest reference to the city's most prominent landmark. She didn't react.

"Do forgive me," she said. "I lost track of time. Please don't let me hold you back from your lovely evening."

I threw a twenty on the bar to cover the drinks and headed for the door. At the exit, I glanced back, expecting her to follow me and try to persuade me to take on her case. Every person is the king or queen of their own realm; their problems are urgent matters of state, their loved ones nobles, the tawdry goods that accumulate in their lives the crown jewels. They have difficulty understanding why nobody else gives a crap about their problems, forgetting others have their own kingdoms to worry about first.

Instead, she sat there—once again the picture of composure—and gave me a breezy wave. "Give my regards to your date."

Her nonchalance riled me, but I was damned if I was going to show it. I clicked the door closed behind me.

3

There was never a safe time in Lost Angeles, but the closest you came was in the golden hour before nightfall, when those who had homes rushed back to lock themselves in, and the bums wrestled for the right to burrow to the bottom of the deepest dumpsters. I didn't know why they bothered; doors, windows, and slimy potato peelings couldn't stop what was coming. They were kids hiding under the bedcovers as the bogeyman's claws grated on the floorboards.

It was a touch after seven when I came out of Benny's, and the flight for the false comfort of shelter was in full swing. Shutters were slamming down on the casinos, bookies, fighting dens, and bars that ran the three miles of Providence Avenue—the main strip in the gambling district of Cajetan. Faces of every shade, hue, and shape bobbed around me, but for all the differences, they could have been related. Nothing creates resemblance more than the expressions painted on the human face—the crinkle of a nose or an asymmetrical smile passed down from parent to child—and these people wore identical looks. Foreheads pinched, lips tight slashes, and eyes unfocused as thoughts turned to making it through the ordeal ahead. Everybody hurried along in silence; even the car engines, throbbing as the drivers sat in the rush-hour traffic, seemed muted.

Only Flo's crew weren't making themselves scarce. They roamed this, his heartland, each day, collecting protection money and policing the streets—if shaking down passers-by, making lewd comments, and ignoring everything that didn't threaten Flo's business interests qualified as such. They needed to be back on station by midnight, which meant taking their punishment where they worked. You could tell his crew by their uniforms: men and women alike wore brown linen suits, buttons undone to allow rapid access to holstered weapons, and black open-collared shirts; a tie was too easy for an opponent to yank on as an aid to a head butt. My clothes were similar, except I went for shades of royal blue rather than brown, and I only wore a jacket in the cool of the night. I didn't wear a tie either, and my blouses were generally black as a matter of expediency. I needed to give off the impression of ready-for-anything calm to clients. The sopping-wet armpit rings and visible nipples a white blouse put on display didn't fit. Wearing white against the sun was pointless anyway—the heat was too intense for a reflective scrap of cloth to make any difference.

I nodded to Sid, a square-faced hood with eyes like pinpricks, as he leaned against one of the gold-painted pillars flanking the faux marble steps leading into the Lucky Deal Casino. He nodded back in that affected I-see-you, you-see-me way the hard boys were so fond of. I had an odd relationship with Flo's gang. I'd stomped on their toes during a couple of earlier jobs. In such situations, payback was supposed to follow. Another downside of not dying permanently was that you could be tortured to death time and again or encased in concrete and buried in the desert to enjoy a living death, so most people were careful not to poke the lions. For some reason, Flo's mob went easy on me. Sure, I got a talking-to and some finger wagging, but nothing more. Somewhere down the line, I must have inadvertently done Flo a big favor. I didn't want to find out exactly how far my line of credit extended, though; these days I was careful to keep my roaming feet off Flo's tootsies.

I'd never met the man himself. Few people had. He took over the racket not long after I arrived. All the other Trustees—the mob leaders who ran the moneylending, weapons, drugs, gambling, prostitution, booze, food, and gas rackets—were high profile, none more so than Hrag Chanchanian, the Armenian American gangster who controlled the sex trade. You could get anything you wanted in his fleshpots: men, women, transvestites, hermaphrodites, and any permutation of the above. There were no laws in Lost Angeles. There was only what you could afford. The sole demographic who missed out were the pedos, although Hrag dressed up his younger hookers in school uniforms in an effort to fill the gap in the market. Hrag spent his time glad-handing the big spenders in his brothels, screaming from the blood-spattered front row of the Colosseum, and swanking around town in furs and a gold-toothed grin. Flo preferred to maintain a layer of mystery. Nobody even knew his second name. He remained permanently cloistered away in his private apartments on the top floor of the Lucky Deal. There were rumors the previous incumbent, a surly Bostonian who'd been unpopular with his crew, was still up there. The tittle-tattle said he spent his days having sundry parts detached from his body in payment for some slight against his successor. I didn't give this story much credence. Flo wasn't known for his savagery. It sounded like the kind of fairy tale a smart gang boss spread to intimidate his competitors.

I left Sid to work on his act and cut left onto Fortune Hill. The road wound up a steep incline, and it was twenty minutes before I sat on a rusty bench in a park, my blouse sodden. It wasn't much of a public space: a patch of piebald grass, a few stunted cacti, and a jumble of empty wine bottles in place of a rockery, all crammed along a thin ridge. The park didn't even have a name. By day, in the real world, parks meant relaxation with the progeny—Frisbees tossed, kites flown, dogs walked, and balls kicked. By night, parks served as dark corners to indulge in illegal or shameful activity. But this city was one big dark corner, shame was in short supply, and there wasn't a single person under sixteen—here, traditional man-woman fucking produced no offspring, and the young seemed to be spared judgment for their sins. There wasn't much call for parks.

What the rundown strip did offer was solitude and a bird's-eye view. The sun, bloated like an overripe blood orange, was kissing the ridges of the hills in the west now. The highway ran through the desert like a knife wound, piercing the scrublands that ringed the city. Where the Styx plunged from the cliffs to the desert plain, spray misted up and glowed red. The watercourse encircled the tower in a wide moat and snaked through the city to the sea in the east, which shimmered off to the distant horizon. The eye couldn't parse the individual houses and blocks that lay low and flat in the deepening gloom, delivering up a pixelated panorama of urban sprawl. Only Desert Heights in the northwest and Avici Rise in the northeast peaked above the peripheral districts, which seemed to be keeping their heads down in the hope of going unnoticed. Downtown, in the financial district, the windows on the upper levels of the tall buildings shone with ethereal orange light. They were midgets compared to the tower, which ascended until it dwindled to a sharp point. The shadow stretched across the length of the city and far out into the sea. I had no idea if the tower ended or if imagining a peak was the sole way my brain could make sense of its vastness.

I didn't know how many times I'd sat upon the bench. Like I told Franklin, I'd lost count. The world upstairs was moving on, but I never asked the newcomers what the date was. If anybody tried to volunteer the information, I put my fingers in my ears and went "lalala." Embracing the fuzziness of time was the only way to stay sane. The uniformity of life helped. There were no seasons here; every day the sun came up at six AM, baked everyone to a crisp, and set at eight PM, as regular as a health nut on an all-bran diet. In the real world, people marked time in their bodies' decay: gray hairs and saggy breasts, chronic aches and pains, and wrinkles added year by year like rings on a tree. Aging didn't apply in Lost Angeles. I was forty-two when I put a bullet in my brain, and that's the way I stayed. Sure, you could grow fatter or thinner depending on how much you enjoyed the sin of gluttony, and if you were careless enough to lose the odd body part without going so far as dying, it stayed off. The moment you died, though, back you went to the form you arrived in.

Then there was the city itself. There were no industries to develop new technologies and no raw materials to do so anyway. Lost Angeles was sealed off, and the gatekeepers controlled what came in. We had what we were allowed to have, nothing more. And what we had, if you discounted attempts at building homemade gadgets, was all early fifties era—from the cars to the telephones to the double-reel motion picture cameras Hrag used to shoot his movies. As we reset, so did the city, as if it were alive itself. Sure, Desert Heights had appeared to be crumbling in my first weeks, but I'd been back since and found the ruin had advanced no further. If fire gutted a building, the next day it returned to normal. Nothing aged or broke down. My car had never gone on the fritz, even though I'd ridden it hard for longer than I cared to remember. Water flowed in the taps, though there were no reservoirs. Electricity crackled in the outlets, though there were no power plants. Only superficial changes took. Bullet holes chipped out of walls remained. If I scratched my name into the bench, it would be there the next day.

This reality had initially presented me with another major head fuck. I died in 1978, so I'd been startled to find that not only was I now in Hell, but I'd traveled over two decades back in time. Nobody knew why Lost Angeles had stopped developing. The city had once moved with the times, according to the few historical documents available. It felt like a moth-eaten movie set, a backdrop against which the sinners acted out a never-ending immorality play for an unseen audience.

That isn't to say things didn't change. Petty empires rose and fell. People went, some of them no doubt to a living hell at the pleasure of some shady character or other, the rest to a more uncertain fate. The Penitents, as they liked to call themselves, believed these vanishings were the result of sinners being elevated to Heaven. They also recommended scourging, self-mutilation, and starvation as a means of drawing God's attention to their contrition, so I didn't take their opinion seriously. My theory on where the disappeared went was less optimistic. And, of course, the parade of sin on Earth ensured plenty of fresh meat. These sinners brought notions of being able to re-create their modern lives. They always failed. That was it for progress. For a society to develop, it needed more than the materials and ideas to do so. It needed hope. It needed the possibility of a brighter future for the current generation and their descendants. It needed the belief that people deserved better. Nobody was suffering under any of those illusions in Lost Angeles. We were lost souls stumbling through an endless desert, afraid to look up and realize the distant horizon was never growing closer.

A blanket of dread had settled over the city, and now the faintest sliver of sun crowned the hills to the west. People would be locked away, muttering feverish prayers to the gods who had forsaken them and hoping that, for once, the wings would beat over their bolt-holes without stopping. I fixed my gaze on the tower and prepared to face my sin head on.

The hills gobbled up the last bite of sun, and the tower seemed to dissolve, dark edges bleeding out into the gloom. It stayed that way for a few seconds. Then, like startled flies taking wing from a corpse, the Torments exploded over the city in a swarm, eating up the gunmetal sky and blotting out the last dregs of light. The leading edges of the expanding cloud dropped black rain on Desert Heights. The screams began, rising above the sibilant hiss of beating wings. There was a beauty there, if you made yourself look: swirling ropes of darkness, knotting and unknotting, unfurling across the sky in incomprehensible complexity. My heart raced, urging the blood through my veins so I could run, hide, or fight. I forced myself to sit still, watching as the cloud reached Providence and Torments peeled off to slather the rooftops.

The swarm was overhead now, the wind stirring my hair as wings frothed the air into a near-solid mass. A single Torment arrowed down so fast that it looked like a widening smudge on the impressionist chaos of the sky. It thudded to the grass ten feet away, spewing up gouts of dirt. It was humanoid in form, the slender body utterly smooth and as black as the tower. The Torment took two steps on clawed feet and raised its head. In the half-light of dusk, its face was a perfect ovoid upon which the blank surface swirled like an oil slick on a swelling ocean. My reflected features emerged: hollow cheeks and sunken eyes, sucked-in lips, and furrowed brow. It was a face excavated of all hope, a black mirror of my soul, my very own *Picture of Dorian Gray*.

I knew the drill. In a few seconds, the Torment would hurtle inside me and show me what I really was. Now I did close my eyes, my fingers clawing the bench so hard that a fingernail snapped. But the shock of shifting planes didn't come. The bench creaked as a weight settled next to me. That was new. I opened one eye.

My Torment was still there, back in a crouch, its face returned to rippling blankness. Its head was cocked as if looking at the person sitting next to me through unseen eyes.

"Smashing view," Laureen said as the Torments fanned over the remainder of the city. "Shame about the weather."

I looked around, searching for the nightmare with her name on it. The park was empty, present company excepted. She looked like she was about to whip out a picnic basket. Nothing was coming for her.

"What the fuck is going on?" I shouted.

"Well, that's gratitude for you," Laureen said, brushing a speck of unseen dust from one polished nail. "Here I am, throwing you a bone, and all you can do is potty mouth me."

"Pardon me if I'm feeling a touch astonished," I said after taking several shuddering breaths in an effort to recover some semblance of composure, "but you can stop them."

"Ah, the legendary powers of observation at work. Impressive."

"Who are you?"

Even as I asked, I realized who, or what, she was. Even though we never saw them, we knew they were there, just as we knew air was there when it filled our lungs. Laureen and her ilk filled the city's lungs, supplying the Trustees with the raw materials that sustained our vices. They had created this city and put each and every one of us in here. There were various nicknames for them—the Architects, the Wardens, the Fuckheads—but they were officially known as the Administrators. This title was nothing but pretty pink paper wrapped around a steaming dog turd. Laureen was a demon. A hot one with a killer dress sense, and not what I'd expected, but a demon all the same.

"I'm Santa, the Easter Bunny, and the Tooth Fairy all rolled into one," she said as my brain fumbled for the strings that worked my mouth. She got up and scratched the Torment's neck. Its blank face nuzzled her wrist. "Here's the deal. I need my missing doo-dah back, and I believe you're the person most likely to get it for me. Since you won't accept money, I'm going to sweeten the pot, much as I'd prefer not to. In return for your services, I'll stop your nightly visits for the duration of the investigation. If you recover the item, I'll stop them for good. What do you say?"

I gaped at her standing there, the creature snuggled against her thigh while the city shrieked. My head was buzzing, my extremities numb as the fight-or-flight reflex receded. I would have accepted a thousand extra punishments for the chance to take back what I did. But I couldn't change the past. I would have taken a hundred physical torments—a decade on the rack, a century in flames, a millennium of needles in the eyeballs—rather than the one I'd been given. All I had to do was nod my head. But I hesitated. The deal seemed too good to be true, the payment too high for a simple case of missing property. More than anything, I didn't know if I could trust her to pay up—she was a demon, for Christ's sake.

"Better the devil you know. Is that it?" she said as I remained silent. "Then let me give you time to think my offer over." A card appeared in her fingers, an act of prestidigitation any shabby street magician could have pulled off. It was somehow more impressive coming from her. She tossed it at me. "When you're ready to talk, come see me."

She took her hand off the creature's head, and my features once more bubbled up on the oil slick of its face. The fight-or-flight response kicked in again, and I realized what a fool I was being. Anything was better than what I was about to face, even if the offer of respite only lasted a few days. I jumped up, the word "yes" rising in my throat. I was too late.

"She's all yours," Laureen said.

Then the Torment was in me.

4

The Nimrod Motel was so seedy that it could have planted an entire field with enough left over for a brownstone full of spinsters' window boxes. It was one of those U-shaped affairs, thrown together from bargain-basement building materials. The closest it came to a swimming pool was a sprawling, axel-cracking pothole in the car park, which the evening's earlier downpour had filled to the brim. The puke-green motel sign reflected in the rippling rainwater as I splashed toward room number three.

My target was an amateur blackmailer who'd gotten his paws on compromising pictures of a high-society trophy wife—two blurry Polaroids from a soft-porn movie audition before she'd snared an aging Casanova with a membership at Hillcrest Country Club. The blackmailer wanted five thousand bucks. My client could have paid up from the change that had rolled down the back of his Chesterfield sofa, but he'd amassed his wealth by being a tightwad. He engaged me for two hundred a day plus expenses.

It didn't take long to identify the perp. He worked as a barman at the club and had wormed his way into the wife's boudoir while the old man was slicing balls around the greenery. She showed her lover the pictures to add a splash of spicy gravy to the cuckold roast. He filched them. The husband knew about the porn career

28

and the pictures. He'd seen the one movie she starred in and figured he'd grab himself some of that action for his own bedroom. He'd bought the pictures and all the copies of the film—he didn't want the set he ran in to know about his new wife's past—but insisted on keeping them instead of doing the smart thing and burning them. He thought somebody had pinched the pictures from the house. I heard this from the wife, who begged me not to tell the old fart the truth. I complied. She'd put so much work into hauling herself up from the streets that I didn't feel like kicking the ladder out from under her. I knew from experience how hard it was for a woman, no matter how capable, to make it in this town.

All I'd ever wanted was to be a cop, like my father. It wasn't hero worship, not entirely. My mother worked as a secretary at a law firm. She was smarter than the blowhard men—all slick suits and strident voices—who fronted the operations. Yet there she sat, looking pretty in front of a typewriter, every clack of the keys marking the death of another brain cell. It shrunk her and prompted the gin habit that killed her. My father, though—he came home full of pride and tales of catching bad guys. He drank because he enjoyed it, not because he needed a crutch to lean on. He slept like a baby, while my mother sat up late into the night, draining bottles that she hid down at the bottom of the trash. I wanted what he had.

By the time I joined up, in 1955, I knew how tough it would be. But I needed to escape the roles my gender circumscribed for me or end up like my mother. I thought I could get my foot in the door, prove my worth on the desk, and become the first woman on patrol. With the naïveté and blind conviction of a nineteen-year-old, I refused to believe that the men who ran the force could be dumb enough to ignore my talents simply because I lacked a pair of balls to trouser juggle while leaning by the coffee station and shooting the shit. I learned quickly. The captain laughed every time I asked to hit the streets, while the beat cops kept offering to provide the hard fuck I obviously needed to convert me from the raging lesbian my aspirations to a man's job told them I must be.

I could see change was slowly coming. A vanguard of women was forming associations and pushing for the right to do real policing. But I also knew that, after one ass pat too many, I would brain somebody with my heavy typewriter. I quit after two years and did the next-best thing. I became a private investigator. My time on the force wasn't a dead loss; I'd learned a lot of the tricks through eavesdropping and amassed a network of female dispatchers who passed tips my way. But I still had to work five times as hard to prove myself, even though I was ten times wilier than the male investigators, who relied on thuggery to get the job done. I was dirt poor for years, but I stuck it out. Self-respect mattered more than a full stomach.

My situation only started to improve when I focused on infidelity. The wives liked dealing with a woman, presupposing more empathy than they got from male detectives—who for all they knew were fucking around themselves. The husbands thought that, being a woman myself, I would better understand the conniving female mind. As I got results, and America's attitude toward uppity women gradually softened, my portfolio diversified. By the early seventies, I finally rose above the breadline. But to get there, I still felt the need to play down my feminine assets. I made myself more mannish in appearance, mannerisms, and speech so I wouldn't be dismissed as just another pretty face.

At first I hated myself, and the world, for it. Then I realized I liked wearing my hair short. It saved me precious time each morning, requiring only a quick finger comb. I liked wearing suits. They were easier to run in, and I didn't have to adjust my skirt demurely when I sat down. Plus I looked damn good in them.

Above all, I liked being able to say whatever the hell I wanted, and screw whether it fit society's definition of femininity. In trying to become someone else, I became myself.

This particular wife didn't have the option to do what I'd done. Given the angles she was pursuing, it wouldn't have paid dividends. So she worked with what she had: shapely pins and a back-achingly huge pair of breasts. Anyway, I wasn't in the kind of business where I could afford to judge people's morals. And even though she'd been doing the dirty behind her husband's back, she clearly made him happy. When the truth hurt, it was better to run with the fiction.

The ex-lover had skipped his apartment, but even that wasn't much of a wrinkle. One of his work buddies, some guy he'd probably pissed off by monopolizing the rich wives, had called me to tell me where he was holed up. It hadn't been challenging, but I was content to take on a low-profile job. I'd vexed some unsavory types recently, chief amongst them Bruno, who ran half the casino action in town. Tommy, an old buddy from my days on the force, one of the rare guys who believed women could be more than dispatchers, had been caught counting cards. Instead of leaving quietly, he'd broken the dealer's nose and stuffed his pockets with chips. After security booted him out, he got wasted and returned to slash the tires of Bruno's vintage Cadillac Sixty Special. As the *piss de résistance*, Tommy smashed the windshield and took a generous leak over the leather interior. Big mistake. Over two decades, Bruno had changed wives four times, but his car not at all. He had hundreds of employees, but every day he washed and waxed the gleaming chrome himself.

I happened to be on my way in to meet a client as Bruno, cheered on by two henchmen, was stomping on Tommy's head. I didn't know the history then—Tommy filled me in later through a mouth of broken teeth—but I could tell from the look of determined savagery on Bruno's face that he wouldn't stop until my friend's skull was as flat as the Caddy's tires. I encouraged Bruno to desist by pointing my gun at his nuts. He didn't buy my argument that I was doing him a favor by saving him from a murder rap. As I dragged Tommy away, Bruno outlined the various ways in which he would make me pay. I wasn't too worried. Bruno tossed out threats like candy, and most of them lasted as long in his memory as a sugar rush.

I wasn't expecting trouble in the motel either. Opportunistic blackmailers usually folded like a skittish gambler in a high-stakes poker game. It would take a few hours to retrieve the smutty images and return them to their rightful owner. I would be home by midnight, giving me enough time to heat up my blood in a hot bath, reading *The World According to Garp*, before Danny came home and heated it up further.

It was my first time in love, which was considered abnormal for a woman of my years. I didn't see how it could have gone any other way. My few lovers had been either guys who, after the initial honeymoon period, started fretting for the American dream of a dutiful wife, two kids, and a suburban home or those who were obviously homosexual but didn't have the guts to admit it so picked the most masculine woman they could find and pestered her for anal sex. I wanted somebody who didn't care how he was supposed to behave, somebody who wore his skin like it was his own rather than a costume society had lent him. Those kinds of men—those kinds of people—were few and far between. For a long time, it seemed like I would grow old with only my ever-expanding library for company. Then Danny came along.

I first saw him in the Criminal Courts Building in downtown LA, where I was slouching in the peanut gallery. It was a good way to pick up work when business was slow. If a guilty defendant somehow got off, the victim and their families still wanted justice.

I would approach them and suggest they call if they needed a pro to find new evidence.

The case in progress was as juicy as a rare steak. Some banker had been playing fast and loose outside the marital bed, so his wife hired a private investigator—not me, which had pissed me off. The investigator delivered a slew of incriminating pictures. So far, so-so. Then, two weeks later, the banker turned up in the emergency room carrying his dick in a paper cup. The wife stood accused of hiring an unidentified lowlife to carry out the back-alley surgery. I could tell there was no angle for me. The husband sat pale and hangdog in the front row. If the wife walked, he'd let the case drop rather than face fresh humiliation. I stuck around because I was curious to lay eyes on the investigator due in the witness stand: one Danny Ainsworth. I'd heard his name but never met him. He was fresh in town from New York and was ruffling feathers by trying to muscle in on established operators, including me.

When Danny took the stand, I didn't see much in him. He wore a nondescript gray suit, jacket unbuttoned to allow his paunch room to flower. He was around six feet, although the stoop he'd developed from hunching unseen in too many doorways shaved off a few inches. His hair was brown, thinning on top, and he'd obviously shaved before the trial; small cuts clustered under his long, thin nose and over his jutting chin. He hadn't even bothered to remove the tissue paper from one. I pegged him for midforties. While the attention of the courtroom was elsewhere, Danny turned to the defendant. His eyes, encircled by crow's feet, had been half-closed, but now they sat open. They were jade green and alive with intelligence. He gave a slight nod. Somehow, I knew then that the woman was guilty and that Danny knew it too. I sat up and started to pay attention.

The prosecutor, a well-groomed woman in her fifties, launched into the usual schtick: all declamations, leading questions, and dramatic pauses. The witness stand could put anybody on edge: the prosecutor hammering you for cracks in the defense case, the judge glowering down, and the courtroom watching every facial tic. As the lawyer harangued him, Danny lounged on his seat like it was a deck chair. After five minutes of easily fielded questions, she was the one to lose her composure.

"Are you saying he deserved it?" she said.

"No," Danny said. "I'm saying he put his dick in so many suspicious holes, it was bound to get bitten off eventually."

Titters raced around the courtroom, but Danny didn't react.

"So you think she's guilty?"

Danny turned a scathing look on the prosecutor. "Am I not making myself clear? I followed this pecker on legs for weeks. He wasn't fussy about who he screwed. He'd hump a fire hydrant if it had pubic hair. Half the women had lovers or husbands, and we're not talking high society. There's at least three cuckolds out there pissed enough to have hacked off his overstimulated dick. I suggest you go find which one of them did it and give him a medal for services to humanity's gene pool."

The courtroom exploded in laughter. The judge banged his gavel enthusiastically even as a slight smile played across his face. That was the moment I knew I wanted Danny. I'd seen investigators smart-mouthing in court before. Their eyes always flicked to the spectators, checking to see how entertained the audience was, puffing up with pride when they got a big laugh. Danny looked steadily at the defendant, his gaze and demeanor reassuring. He wasn't playing it for laughs or looking for admiration. He was stating his opinion and sticking up for his client. I slipped out of the gallery to splash some water on my flushed cheeks. Here was a man who didn't give a rat's hairy asshole what anybody thought. I had to meet him.

When he came out, I was leaning against the window across from the courtroom, trying to look calm and collected.

"Seems like we went to the same charm school," I said.

"I don't talk to the competition," he said without breaking his stride.

I scurried to catch up. "Who says I'm competition?"

"I do, Kat Murphy." He caught the flicker of surprise on my face. "Yeah, I know who you are. I did my research. You're allegedly one of the best in town. And I do say allegedly. I followed you last month to see if your reputation was deserved. You didn't notice."

"Predators look forward. Only prey look back."

"Yeah, and plenty of predators get bitten in the ass by rivals."

Blood was rampaging around my veins, and my breath was short. I didn't know whether I was angry, horny, or tired from matching his fast pace. All three, I decided.

"I suppose you've got three-hundred-sixty-degree vision," I said, struggling to keep my voice even.

"I can spot a tail, if that's what you mean."

"How about I tail you? If you don't spot me, you let me buy you dinner."

He halted, a slight smile on his face. "Are you hitting on me?"

"I only want to swap notes," I lied. "I can give you the lay of the land here. You can let me know how you do it in New York. We'll both learn something."

We stood in the middle of the corridor, gazes locked as human traffic flowed around us. His scent lit up all the right parts of my brain. His nose twitched too, and I was sure he was feeling the same sensation as me.

"I'll play," he said eventually. "Follow me for a full day at some point in the next week. If I see you, we're done. If I don't, write me a report about what I did to prove you were there. Manage that, and I'll buy you dinner. You'd better change that nasty perfume, though, or I'll smell you from a mile away."

He strode off, leaving me standing there, sniffing my collar.

Three days later, I followed him. He didn't do anything special: grabbed lunch at a burger joint, met a few clients, and retired to his apartment around seven not to emerge. He saw me. I know he did. But he didn't let on. We had dinner and then, well, you know how it goes. All love affairs are the same, save for the details. We did the courting dance, swapped life stories, and built our cases to justify listening to what our bodies had been telling us from the beginning. I didn't know I had so many holes in my life until he filled them.

This amazing man, who'd been in my life for three years, was out on a job of his own while I prepared to reel in the blackmailer. He'd told me to expect him around one in the morning. I didn't know what he was working on. We didn't compare notes, because we never stopped seeing each other as the competition. A few months after we got together, I told him about a potentially lucrative case. He scampered off to see my prospective client and offered a discount on my rates—bad-mouthing my methods, results, and personal hygiene in the process. I was pissed, but the makeup sex was so spectacular and he was so endearingly delighted about putting one over on me that I took it and learned to clam up about work. Even now, it was difficult to ask him what he was working on, even though something was clearly bugging him. He'd been off the last few weeks, not his usual sharp-tongued self. Sure, I'd asked him if everything was fine, and he'd said I shouldn't worry, but I couldn't probe for details. When this evening's work was done, though, I planned to broach the subject properly. I couldn't stand to see him lose his spark.

The light was on in number three, so I sidled noiselessly along the wall. I'd already slipped the owner twenty bucks for the spare key to the room. As I edged toward the door, the power went off in the whole motel. Lights still sprinkled the rest of the city, and the urban glow dimmed the stars that had appeared once the rain cloud had retreated. The shoddy wiring had probably blown a fuse when somebody turned a hair dryer on a wet patch on the bed. A couple of guests bustled out and headed for reception. Nobody emerged from number three. I figured the blackmailer had fallen asleep in front of the TV, which would make my job easier. Nothing gave a soft touch the heebie-jeebies more than spluttering awake to a cold circle of steel chilling the forehead.

I slid out my gun and listened by the door. Nothing stirred. The key grated softly as I slipped it into the lock, and the knob creaked when I eased it to the left. There was still no sound, so I shoved open the door and stepped in. A muzzle flash and dull crump came instantly. My own clumsiness saved me. I'd tripped over the doorframe, tipping forward and to the right. Instead of blowing open my chest, the bullet caught me on the left shoulder. I half-fell, half-dove forward, getting a mouthful of foul carpet for my trouble. The muzzle flash had lit up the room for a split second, illuminating the single bed that now provided me momentary cover from the shooter. There was no pain yet, just a seeping wetness down my arm and a numbness spreading across my chest.

He'd heard me coming and panicked, the dumb shit. What did he think I was going to do, kill him for the sake of some dirty pictures? I wanted to negotiate, to try to calm him, but it was too late. The adrenaline rush from pulling the trigger would have strung him even tighter, and talking would prompt more gunfire in my direction. I had some experience on that front, testified to by a dime-sized lump of scar tissue on my thigh. I'd gotten lucky that time—the shooter had gone on the lam instead of finishing me off. I wasn't about to make the same mistake twice. As much as I didn't like it, this was going to end with one of us coughing up blood; the sooner I acted, the less likely it would be me.

I rolled out from behind the bed, ignoring the burning sensation in my shoulder. Another flash propelled another bullet, which thudded into the floor by my ear. I aimed at the afterimage and pulled the trigger three times. He got off another shot, but the barrel was pointing up as he fell. The bullet punched a hole in the ceiling. My ears were ringing from the gunshots, but I heard him spit out a whimper. The stink of blood and shit perfumed the air as the body hit the floor. I rose to my feet in stages. Blinking away the spots of light from the muzzle flashes and keeping the gun trained on the dim outline of his prone form, I crept closer. He was alive but wouldn't be for long; his breath came in a burble. It was all so pointless. He was going to die for the sake of a lousy score he would have blown in a couple of months.

Still, I had a job to do. Footsteps were slapping the wet concrete outside, and shrill voices were shouting for someone to call the cops. I could smooth things out with the LAPD. It would be time-consuming and annoying, but I wouldn't go down. My license was up-to-date, and the department knew me as somebody who didn't open fire without good reason. They would chalk it up to self-defense. Hell, I'd never even killed anybody. I'd had occasion to shoot at people, but through the vagaries of chance or bad aim, none of my bullets had struck anywhere vital. Finally, I'd claimed my first life. I didn't know how I felt about that and didn't have time to get angsty. I couldn't let the cops get the pictures. Honesty wasn't a universal commodity on the LA force, and there was a chance one of the officers would pick up where the blackmailer left off.

I pulled out my pocket flashlight and clicked it on. Smoke and particles of gunpowder drifted in the thin beam as it swept across the carpet and lit up the face of the man I'd shot. The flashlight fell from my numb fingers just as the lights clicked back on. There lay Danny, blood pooling underneath his body and staining his cheek. His eyes were drowsy, the pupils jittery as he looked at me.

"Kat?" he said, his voice obscenely wet. "How did you find me?"

I closed my eyes against the harsh overhead light and counted to three. I told myself that when I opened them, he wouldn't be on the floor, sandwiched between a peeling plastic chair and a sagging bed. It would be the blackmailer, his stomach and chest ripped open, dark blood oozing from his lips. Not Danny. But when I let the light back in, Danny was still dying. I fell to my knees and cradled his head in my lap. He didn't need to know he'd almost killed me. He didn't need to know I'd killed him.

"I tailed you," I said, forcing the fiction out through clenched teeth. "Like when we met. I came in when the fireworks started."

He somehow managed to lift his hand and curl his fingers through mine. "I didn't see you. You're getting better."

"No, you're getting slacker."

He smiled, lips smudged red like we'd been kissing all night. "Did you get him?" he asked, eyes growing suddenly sharp.

"Yes."

He frowned and tried to crane his neck to look for the body. I held him tighter, but I couldn't fool him. I never could.

"Oh, Kat. It was you."

"I didn't know," I said, barely able to see through the tears. "I swear I didn't know."

"It wasn't supposed to be you," he said, and the light went out of his eyes.

I knelt there in the blood of the man I loved, the man I'd killed, for as long as it took to absorb the weight of my crime and loss. I rolled him onto his back and buttoned the jacket over his big belly to hide the wounds. I sponged his face with toilet paper wetted from the tap until the blood was gone. I kissed him on the lips one last time. I sat in the chair and picked up my Colt.

Somebody had arranged for this to happen, but not this way. The lights had conveniently gone out as I arrived, so Danny couldn't see his target's face. He would have been safe in the shadows with a clear shot at the silhouette in the doorway. He fired the second the door opened. He must have been in fear of his life. That was why he'd been behaving so oddly of late. Somebody had been coming to kill him, or so he'd been told. But the somebody who came, courtesy of an anonymous tip-off, was me. I was the one meant to die in this room at the hands of my lover. Bruno had set this up. I'd lit his fuse and ignored his threats in my arrogance, misreading how angry he really was. But I was the one who'd dodged the bullet that should have killed me and so spared Danny. I was the one who'd pulled the trigger.

This was all down to me.

Sirens were growing in volume. The police would be here soon. They wouldn't punish me. Nobody would. Except myself.

I put the gun deep inside my mouth and pulled the trigger.

5

The Torment spat me out onto the hill, where I lay puking and shivering as it joined its black brothers to wheel back toward the tower. The back of my head tingled as if the bullet had just exploded out in a shower of bone, but that was nothing compared to the razor claws of shame and grief tearing my heart to ribbons. These visitations brought neither nightmares nor visions. They plunged me into vivid Technicolor reality. Each night I lived it all again—every sight, sound, smell, and emotion. Only when I found myself back in the park did I recall where I was and the life I'd been living since I lost Danny.

I did what I always did. I took deep, shuddering breaths and tried to conjure up happier images of my lover: his triumphant grin as he reduced me to one sock in a game of strip poker while he'd lost nothing more than his jacket; his flushed cheeks after a blistering quickie down an alleyway; his hat blowing off in the wind as we drove to Santa Monica beach, bopping me in the face and, to peals of laughter on his part, making me veer into a bollard. But the images were fuzzy and fleeting; his pale, blood-soaked face kept forcing them out. I tried to tell myself I couldn't have done anything differently—the motel room was pitch black, I came under fire, I didn't know it was him, I was defending myself. The sole mistake I'd made, I argued, was that I didn't find Bruno and torture him to death before decorating the wall with my brains. Above all, I tried to convince myself I'd spared Danny this pit. If his bullet had hit its mark, he would have ended up in Lost Angeles sooner or later and been forced to relive the moment he killed me. Instead, he was somewhere better. He had to be.

None of my justifications erased the fact that I'd killed him. None of them made me any less guilty. I'd failed, as both a lover and a detective. I hadn't tried to find out what was bothering Danny. If I had, he might not have ended up in the motel room that night. I'd written off Bruno's anger too easily. I hadn't even told Danny, so foolishly confident was I that there was nothing to worry about. I hadn't been alert, hadn't questioned the tip-off or why the lights had gone out at such a convenient time. Being in love had made me soft, had cast humanity in a better light than it deserved. I should have seen that my personal contentment hadn't made the slightest difference to how shitty people could be to each other. His death was my fault.

That was the genius of the punishment. With time and distance, people can justify or soften any act. We tell ourselves a story that casts us in a better light until it replaces the memory. There was no distance here, no other story to be told. You always knew exactly what you'd done. When Lost Angeles snapped back into solidity around you, so came the knowledge that you would have to suffer your sin again, and again, and again. If there had been some way to kill myself again for good and surrender to the void, I would have taken it, as would many others. I knew people who'd tried to obliterate their bodies in such a way so they couldn't regenerate: grenades strapped to head and torso, a long dip in an acid bath, thugs paid to hack off limbs and heads and scatter them far and wide. The city reset them anyway, delivering them back to where they died, looking as they had the day they first woke up in Lost Angeles. Nobody I knew of had ever found a way to escape the Torments. Until now.

Laureen's card lay where it had fallen, propped up against a used syringe. I crawled over and snagged it on the second clumsy attempt. The card was printed on thick embossed paper and read in black ink,

Laureen Andrews
Chief Administrator, Lost Angeles
7 Arcadia Drive, Avici Rise
244-3876

I slipped the card into my wallet and found enough strength to get to my feet. I staggered down the hill, making for Benny's to gulp down the nightcap I always took in an attempt to rinse the foul taste of sin from my mouth. The city was remembering itself as I wobbled along Providence. The Penitents were out already, laboring under the weight of sandwich boards and placards exhorting sinners to repent. One of them stood in the middle of the street, flailing at his bare back with a whip no doubt purchased from one of Hrag's stores. The doors were open at the Lucky Deal. Sid stood outside, trying to plaster the hard look back on his face. The first customers of the night were trickling in, ignoring the cries of the Penitents. Male and female hookers draped the lampposts like fleshy tinsel, exposed skin glistening sickly in the sodium light. Their glassy eyes looked through me. Benny stood outside the bar, staring at the shutter pole in his hand as if he'd forgotten its purpose. The whole street, the whole town, reeked of sour fear sweat. The smell would fade soon enough as the nostrils adapted and the citizens of Lost Angeles set about erasing old sins with new.

I didn't get what they—Laureen and her associates—were trying to achieve. They were punishing us—that was clear from the Torments. On the flip side, we were free to indulge in every passion, vice, and sin the mind could conjure up. There were plenty of shameless assholes out there who seemed able to shrug off their transgressions and gleefully wade back into the human sewer. The Torments released us at midnight precisely. By two AM, the city would be back in full swing. This was supposed to be Hell, but for some it appeared to be Heaven. And I always wondered what the Torments showed the real monsters: the serial killers, pedophiles, and rapists. For them, reliving their sins would be a daily Christmas present. Lost Angeles made everybody worse; no matter the sin that brought you here, you had to learn new dirty tricks to survive. Give Franklin a few years, and he would be selling his sweet cheeks to the sodomites out in Astghik or toting a gun for one of the Trustees.

I nudged Benny to snap him out of his torpor. He almost belted me with the pole before he realized he wasn't under attack. I didn't wait for him to get the shutters fully open, entering the bar and pouring myself a stiff one. The drink wet-slapped my brain, shocking me part of the way out of my daze and returning some color to my cheeks. I turned Laureen's card over in my fingers. If I took the job, I would be making a deal with the devil, or at least one of his subordinates. Even though instinct still told me I was going to have to wade forehead-deep through a river of shit to see this one through, the payment was too big to turn down. Wounds needed time to heal, but the Torments ripped open the scab every night. If I could get some respite, maybe I could reclaim my memories of Danny as he'd been, not as I'd last seen him. I could never get him back, never wipe away what I'd done, but maybe if I remembered the good stuff, I could find as much peace as was possible to find. Maybe I could even find a way to forgive myself.

I would go see Laureen in the morning.

6

Avici Rise was a gated community—a fancy way of saying poor people weren't welcome except to clean the houses and pools or dirty up the residents' bodies and souls in exchange for a sliver of the money pie. The rise in question overlooked the Styx Delta, where the widening river foamed over rocks and boulders to spill into the sea, smearing the dark waters with an orange brush. The city hugged the curving shoreline, fading off into the shimmering heat haze. From up here, it was almost pretty. Shame nobody inside could enjoy the view. A twelve-foot wall topped with barbed wire ran around the perimeter, interrupted by the wrought-iron gate in front of which I now idled, looking like the sort of undesirable the barrier had been built to keep out.

The guard stayed put on the other side of the bars, giving my dented Chevy a look so hard, I was worried the fender might fall off. He was probably afraid my old jalopy would drop flakes of rust along the pristine driveway or pollute his crisp lime-green uniform with a cloud of gritty exhaust fumes. I could have afforded something swankier, but it would have been a waste of money. Unless you paid the right guys, and I didn't, a nice car would last as long as a box of free doughnuts in a precinct break room. My Chevy looked like it could go a few hundred feet tops before coughing to a halt and belching flames from the hood, so nobody would steal it. Looks were deceptive, though. The powerful engine could propel the old hunk of steel close to one hundred, and the reinforced windscreen could stop a slug.

I rolled down the window, stuck my head out, and tried to rearrange my features into a trustworthy expression. "I'm here to see Laureen."

The guard sniffed and turned side-on so I could see his piece. Guns didn't carry the same menace as in the world above, but a bullet to the forehead still caused inconvenience. And, depending on the patience of the gunman, he could always repeatedly shoot you dead until you got the message you weren't welcome.

"Is Ms. Andrews expecting you?" he said, putting a great deal of emphasis on her second name to show how inappropriate he considered my use of her first.

I could have called her, but I'd chosen not to. She'd dropped in on me unexpectedly. I wanted to return the favor. "Not at this precise moment, but she told me to drop by anytime. We're best friends, as of yesterday."

I pulled out her business card, licked the back, and stuck it to the inside of the windshield. He leaned in close enough to eyeball the card through the gate.

"That could've fallen out of her bag," he said. "You could've found it in the gutter."

"Same place they found you, then. How about you call ahead and tell her I'm here, and I can let you get back to sleeping or picking your nose. In fact, you look like the kind of capable guy who can do both at once. Is that how you got the job? Told them you could multitask?"

He bit his lip and narrowed his eyes in concentration, searching for a response. When he didn't find one, he left me hanging long enough to show he was still in charge. Security guards were the same everywhere. If this were the sea, they would be shrimp, so they took every opportunity to flaunt what scraps of authority they had. I found guards to be as useful as a toothbrush in a retirement home. I'd worked a lot of robberies, and half the time, the guard had taken a backhander to let the thief in. I could understand why. Put a working stiff on a stingy wage next to disgusting wealth, and he was bound to line his pockets when he got the chance; it was like a zookeeper asking the chimps to keep an eye on the banana stash. He finally took my name and disappeared into his booth. He emerged a few minutes later and grudgingly buzzed me in. The gate swung open soundlessly, and I cruised through.

Arcadia Drive spiraled inward through bungalows and mansions set in acres of bright-green grass upon which sprinklers revolved, throwing up minirainbows in the morning sun. I could almost have kidded myself that I wasn't in Lost Angeles were it not for the Black Tower, which split the sky every time I made a circuit and faced back to the west. At first glance, Avici Rise looked like a standard millionaire's ghetto. I'd seen plenty such places up top. When I was younger, I'd always considered money something that would, in the unlikely event I ever made enough, buy more freedom. As I grew older, I saw that money built a gilded cage. The more people amassed, the greater the fear of losing their wealth grew, and so they locked themselves away from the impoverished hordes. It never seemed like much of a life to me. I'd always preferred to live amongst the filth, noise, and vibrancy of the real world. The kids who rolled in the muck had the most fun. Things were different in Lost Angeles; I found myself envious of the peace of this slice of cut-grass suburbanity.

Avici Rise was the sole place in the city I hadn't explored, which now struck me as weird. Rich people needed detectives as much as the poor—probably more—yet I'd never been called up there. In fact, I'd never met anybody who professed to live there—the Trustees, the richest people in town, lived in their districts. Somehow it had never occurred to me to probe the mysterious residents of this prime real estate. I wasn't the only one. We all knew Avici Rise existed. You couldn't really miss it. But we only talked about the place in vague terms, if it all. Avici had a way of slipping out of your mind. Now that I was through the gates, this inability to focus seemed more than weird; it seemed downright suspicious, especially since I now knew an Administrator lived here.

I'd always assumed the shadowy figures running the city resided in the tower, where we could never see them or get to them. Maybe they all lived in Avici Rise. Mind you, if the residents were demons, they didn't look or act particularly demonic—unless the Bloody Mary I saw one purple-haired old lady drinking on her porch contained real blood from a real Mary. The only unusual element became visible as I circled inward: a miniature replica of the tower, around thirty feet high, set in a communal garden. I'd never seen another like it. Either these people so loved exclusivity that they had to have their own tower in order not to have their posh Torments mingling with those of the scumbags, or this was a sign my strengthening hunch about the community was correct.

The moat around the Black Tower served as a barrier to approach—not that anyone in their right mind wanted to get close—but you could walk right up to this one through sculptured flowerbeds teeming with red, white, and yellow roses. I parked the car by the curb and waded through the blooms. A lot of people would have hesitated, but life had taught me that opportunities to learn things you weren't supposed to know rarely cropped up twice. Those who recognized this and acted accordingly tended to succeed. Mind you, sometimes they also found themselves drifting to the bottom of the river in concrete slippers.

As I approached, my legs grew heavy. A cold, invisible hand seemed to press against my chest. The sun faded like a light on a dimmer switch. The scent of the flowers, which had been sweet and heady a few seconds before, turned dark and cloying like a bouquet left to rot on a grave. A sick bubble of dread rose in my throat, shortening my breath, but I pushed on until I stood within touching distance. The surface was as black as it seemed from a distance. I couldn't tell what materials had been used in its construction—there seemed to be no joins or welding marks—and I couldn't persuade my hand to reach out and touch it.

I circled the thing, suppressing the growing conviction that I needed to scoot before I woke something nasty. Around the back, the flowers were trampled flat in a trail leading between two houses and toward the west of the compound. I saw faint markings etched into the base of the structure. They were a slightly lighter shade of black, so I had to hunker down and tilt my neck to make sense of the carving: a line drawing of a long-snouted creature with sharp teeth, reptilian eyes, a mane, forelegs that appeared to end in paws, and a fat hind section with dumpy feet. It looked nothing like a Torment. In fact, it looked ridiculous, like some mad surgeon had stitched together a crocodile, a lion, and some other random animal parts from around the lab. Something about the drawing set my skin crawling, and I thought I heard furtive movement from within the structure. I gave in to my body's primal response and hurried off on the verge of a run. Once I'd reached a safe distance and the sun had dialed back up in brightness, the dread backed off, and my heart rate started to drop. As my mind began functioning properly again, I realized what this tower and its big brother were. They were kennels for pet monsters, nothing more. And the demons holding the leashes lived around me, here in Avici Rise.

I jumped into my car and gunned the accelerator, the roar of the engine in the quiet green space as appropriate as a belch in church. I didn't care. These shitheads didn't deserve peace, not when they were visiting so much suffering on the city below. I made the last two circuits around the spiral at pace, squealing the tires and attracting dirty looks. Laureen's pad was near the center, a two-story real estate agent's wet dream of white wood panel, gold trim, and sun-facing windows. I screeched to a halt and gave the engine one last rev before killing it. Now wasn't the time for anger. This was the most important case I'd taken on; I needed a clear head. I closed my eyes, took a deep breath, and stepped out to where Laureen was waiting for me in the driveway, dressed in a yellow summer frock that showed more shoulder than an all-you-can-eat Sunday roast.

"Ms. Murphy," she said. "I'm surprised it took you so long to get here from the gate considering you appear to enjoy a second career as a drag racer."

"Better than being a drag queen, like you."

"I see your social skills haven't improved."

"You're not hiring me for my social skills."

"True. Nonetheless, I'm glad you decided to join me."

If I'd had balls, she would have had me by them, and we both knew it. But my talkative gut informed me that she needed me more than she was letting on, despite throwing me back into the Torment's embrace. She'd done that to make a point. I'd been nothing but rude to her from the moment we met, yet here she was, still smiling and taking my lip. I decided to push it further and see what I could find out about Lost Angeles from the horse's mouth. I'd read all available material on the city, which was hardly extensive, and had tried to pick the brains of the Trustees I knew personally. They wouldn't talk, and nobody else knew more than I did. Now that I had the opportunity to dig deeper, I wasn't going to waste it.

"Is that what you always look like?" I said.

"You don't approve of my dress sense? I thought this was a fetching outfit."

She gave me a twirl, skirt billowing up to expose thighs so taut that they could each have held a degree in nuclear physics.

"I meant your face. Your body."

"I see what you're getting at. You were expecting something in scales and sharp teeth, perchance?"

"It had occurred to me."

"Scales are so last year, plus it's very impractical when one wishes to power dress. Nothing ladders a good stocking like an unclipped claw," she said with a sly grin.

"You're yanking my chain."

"I am indeed. We aren't monsters. Nothing is what you think it is, Ms. Murphy."

"Yeah, I'm beginning to get that feeling. And call me Kat. Ms. Murphy makes me sound like a brothel keeper."

"Kat it is. Shall we proceed inside?"

She turned, closing the door on further questions. I trotted along obediently. The interior was blissfully cool, the open windows and doors channeling a light breeze through the spacious interior. I had to hand it to her; she had taste. The walls were sunflower yellow, the hand-carved furniture artfully and sparsely arranged over the white tiles. What really lit my lemon were the rows of shelves dominating the far walls. On them sat books. Hundreds of them. I could almost smell the vanilla tang of aging paper. I may have dribbled.

I was a book whore, always had been. Many of my early memories of my father were of sitting on his lap and turning the pages as he read. When my mother was home, he stuck to stories appropriate for a little girl: anthropomorphized animals and princesses longing for a prince to sweep them off their feet. When she went out drinking with her friends, he read me pulpy novels filled with tough cops and world-weary detectives, cigarettes and gun smoke, and dames with abnormally long legs. As I grew up, I expanded my reading to books of all stripes: history, philosophy, biographies, politics, whatever. Most cops and detectives passed the time on stakeouts with a hip flask, a pack of smokes, and a headful of dreams. I stuck my nose in a book. I'd even created a modified flashlight, taped around the edges so the beam narrowed down to a thin point and allowed me to plough through my latest read without anybody seeing the glow of light in the car or bush I'd set up in. No matter what or when I read, I always imagined my father's warm breath on the back of my neck and the vibration of his chest against the small of my back.

In Lost Angeles, books were at a premium. Sure, people created their own—either handwritten or typed out on shoddily bound newsprint run off the sole printing press in town, rented out by the *Lost Angeles Chronicle*, a newspaper so named because it was chronically bad. But the quality of the books was variable, to put it kindly. I could guess why books—alongside music and art—were one of the few things the Administrators didn't lay on in plentiful supply. They let you leap into somebody else's head and escape the reality of your dismal life for a few hours. They made you want to be a better person. They gave you succor, hope, and respite—none of which the damned deserved. Books from the real world were so rare as to be largely out of my price range.

As Laureen swept through the living room and mounted a broad staircase illuminated by an atrium, I cast a last longing glance at the shelves, which were too distant for me to read individual titles. Biting back my resentment at her flaunting of this unattainable wealth of words, I followed. Into the bedroom she went and sat down on the edge of a luxurious four-poster. She slid a fingernail under a catch on one of the posts, pulled open a disguised panel, and pressed a button. A hatch popped out of the polished floor at her feet. She bent over and dialed in a combination on the concealed safe, blocking my view with her legs.

"That was where I kept it," she said, moving away to allow me access.

"Mind telling me what 'it' is?"

"An Earth-shaped box carved out of mahogany. It's very old and very valuable."

I hauled open the safe. The hatch was six inches of steel, which was standard. The addition of a lead lining wasn't. Inside sat a carved globe about the size of a large grapefruit mounted on a wooden plinth. It could have been mahogany. It could have been plywood. I wasn't an expert on wood. Since Laureen had referred to the item as a box, I assumed there had to be a way to open the thing. However, there appeared to be no lid and no obvious catch. All in all, it didn't look impressive or valuable. Even the carving of the continents looked rough. In fact, the box looked exactly like the kind of overpriced tat rich idiots brought back after they'd swanned off to Africa on safari. What was most surprising was that it was there.

"It's still here," I said. "Case solved."

"That's a replica. I had it made after the real one went walkies."

"And why would you do that?"

Laureen came to stand beside me. She smelled of lavender, which wasn't the most demonic of fragrances.

"Do you always ask so many questions?" she said.

"Call me old-fashioned, but it's part of my method for getting to the truth. Did anybody else know the code to the safe?"

"No."

"Was anything else stolen? In the safe or out?"

"No."

"Seems to me you've got a whole lot of expensive stuff lying around the place. I'm wondering why they only took the box. Care to tell me why it's so important?"

"Not particularly."

"Care to tell me anything useful at all?"

"There was a note. I received it yesterday morning, two days after the burglary. An unknown personage rode up on a motorbike, threw the envelope at the guard, and disappeared again."

"Now we're getting somewhere. It's ransom. Why don't you pay up? Seems to me you've got the cash."

Laureen rummaged around in a writing desk and handed me a piece of paper bearing two sentences: *All sins forgiven. You will be informed of who and when.*

"I don't have the power to forgive sins," she said. "So I can't pay up. And given that everyone in Lost Angeles is a sinner, the thief could be anybody."

I handed the note back. "Not that I want to talk myself out of a job, but why come to me? Can't you sic your pets on the city to find it?"

"I could send the Torments out to disassemble this city brick by brick, particle by particle until I found it, yes. But that would cause a fuss."

"Wait it out, then. If this person wants their sins forgiven, they'll have to reveal themselves at some point. I expect they're busy racking their brains trying to figure out how to make sure you keep to the deal before giving themselves away. Once you have the name, you could at least focus your operation, apply some leverage."

"That would still be too visible."

"So you need this theft to be kept quiet, which is why you've gone off the books. Let me take a stab in the dark here: this box isn't yours. It belongs to what, for the lack of a better word, I'll call your company. Your boss doesn't know you've lost it and wouldn't be all smiles when he found out, right? That's why you had a replica made, so you can try to fool him if he pops around for cocktails and asks to see it."

As I spoke, I realized who her boss was. Satan. No wonder she wanted to keep the loss under wraps. If he was anything like your typical evil mastermind, he probably didn't have much patience for incompetent underlings and boasted many more ways to make them pay for their failings. Laureen needed me as much as I needed her. Maybe more.

"If you're trying to convince me of your powers of perception, save it," she snapped, proving I'd hit the nail on the head. "The job's yours already, unless you enjoy spending every night reliving your squalid sins." I said nothing. "Thought not. So let's get on with the business at hand, shall we? Give me your analysis."

I scratched my nose, staring into the open safe. Once you peeled away all the demonic trimmings, I'd done this kind of gig dozens of times. "They knew exactly what they were looking for, where to find it, and how much leverage it would buy them. Sounds like an inside job."

Laureen nodded, her face grim. "That's what I'm afraid of. Only a select handful of Administrators know about this object. Somebody in here helped a third party steal it."

"How do you know one of your pals didn't take it themselves?"

"An Administrator would know I can't forgive sins. So the ransom note would make no sense."

"Maybe the note's a smokescreen. Whoever took the box might be trying to get you the chop so he or she can take your job. She's asking for something that can't be delivered and has no intention of returning the box."

"That doesn't make sense either. If it were about shunting me out of the way, the thief would have tipped off my boss by now."

"So what's the motivation?"

"I am floundering in the dark in that regard, which is why I came to you. All I know is that we, by which I mean all the Administrators, were in a meeting when the box was stolen. That means the thief had inside knowledge of when the compound would be deserted. And said sneaky worm wriggled past the extra layer of security we lay on for such moments, quite unmolested. That shouldn't be possible unless an Administrator made sure the coast was clear."

"You mean your guard dog? I saw its kennel."

She frowned, her nose crinkling. "So you had a poke around before you came to see me?"

"What can I say? I have a compulsion. What is it?"

"Something you should be very afraid of."

"I'm afraid of everything. I live in Lost Angeles, remember?"

She put her hand on my arm. "I know you think you've had it rough. But there are worse horrors than those you've encountered. This is one of them. Take my advice: save your powers of curiosity for the investigation and pray you never meet it."

Maybe I was being paranoid, but I could sense an implicit threat: get too smart or blab about the box being lost, and you'll meet the beast. I remembered the feeling I'd had when I stood by the small tower, the way my body had screamed at me to run and never look back. I was never one for taking advice or caving in to threats, but on this occasion, I had the feeling that doing so would be the wisest course of action.

"Does God listen to the prayers of the damned?" I asked.

She released my arm and smiled. "Don't you know God loves sinners?"

"Doesn't feel like it from where I'm standing."

"Try kneeling. I hear he likes that."

"Very funny. So, do you have any names for me? Workmates you've had arguments with? Anybody who seemed jealous?"

"No, and I don't want you interviewing any of the other Administrators. That would tip them off something was up."

"Fine, what about the guard? It's always the guard."

"The guards are Administrators too, low level. They know nothing about the box."

"So basically you can't tell me what the box is, you can't tell me who might be involved from your end, and you can't give me any clue as to why they may have helped the thief."

"That's about the size of it. Oh, and I need the box back within ten days. Don't bother asking why, because I won't tell you. Are you up to the job?"

I suppressed a sigh. Demons, or at least Laureen, weren't so different from people. Her behavior was typical of clients. They often had something unsavory to hide and tried to tie your hands in the hope you could get them what they wanted without stumbling over their nasty secret. Fat chance. When you let a bloodhound follow a scent around your house, the first thing it always did was snuffle around in the dirty laundry.

"Can I trust you to keep your end of the deal?" I said.

"You want a contract signed in blood? You have my word. Starting tonight, no more torment for you."

Her word was going to have to do. Even if she welched once I found the box, I would have enjoyed a week or so of blessed relief and an eye-opening whiff of Lost Angeles's stained underwear. That was more than I could have dreamed possible the morning before. And despite the fact that she'd been almost entirely useless as a source of information, I knew where to start looking. Only a specialized thief could have cracked the safe, and I knew a man who could point me in the direction of that thief. If I was lucky, the trail would end there. If not, I'd do whatever it took to get my hands on the thing.

"I can find it," I said.

7

Noon had yet to arrive when I left Laureen's armed with the pop-gun's worth of information she'd divulged. She had me operating on a need-to-know basis. She didn't realize I did need to know. Everything. It was a character flaw of mine. I'd suppressed my curiosity as best as I could in Lost Angeles for the sake of my sanity. Now the itch was coming back. There was more to this than she was letting on. Boxes themselves tended not to have any value; it was what people squirreled away inside them that counted. I was keen to know what a demon kept in a sealed box in a hidden lead-lined safe. Clearly something very important. Perhaps something very dangerous.

I motored down the hill, away from the tranquility of Avici Rise. A sandstorm had kicked up, driven by searing gusts that made the Santa Ana winds feel like the gentle waft of a lover's breath. From above, I could see the red cloud swirling into the city's every nook and cranny. It was strange. Even though the haze enveloped the city, my mind felt clearer than ever. Avici was at my back, but the memory of the place no longer squirmed away. Meeting Laureen had lifted the blinkers that kept me focused on my plodding feet. It was time to start unpicking the city's secrets.

I hit the cloud halfway down. The dust devils danced and writhed in the corners of my vision. You grew used to them, knowing they could do no more than gum up your eyes and clog your nostrils, but it was still unnerving and murder to drive in; I'd nearly run over half a dozen people by the time I swung into Diyu.

You could buy drugs anywhere in the city through handy street-corner dealers. Yama, who ran the drug trade, paid a slice of the proceeds to the other Trustees—this was the standard deal, each paying the others to allow them to sell their wares in areas outside their control. Diyu, however, was the go-to district for the hardcore junkies, those who were trying to medicate themselves out of their misery and didn't mind lying around in their own and other people's filth while they did so.

Yama wasn't the kingpin's real name, but his chosen moniker reflected his rampant megalomania. Yama was the ruler of Hell in Chinese mythology, and while the drug lord certainly didn't control the city, he harbored ambitions to do so. There had been several wars, the last of which had ended in an uneasy truce. I, for one, was grateful. The fighting had become so intense that you couldn't go outside without dodging bullets, clubs, and swords as the rival gangs killed each other over and over in a monotonous and pointless cycle. The streets ran with blood, which at least meant the shoeshine boys did a roaring trade. Yama gave up the ghost when he finally got it into his skull that you couldn't win a war in which nobody died. Besides, the constant fighting was bad for business. Everybody knew he was still plotting, though. If he could find a way to tip the odds in his favor, he would be back on the rampage.

I drove down the main drag, past comatose smack heads lying facedown in the gutter or pillowing their lolling necks on piles of trash. Fat rats strolled openly, one of them pausing to nibble at the toes of a seminaked woman spread-eagled in the middle of the road. Even through the rolled-up windows, the stench of unwashed bodies and human detritus brought me to the verge of barfing. While the other Trustees made an effort to keep their districts clean, Yama didn't bother—at least not on the streets where the junkies swarmed.

The dealers worked out in the open, selling baggies and pre-prepared syringes from stalls set up along the sidewalk. Each stall had its own security: two impassive individuals dressed in T-shirts and trousers, each carrying a machine gun and a sword. The streets were for those who couldn't afford to pay for access to one of the dens where you could hire a thin mattress and stretch out to enjoy your trip to la-la land in relative safety. As I crossed the old stone bridge over the River Styx, two emaciated guys finished emptying the pockets of a third equally pitiful-looking junkie and tipped him headfirst into the river.

Diyu was second to Desert Heights as the most festering sore in Lost Angeles. Most non–drug users avoided the district unless they wanted to remind themselves they could be much worse off. Peeping on the misfortunes of others often perked people right up; I'd always wondered why more doctors didn't prescribe a trip to Skid Row instead of a Mother's Little Helper for dissatisfied and harassed housewives up in LA. Maybe that would have helped my mother. But I wasn't here for a pick-me-up. Diyu was where Enitan George, the best fence in the city, had set up shop. Enitan was the man to see when you wanted to get your hands on something in particular or when you needed to offload hot goods. He served as a middleman, hooking up buyers with sellers and taking five percent off each for his trouble. While there were nicer places to base a business, Yama offered the best protection. His minions were ruthless, ferocious, and conversant in dozens of inventive means of torture. As a result, nobody messed with Enitan, even if they were sure their prized possession had passed through his hands. In return, Enitan never got involved with anything stolen from Yama. Missing property was a solid business for me, and I'd filled Enitan's pockets in exchange for tip-offs on enough occasions to make his tongue loosen at the very sight of me. He was also my best friend.

His shop butted up against the banks of the Styx on the southern edge of Diyu. I parked outside on the narrow potholed street, where I could see the car through the window—nobody in their right mind would steal my Chevy, but junkies weren't renowned for their clarity of thought and would pinch the scabs off a leper's back given half a chance.

The bell tinkled as I opened the door into the cave of junk, rubbing the sand out of my hair. Enitan doubled up as a pawnbroker and bookseller. His shop brimmed with unsellable goods: guitars that never held a note; plastic jewelry that melted in the midday sun; copies of famous artworks; bits, bobs, and utter crap. Pretty much everything on sale was handmade by sinners dissatisfied with the lack of ways to uplift the human spirit. Enitan claimed he was fascinated by what people made, said it demonstrated that human ingenuity could survive even down here. I suspected he was simply a soft touch and took pity on the desperate characters who sold him their trash. There were quality items out there—paintings and instruments crafted by real artists from salvaged materials—but they cost serious money. None of the good stuff made it to Enitan's.

The one market Enitan had cornered was literature. He'd built up a library of books, many of them written by literary sinners who, like me, were upset at the paucity of the written word in Lost Angeles. The majority were copied from memory, although there were books allegedly rewritten by the real authors—what with many artistic types being suckers for suicide—as well as new works set both in the city and in the world we'd left behind. Escape again, this time on the part of the author. I'd read nearly every book in his library, buying some and borrowing others. There were books from beyond my lifetime, which was how I knew the world upstairs had advanced rapidly. They were full of references to modern distractions: high-definition televisions, game consoles, phones that boasted the power of a 1970s supercomputer and allowed people to disappear into virtual worlds. I thought these inventions could be why Lost Angeles stopped developing when it did. So many human advances seemed to be in entertainment, which were diversions from the grind of life and therefore off-limits. Mind you, this theory didn't fit when you considered that alcohol, drugs, and sex—three of the oldest distractions known to humanity—were freely available.

I was able to read the post-1978 books because Enitan understood his market. He was aware of the exact date upstairs but also knew few people wanted to find out that information. He redacted the dates from more modern books so readers need never know how long they'd been trapped in Lost Angeles. Some of the books were good, a rare few excellent. Plenty were badly written and of suspect accuracy. For example, I was sure *Of Mice and Men* didn't end with George and Lennie spit-roasting Curley's wife in the barn and then driving off to raise rabbits and indulge in nightly threesomes. Not that I was complaining about that one. I always preferred a happy ending.

Enitan didn't seem to belong here. I'd read Dante's *Inferno*, and if that was anything to go by, you could be lobbed into Hell for minor infractions such as persistent flatulence or kissing with tongues out of wedlock. I always tried to convince myself that the fence's sin wasn't as bad as mine. I was probably kidding myself. Lost Angeles didn't strike me as a place for minor sinners. It was for the big hitters. All the same, I couldn't imagine what Enitan had done. He came across as such a nice guy and didn't strike me as the suicidal type.

He looked up from his usual position bent over a book and flashed me a toothy grin. He was shaped like a watermelon with a tennis ball glued on top, and it took him a couple of rocks to build enough momentum to stand up on his bandy legs. Enitan didn't set much stock by the rule of not talking about your real life. He'd told me some of his history: how he'd been a doctor in Nigeria and moved to Texas with his wife and grown children in the late 1960s to escape the brutality of the Biafran War. He still preferred traditional Nigerian dress, which he sewed himself. Today, he was wearing a particularly elaborate concoction: purple with embroidered flowers, a beaded neckline, and voluminous sleeves. It was my understanding that you were supposed to wear the billowing robe over trousers, but Enitan preferred to go without, to "provide a refreshing breeze in the nether regions." Maybe that was his sin: going commando on the Sabbath.

"Kat, it has been too long a time," he said, stomping down the narrow aisle between the tottering stacks of goods to give me a welcoming hug. "Still putting your nose where it does not belong?"

"Still putting other people's things where they don't belong?"

"All property is theft, my dear."

"In which case, you won't mind if I steal your cash register," I said, ducking out of his embrace and wandering over to the metal behemoth on the counter.

"You will never lift it. Your muscles are softer than my grandmother's overcooked beans."

"Then I'll steal the money from inside." I rang the till open to empty drawers. "Somebody already clean you out?"

"What can I say? I bought too much merchandise this morning."

"Let me see if I can fill her up a little." I pulled out a twenty, snapped it, and placed it in the till.

"So you wish to buy something? Most excellent. Can I interest you in *War and Peace*?" He indicated the tatty manuscript he'd been reading. "I received it yesterday."

I flicked through the pages. The manuscript seemed thin. "Isn't *War and Peace* supposed to be longer?"

"The man who reauthored it liked war so much, he left out all the peace. It makes for a more exciting read."

"I'll pass. I'm after a different kind of information. About a job somebody carried out three days ago."

"Of what manner of job do you speak?"

"A burglary up at Avici Rise. One item stolen, a box of supposedly great value. The thief would need to be skilled. The safe was high-grade steel with a concealed-entry system."

At first Enitan looked confused, as though he'd never heard of the place. Then understanding came into his face, and his lips curled up in a dreamy smile. "Ah, Avici Rise. Of course. I am sure they have all kinds of wonders up there. It is a great pity he did not visit me. I have not brokered such a job."

"Heard anything through the grapevine?"

"Nothing about a robbery." He rubbed his head and raised one eyebrow. "A skilled thief, you say? Something did occur that may be connected. Yesterday, a fine woman named Alexis Black came to see me, looking most upset. I was forced to give her a hug."

"Was it one of your special rhythmic hugs?"

"Do not be so dirty of mind. This was a damsel in distress. Ms. Black is the partner of Sebastian Vega, a splendid thief whose acquaintance I made recently. Acrobatic. Silent. Technically adept. He disappeared a few days ago. She wanted to know if I had seen him."

I wasn't convinced of the connection. Rapid and unexplained vanishing acts weren't rare in Lost Angeles. People would go off for their nightly appointments with the Torments and never come back. There were never any witnesses, as everybody was busy reliving their own sins. Within a week, the possessions of the disappeared would be divided and their homes taken by whoever got there first. Soon, it would be like they'd never existed. "People disappear all the time."

"True, but the people who disappear have normally been here for some time. Sebastian is new. His absence could be considered out of the ordinary."

"And you think he could get into a high-end safe?"

"Indisputably."

While the lead was thinner than a high-society girl on a vomiting diet, it was the sole one I had. I figured I may as well check it out. "Do you have an address?"

"Alas, no. He came and went as he saw fit. He revealed little interest in more regular work. I can tell you where Ms. Black works, however." He looked significantly at the till.

"Come on. Twenty bucks is more than enough for speculation."

He rubbed his shaven skull and grinned. "A man can try. I did actually tell her to go see you about her missing amour. I assume she did not. She works in snuff movies."

I grimaced and stuck out my tongue. Although I'd never seen any examples of Hrag's "art," I knew all about the racket. It wasn't exactly underground; there was plenty of demand for such perversion. Hrag wrote and directed the films, filming them by night at his studio in the red-light district of Astghik. Apparently, he preferred to shoot after the visits of the Torments. His actors found it easier to appear distressed. He ran the horror shows to full houses in his cinema every night.

"And how would you know that?" I asked Enitan.

"Please, Kat," Enitan said, pouting. "You know me better than to think I would be interested in such obscenities. A customer happened to be browsing my wares when she entered. He recognized her. She is a big star. He even got her autograph. She mentioned they were shooting a new feature at the moment. This is how you will find her."

After a brief moment's hesitation, I withdrew another twenty. Enitan was the most learned man I knew, even if his secondhand source materials could be unreliable. I thought I could squeeze more out of him with the right lubrication.

"While we're talking—I don't suppose you've come across any mentions of a carved wooden box in the shape of a globe?"

"This is the object you are searching for, I assume? I am sorry. I have no knowledge on this subject."

"How about this?"

I scribbled a picture of the creature I'd seen on the small tower. The drawing came out looking like the product of a four-year-old's crayon. Nonetheless, Enitan's brow crinkled in recognition.

"That does look familiar," he said. "Let me peruse my books and see if I can come up with anything. Is this related to your case?"

"Not exactly, but you know me—I never pass up a chance to expand my knowledge."

"Then allow me to give you *War and Peace* on the house," he said, pressing the manuscript into my hand.

I took it, giving him the second twenty in return, and rolled the book into a tight wad. I'd noticed a junkie sniffing around my car, and the manuscript would come in handy to beat him around the head with, even if it wasn't as chunky as it should have been.

"I will call if I find anything," Enitan called after me as I ran out the door and set to with my work of literature.

8

I'd always been the kind of girl who chose her apartment based on its proximity to her favorite bar, and there'd been no reason to change when I died. You never knew when you were going to need a friendly voice or stiff drink, plus a local bar was a relatively safe place to meet people you didn't trust. In my case, that covered pretty much the whole city.

Once I'd earmarked Benny's as my haunt of choice, I'd set to work earning enough dough to escape Desert Heights. Building up work was easier than it had been upstairs. There wasn't much competition. The other good PIs appeared to have been more virtuous than I and hadn't fetched up in Lost Angeles. Presumably they were having a jolly old time listening to harps and sipping fluffy cloud cocktails in Heaven. The jobs here weren't much different from those upstairs: people still wanted to know if their partners were screwing around; they still grew attached to bric-a-brac and wanted their prized possessions back when they got pinched; and gangs still kidnapped loved ones—love did still exist, even for the likes of us—for ransom. The only cases I didn't pick up any longer were those looking into missing persons and murders. When somebody vanished without a resultant attempt at extortion, people accepted they were never coming back. And there wasn't much call for murder investigations when the victim could sit up a few minutes later and point to the offender.

I'd quickly built up a steady income and could afford a place off Providence, no more than five minutes' walk from Benny's. I'd stayed there ever since.

After I'd beaten off the junkie outside Enitan's, I headed back to the apartment. I had nothing to do until Alexis was on set, and I wanted to catch a nap so I would be fresh enough to think clearly. The second-floor apartment, rented from Flo's regime, overlooked an alley popular with hookers, muggers, and mugger-slash-hookers, all of whom I knew by first name. A few of Enitan's artworks, those not too obviously painted by a myopic monkey, added splashes of color to the walls of the living room, which doubled as my office, and reauthored novels filled my bookshelf. The best in this collection were near-perfect copies of all of Virginia Woolf's novels. According to Enitan, these were so accurate because the lady herself had rewritten them following her suicide. I couldn't check up on the veracity of this claim, because in Enitan's telling, the author had conveniently disappeared before I arrived in town. I possessed but two real books: scruffy paperback copies of *The Big Sleep* and *The Maltese Falcon*. These I kept under the loose tile beside my savings. They'd set me back a thousand dollars each, but they were worth every cent—they'd been my father's favorite books. When I reread them, as I often did, I felt his breath on my neck stronger than ever. At those times, I could almost forget I was living in Lost Angeles.

I'd also acquired a chalkboard, upon which I drew diagrams of particularly convoluted cases. I marked up a few notes and lines connecting the parties I'd identified so far—which consisted of Laureen, Sebastian, Alexis, and the mystery inside guy. I had a feeling that by the end of this particular investigation, the board would look like the work of a junked-up spider.

I lay down on my single bed, but sleep wouldn't come. Tonight would be the first that I wouldn't have to revisit the Nimrod

Motel. Better memories of Danny were crowding around the edge of my consciousness, but they wouldn't quite materialize fully, always dissolving back into the motel room. Around six, I swung my legs out of bed, grabbed my gun, and wandered over to Benny's for my habitual early evening bracer. The usual suspects filled the booths, and the atmosphere was already turning grim. I felt strangely guilty that I would be spared.

After a while, the door swung open. I was surprised to spy Franklin, looking considerably less shaken than the previous evening. He marched over and stuck out his hand. "I wanted to say thank you for last night."

His bones felt as delicate as a bird's wings as I took the proffered palm. "Thanks? Did you forget you ended up with a punctured eyeball?"

"No. But you tried to stop them. That makes you a hero in my book."

"Next time I'll bring my cape and tights. Maybe they'll help deliver a better outcome."

He laughed far louder and longer than was justified. "Can I get you a drink?"

"Do you have money? Benny doesn't do tabs until he knows you're good for it. The man's got no faith in humanity."

Benny looked up from the glass he was cleaning with the aid of some saliva. He did a lot of that kind of thing. Not because he was bar-proud; if that were the case, he would probably use water like a normal, hygienic human being. He was trying to keep his hands busy so they wouldn't turn to the bottle so often. Half of the booze in the bar went down his gullet instead of to customers; most of the time his eyes looked as smoky as the windows.

"I got faith in humanity," he said. "Just not the sort living in this shithole."

"Ah," Franklin said, his lower lip drooping. "I'm broke. Maybe I could wash some dishes?"

"I don't do food," Benny said. "Cuts into drinking time."

"I'll buy," I said. "What's your poison?"

"I'll have whatever you're having."

I ordered two Ward Eights. He took a long gulp of his. I sipped mine. "So, have you run into any more trouble?"

"No. I stayed in my room all day and came straight here."

"Take my advice: spend the next few weeks getting killed as many times as possible. Insult every gorilla you see. Stand in the middle of Route 666 during rush hour. Jump off every high building you can climb. The sooner you get used to it, the easier it'll be to deal with."

"Wouldn't I be better off learning how not to get killed?"

I looked at his scrawny frame and bookish features, which screamed "victim" in neon letters six feet high. I said nothing.

"Maybe you could teach me," he continued. "You seem tough."

"I'm not tough. I'm just dumb enough to get into trouble and just smart enough to get out of it."

"What do you do for a living?"

"I'm a private investigator."

His eyes lit up, and he tapped his foot off the barstool like a dog that had caught a whiff of a juicy steak. "Wow! I always wanted to be a private dick. I was something of an investigator myself, you know."

"What did you investigate? Who stole the cookies from the dorm room?"

He forced out another laugh even though I was insulting him. It was amazing what people were prepared to put up with when they were on the make, and Franklin definitely wanted something. Maybe he saw me as a protector or mentor. If so, he was looking in the wrong place. "I know I look young, but I'm twenty-five. I am—was—a religious historian. You'd be surprised how many mysteries there were to be unraveled in all those old texts. I was good at following the threads. Maybe I could help you out."

I massaged my temple and took a bigger hit of my drink. The kid wanted to be my sidekick. That was what I got for trying to be nice. He probably imagined us skipping around town, fending off bad guys, getting into wacky scrapes, and "unraveling mysteries." I imagined throwing him out of the Chevy after fifteen minutes and watching him bounce himself bloody along the highway.

"What are you working on now?" he said, breathless. "I bet it's a big conspiracy. Is there a woman involved? There's always a woman, right? Or maybe not, since you are a woman . . ."

I raised my palm to cut him off. "Listen, kid. You seem nice. That's the problem. You're not cut out for this line of work. You need to be an asshole to get results."

"I can be an asshole," he said, adding as an afterthought, "you big, smelly bitch."

"Nice try, but no cigar. Everybody's born with an asshole, but not everybody can be one. It's a God-given talent."

"I could do the research. Be your backroom guy."

I was beginning to understand why the big goon and his pals had been so set on roughing him up. They'd probably wandered in for a quiet drink, and Franklin had started trying to recruit himself as a professional thug, citing his experience at issuing smackdowns in debate club. I drained my drink and threw some cash on the bar. "I work alone."

"That must be lonely. Don't you ever feel like having some-body to talk to? It can be useful to bounce ideas off other people."

"If I get lonely, I talk to my superhero alter ego. Find yourself a line of work that suits you better."

I left before he could open his flapping mouth again and set off along Providence. I hoped he'd gotten the message and wouldn't come back to Benny's to bug me. I wasn't going to be driven out of my favorite watering hole. Benny had been good to me when I'd arrived. He'd extended the line of credit far beyond what the piece-of-shit car was worth, which kept me in booze until I got my feet under me. Under the gruff exterior, he had a good heart. Well, a not entirely warped heart. He and Enitan were as close to family as I had down here. If the kid did prove to be a cling on, I'd have to find some way to get rid of him.

My feet, locked into the daily routine, had been taking me toward Fortune Hill. I stopped as I remembered that the situation had changed. Sure, I could go up to the park, sit on the bench, and watch the Torments swoop, safe in the knowledge that none of them were headed my way. Provided, of course, that Laureen was true to her word. Or I could stay down on the streets and see what happened when a Torment transported somebody to their own personal nightmare. Curiosity won, so I installed myself in a doorway across from the Lucky Deal as the crowds scurried home. Sid was outside as usual, leaning on the gold pillar. He didn't notice me, too intent on casting nervous glances to the northwest.

As I waited, a lingering Penitent caught my eye and tottered toward me. He'd clearly been on the starvation diet. Glittering blue eyes burned fervent in his skeletal face, and he dragged his placard along the ground, too weak to hold it up. He opened his mouth to speak, but I got there first.

"Let me guess. I should repent, right?"

"Yes!" he shouted, his voice surprisingly strong. "Repent! Do not sell your body to the fornicators. Surrender yourself to God, and you will be saved."

I snorted. "Do I look like a prostitute to you? I'm not exactly putting the wares on display."

His gaze flicked down at my trousers and buttoned-up blouse. "My mistake," he said at a normal volume before getting all shouty again. "Repent nonetheless, sinner!"

"I've done nothing but repent since I got here, and a fat lot of good it's done me. God doesn't give a shit about anybody in this city." I pressed ten bucks into his hand. "You don't need to punish yourself. Lost Angeles does it for you. Do yourself a favor when you wake up and buy yourself a decent meal."

He stared at the money, face contorted with longing as his stomach rumbled. He balled up the ten spot, dropped it, and began punching himself in the traitorous gut. He continued to do so as he weaved away through traffic to harass the last of the crowds.

Soon enough, the streets were empty. I couldn't see the tower from where I lurked, but when the last ray of light had slid off the facade of the Lucky Deal, I heard the thrumming of wings. Sid fell to his knees and crossed himself. I'd never taken him for a religious man. It was a bit late anyway. Hundreds of Torments thudded onto roofs, ledges, and sidewalks. They perched above and around like crows, flicking their wings out of existence, and then melted through whatever obstacle stood between them and their targets. My heart lurched as one dove in my direction. For a moment, I cursed Laureen for a welcher, but the creature turned in an arc halfway down and landed in front of Sid. His eyes were squeezed shut, his lips moving as he recited a prayer. Sid's reflected face oozed out of the tar, lips moving in synchronicity. The Torment stalked forward until it came nose to nose with the praying man. Then, like two reflections melding in a funhouse mirror, the Torment oozed into him and was gone. Sid toppled sideways and lay still.

After a few minutes, I stuck my head out and looked up, like a woman sheltering from a thunderstorm checking to see if the rain had passed. The sky was clear. Laureen had kept her side of the bargain. I wanted to yell my freedom at the top of my lungs, but Cajetan was eerily quiet, the screams that had heralded the approach of the beasts now stilled. It felt wrong, almost sacrilegious, to break the silence—so much so that I tiptoed over to Sid's prone form. Every muscle on his face lay slack, and his chest appeared still. When I leaned in to check for breath, wondering if the Torments tore our souls out of our bodies and left them lifeless for the duration of the punishment, his eyes snapped open. Black viscous fluid, seething like boiling oil, coated the eyeballs. Images formed in the shifting, shining surface: a cramped basement with a single foldaway chair and a low table, one man looming over another, a tight huddle of three figures pressing in behind. As I leaned closer, a black tendril wavered out as though searching for me. I leaped back, and the questing strand collapsed into Sid's hideous black gaze.

His hands flexed as he whispered, his voice racked with pain, "I'm sorry, Petey. I got no choice. You know that, right?" Then his voice grew loud and strong, full of forced bravado. "Tie him to the chair real tight. He's gonna squirm some."

I backed away. Sid was trapped in there, reliving his worst sin, the one that filled him with shame and regret. I didn't want to see, didn't want to hear, didn't want to watch his face writhe in sorrow as he went through it all again. It felt wrong, like eavesdropping at a confessional. I knew I wouldn't want anybody to stand over me and watch as I suffered. I'd been considering wandering the city for the next four hours to take it all in, but I'd already seen enough. I rushed home, ignoring the few other twitching bodies caught outside when the storm came. Voices mumbled and shouted from my neighbors' apartments as I took the stairs two at a time and fumbled to unlock the door. I dropped onto my bed and wrapped a pillow around my ears. Broken and shattered shrieks, a hundred times worse than those that emanated when the Torments first made their approach, began to echo around the city.

Every city has its own character and energy—its own soul, if you want to get all philosophical—charged and kept alive by the thoughts, dreams, and actions of the residents. In most places, the basic goodness of ordinary folk outweighed the darker desires and acts of the few, and so you got a good vibe. In some cities, where crime and vice proliferated, you felt a shadow that told you not to let your guard down, although never anything strong enough to overwhelm the spirit. But sin defined Lost Angeles; it soaked into every stone, vibrated in every molecule, and tainted the air. The appalling weight of the sin, concentrated by the simultaneous torture, pinned me to my mattress.

I needed to escape, to drown out the screams somehow, but I could barely lift my hand to wipe the sweat from my brow. Had I owned a record player, I could have turned it up full blast and smothered the worst of the anguished cacophony. But like I said, music wasn't readily available in Lost Angeles, save for the ropy bands who played their homemade instruments in the casinos and clubs. I hurried to the toilet to pry up the loose tile and retrieve *The Big Sleep*. Back in bed, I tried to focus on the words and conjure up the comforting spirit of my father. For once, it didn't work.

9

I rolled down Providence at one in the morning, heading for the dingy underpass that led to the other side of Route 666 and into Astghik. My vision was blurry, my mouth was parched, and my chest was tight after hours of listening to the fractured howl of a city under the thrall of the Torments. In some ways, I felt worse than I did after emerging from killing Danny. At least that was a familiar pain, one resulting from my actions alone. I owned it, and it owned me. What I felt now was a psychic hangover induced by the collective bludgeon of millions of living nightmares of violence, treachery, greed, and sorrow. I concentrated on the simple act of driving in an effort to clear my mind. I would need to be focused when I spoke to Alexis. If her boyfriend had been involved in the robbery and had gone into hiding to avoid repercussions, she would be reticent to talk. I would have to find the correct angle of approach and be charming, which wouldn't be easy in my current black humor.

Once through the underpass—which was littered with the tattered bedding and cardboard lean-tos of the homeless—Providence turned into Chanchanian Way. Hrag was no shrinking violet, so when he took over the sex trade, he set about changing the names of the district and its streets. As Hrag was fond of telling anybody who would listen, he'd renamed his district after the Armenian goddess of love. God knows why he chose her, as there was precious little love on show around Astghik. Maybe there wasn't a goddess of panting perverts in Armenia.

This was a conceit not uncommon among the Trustees. Before Yama's time, Diyu was known as Swedenborg, thus named by the maniac of Swedish descent who'd run it until he'd joined the list of the missing. The Seven Gates, where Adnan al Kassar dealt in guns, bombs, and other assorted weaponry aimed at turning people into gloopy piles of flesh, was once named Irkalla. Under the control of Sofia Busco, the district that handled the city's food supplies became Il Terzo Livello. The financial district, where Wayne Beat ran everything from small-time moneylending concerns to big banks, was once called Mammon. He changed it to the FD, presumably to add some gravitas and make him seem less like the grasping swine he was. Two of the seven Trustee-run districts—Eleutherios, where Jean-Paul Guyot took care of the booze, and Cajetan, named after the Catholic patron saint of gamblers—had retained their names for the duration of my stay. Only Tyrell Jackson, who controlled the gas trade, didn't have his own turf. He didn't need one, as gas stations had to be spread geographically.

The perverts were out in force already in Astghik, drooling in lines outside the brothels, cinemas, and peep shows that screamed their wares in multicolored neon lights: bondage, orgies, gang bangs, torture, necrophilia (you had to be quick on the draw, as the object of lust didn't stay dead for long), and pretty much any peccadillo money could buy. The customers were mainly male, which meant the few women seeking pleasure spent much of their time fending off sleazy propositions. Hrag's boys kept the most persistent johns in line—the women's money was as good as the men's, and he wanted all his customers to feel comfortable. One of them was busy dragging a red-faced and yelling octogenarian in erection-tented sweatpants away from a stunning blonde dressed in a long overcoat that didn't quite hide the fringes of her black leather S&M outfit.

Hrag, who fancied himself a fashion designer, decked out his crew personally. Around their uniformly bulky necks, they sported heavy faux-gold chains, which also served well when somebody was in need of a punitive choking. They wore black leotards, ideal for fighting, as the tight fabric gave nothing to grab onto. Mercifully for my eyes, metal codpieces obscured their groins. Knee-high purple boots added a splash of color to the ensemble, and the pierced left ear of each contained a wide stud upon which a portrait of Hrag's mug grinned. The outfits were so farcical, like pimped-up versions of Alex's gang from *A Clockwork Orange*, that anybody who saw them should have laughed. Nobody did.

The studio was set off from the main hub of sexual affray, but some johns were lined up outside. Hrag never passed up a chance to make cash, so those who liked to watch their sexual violence in the flesh could pay to spectate from the peanut gallery. I lashed out ten bucks for the privilege of mounting a narrow set of metal stairs to the rows of benches overlooking the bright studio lights. I selected a spot in the far corner at the front and gave it a good inspection for sticky patches before gingerly lowering myself to a seated position.

Hrag sat in the director's chair, his blond hair gelled up into spikes so it looked like a crown. He was bawling into a megaphone with such venom that his tattooed neck had turned scarlet. On set, amidst bales of hay and makeshift wooden stalls, a makeup artist was putting the final touches on a slender woman with copper-red hair. She had a creamy complexion and a natural blush to her cheeks. The makeup artist was applying white powder and smudging mascara around her eyes. The actress wore a matching lacy black bra and panties that showed off her athletic body. I dreaded to think what flimsy plotline Hrag had concocted to bring about such a state of undress. Offstage, a hulking brute in dungarees, an obviously fake hunchback, and a clown mask was preparing for his role, rolling his neck and theatrically brandishing an axe. Finally, everything was ready, and the crew scuttled off to their places.

"I want real emotion," Hrag shouted. "Fear. Rage. Lust. Nail it into the motherfucking ground. Make my guts churn. Alexis, remember this is sexy time. I want every paying customer rigid."

"*Hunchbacked Axe Clown Rape-Murder Gang Vengeance*, scene sixteen, take one," a flunky yelled and snapped his clapboard.

I grimaced. Hrag was as subtle as a bull in a red-cape factory, so I hadn't been expecting much in the way of nuance and sparkling dialogue. The title suggested the film would be worse than I'd thought.

Alexis explored the fictional barn, looking for places to hide in a way that involved lots of bending over. She finally settled on one of the hay bales and crouched behind it, a tuft of hair sticking over the top. Somebody snapped a piece of wood offstage, a pitiful attempt to simulate a door being kicked in, and the killer clown blundered onto the set. He slung the axe over his shoulder and undid the catches on the dungarees.

"I gots me a big old present fer ya, girly," he cooed, hamming up the country bumpkin accent as his dungarees fell to the floor to reveal his bare ass. He'd obviously been hired for his size, not his acting skills.

I got up to leave, feeling nauseated. Now that I knew what Alexis looked like, I didn't have to witness whatever horrific scene was about to unfold. When I reached the back of the gallery, however, the door was locked. A light above the exit glowed red. I turned around, looking for another way out, as the clown sneaked up to the hay bale behind which Alexis was so ineptly hiding. The perverts were leaning forward, all pink and sweaty. If I'd had the axe, I would have used it to detach some genitals. The sick bastards were all hot and bothered at the thought of seeing a beautiful young woman raped and chopped to pieces.

As I was about to squeeze my eyes shut and put my fingers in my ears, Alexis somersaulted out from behind the hay bale, sailing clean over the axe clown's head. In her hand flashed a wicked steel hook of the kind country folk leave lying around in barns for no discernible reason other than to provide handy weapons for B-movie plots. Alexis landed in a stance of perfect poise and grace and swung the hook into the clown's meaty calf. Blood spurted, and he let out a roar of pain far more convincing than his dialogue, largely because it was real. Alexis yanked the hook out, bringing a fresh red spray. He flailed at her with the axe. She swayed, all lithe and sinuous muscle. The blade whispered past her ear. The hook flashed again as she buried it in his wrist. The axe fell to the floor. She kicked him in the chest, sending him sprawling onto his back.

"Your gang of hunchbacked axe clown rapists done raped and killed my sister," Alexis spat, bending over to pick up the axe. "Now I'm gunning for all y'all. I'm gonna make me a necklace outta your dicks."

"Please!" the clown yelled, arms crossed in front of his face. "I gots me a family!"

Alexis turned side-on, giving the camera a lingering look at her heaving, blood-smeared cleavage. "Not for long," she said, advancing.

Now I did close my eyes. The meaty thuds and screams were almost as bad as watching.

"Cut!" Hrag yelled.

The crowd cheered. I opened my eyes to see that they were on their feet and applauding. Down below, Alexis was now wearing the clown mask and holding the axe aloft, her firm thighs spread-eagled into a killing stance. Once she'd milked the applause, she bowed to her fans. I blinked in unison with the rest of the spectators, and the axe clown gasped back to life. Alexis bent over to help her fellow actor, gore-splattered and groggy, to his feet.

"Brutal work, people," Hrag shouted into his megaphone. "Take thirty while we change the set."

The door clicked open, and the audience filed out, chatting happily amongst themselves and pulling out notebooks. Autograph hunters. It seemed Alexis was as big a name as Enitan had said. I tagged along with the throng, down the stairs and up a corridor until everyone butted up against one of Hrag's toughs, who looked like he'd pumped enough iron to build the Empire State Building.

"No autographs at the moment," he said, prompting a murmur of disappointment. "Ms. Black needs to rest before her next scene."

The starstruck crowd trooped away. I stayed put. "I need a word with Alexis."

"No autographs, I said."

I pulled out a twenty. He shook his head. I sighed and added a second. This job was going to end up costing me. I should have haggled for expenses too. He glanced up and down the corridor, magicked the money into his codpiece, and waved me through. "Ten minutes, then you need to beat it."

I knocked on the door of Alexis's dressing room and went in without waiting for an answer. She had one long leg up on the table and was massaging her calf.

"No, you can't buy my panties," she said without looking up.

"I was thinking of a swap."

She looked up, eyes narrowing as she took me in. "You're not one of the usual droolers. What do you want?"

I hadn't been able to think up a soft approach, so I jumped right in. "I'm looking for Sebastian."

She whisked her leg around, so fast that I had no time to react, and landed a ferocious blow on my temple. She took advantage of my stagger to sweep my legs out from under me. I had barely landed before she was sitting on me. She wrenched my arm up my back to the point of breaking. "You idiots don't give up, do you? I told your pals I don't know where he is."

"Lay off," I said, keeping my voice low. The last thing I needed was Hrag's guy busting in and joining the party. "I'm not here to cause trouble."

"That's good, because you're very bad at it. Tell your boss if he sends anybody else, I'll set Hrag on him. He doesn't like anybody messing with his star. Now get the fuck out of my dressing room."

She released my arm and stepped on my head on the way back to her dressing table. I rolled over to rub my aching shoulder.

"I get the feeling Hrag sets *you* on people who mess with him," I said, clambering to my feet and backing off to a safe distance. "Where'd you learn to fight like that?"

"Hrag talent spotted me in the Colosseum, which I tell you by way of giving you another reason to get lost."

"You've got me all wrong. I'm a private investigator. My name's Kat Murphy." Now she looked up. "You know Enitan. He told me I should come see you about Sebastian."

"And he told me where I could find you. Seems we were meant to be. Why didn't you come? Too busy cracking heads?"

"Something like that. Are you here touting for work?"

I was about to say no, but I realized this, bless Enitan's cotton socks, was my angle. Getting her to hire me would be the best way to make her talk. Plus it would cover some of my expenses for the many more bribes I would likely have to pay as I searched for Laureen's box. "If you want him found, I'm your woman."

"How much do you charge?"

I looked around the dressing room. It was spacious, with a big silver mirror and a leather sofa. A bottle of champagne sat on the table, and the dresses hanging in the wardrobe looked plush. "Five hundred bucks a day," I said, quoting her twice my usual Lost Angeles fee.

"At that rate, I'd have thought you could afford better clothes." She hesitated. "Are you as good as Enitan says?"

"Worth every cent and then some. Tell you what. Since you gave me such a warm welcome, I'll give you a free consultation in return. Then you can decide if you want to engage my services."

She slipped into a fluffy dressing gown and cinched the cord. "Okay, hotshot. Strut your stuff."

"When did Sebastian go missing?"

"A few days ago."

"Any sign of struggle at the apartment? A ransom note, maybe? Any floozies he may have been kicking around with?"

"Nobody cheats on me," she said, turning to face me and letting the robe fall open to display her credentials.

"Can you think of any reason he might have gone off on his own?"

"You got a business card? You could be pretending to be Murphy."

I showed her my credentials, which were way less impressive than hers. She looked at the card, took a swig of champagne, and said, "He was hired to steal something. I could tell it was a big job. He gets excited at a challenge. He came back all smug, so I knew he'd pulled it off. I went off to work. When I came back, he was gone."

"My aching head tells me somebody else came looking for him."

"Some thugs. They said he'd been well paid to steal 'the box,' whatever that is, and he'd better cough it up or else. They didn't believe me when I told them I had no clue where he'd gone."

I suppressed a grin. Enitan had put me on the right track after all. "I take it they tried to convince you."

"They tried. I convinced *them* that wasn't a smart move."

"I'll bet you did," I said, rubbing my temple. "What did the guys look like?"

"Thuggy."

"That's not really narrowing down the field."

"I'm not very good with faces."

Alexis's version of events explained something that had been bugging me. If this had been a straight ransom job, the thief would have left the note in the safe once he'd stolen the box instead of delivering it the next day. The original buyer had wanted it for another unknown purpose. Once Sebastian had either realized his prize was worth more than he'd thought or passed it on to somebody else who knew its true value, the ransom note had been delivered.

"Sounds like we have two possibilities. Your delightful boyfriend decided to keep the ill-gotten goods for himself, or he found himself a better-paying buyer. Either way, he made himself scarce, before the guy who hired him cottoned on, and left you to face the music."

"Sure seems that way."

"So why do you want to find him? Seems to me you're better off without him."

Alexis flexed her biceps. "I want to break every bone in his cowardly body."

Sebastian had dunked himself in a whole septic tank of crap. Laureen, the unknown party who'd hired him, and now Alexis were all gunning for him. I didn't know which one he should fear the most.

"Sounds like you have good cause," I said. "Does he have any bolt-holes you know of?"

"No, otherwise I'd have gone there myself."

"How about habits? Places he likes to hang out?"

"He's a big gambler. We met in the Colosseum. He loves the fights. But he wouldn't be stupid enough to go there if he's got people looking for him."

"Do you have a photograph of him?"

"I burned it."

"How about a description?"

"Tall. Mexican by birth. Wears his hair long. Handsome and he knows it."

"Any distinguishing features?" I was thinking if he was still around, he would most likely be in disguise. Plus her description was so vague, I could have picked out half a dozen wrong guys. I was beginning to wonder if she was shortsighted.

"His left pinky is missing above the first knuckle. He always keeps his fist clenched to hide it. Did I mention he's vain?"

"You alluded to it. You don't seem to like him very much."

"I did like him. Until two days ago. Now I've realized he's a louse."

"Most men down here are. If he's out there, I'll find him."

She crossed her arms. "I didn't say I was going to hire you."

"I thought you wanted to get your mitts on his worthless hide."

"Normally I get paid to beat men up, not pay for the opportunity to do it. Forget it. He's not worth five hundred a day. He's not worth two cents a day. He'll come slinking back when he thinks the coast is clear. Then I'll mess him up. Sorry to have wasted your time."

"You haven't wasted my time. I enjoy being kicked in the head and sat on."

The actor Alexis had killed, still in his pillow-stuffed dungarees, stuck his head in the door. From the way his voice dripped honey, he didn't seem to hold his murder against her. "Hrag needs you back on set in a few, sweetie."

"Be there in a minute," Alexis said.

"I'd better leave you to it. You need to get back to work, and I've got a hunch to follow," I said, nodding in the direction of the departing actor.

I left her sitting there, a smile on her face for the first time, and headed back to the car, feeling better than I had an hour before. I was bummed not to have doubled up on payment for the investigation, which meant I would have to dip into my savings to finance the operation, but now I knew for sure Sebastian had stolen the box. And while I didn't have a lead on who'd hired him, that was okay. Laureen only wanted her precious box back, and if the trail on the original buyer led back to another Administrator, that could prove uncomfortable for yours truly. All I had to do was follow the breadcrumbs to the box, and Alexis had kindly dropped the next one for me.

It was unlikely that Sebastian had realized the box could bring him more than cash, and he was the one trying to have his sins erased. He was a hired hand, nothing more. His employer wouldn't have told him he was stealing from the Administrators—if Sebastian had any sense, that would have scared him off. More likely he'd double-crossed whoever had hired him. In that case, he would turn up. Gambling was an addiction like any other. If my guess was correct, the money would be burning a hole in his pocket. That was presuming the buyer hadn't snatched him to keep him quiet, and he hadn't disappeared like so many before him. I didn't want to give that line of thought much credence; it would put me back to square one and force me to track down the muscle who'd paid Alexis a visit.

Maybe Sebastian would turn up at the Colosseum. Maybe not. Either way, it was worth a few hours to hang around and keep an eye out for him. If I found him and got him to spill the beans, I'd be one step closer to retrieving the box and getting the Torments off my back for good.

10

The next night, I hung around the Colosseum looking for a nine-fingered Mexican, which coincidentally was the name Benny had given to a potent tequila cocktail of his own devising. Even if Sebastian did show his face, spotting him would be as gargantuan a task as staggering home after indulging in a few of Benny's eye-watering concoctions. The Colosseum was a near-scale replica of the Roman amphitheater of death. It held close to forty thousand bawling spectators when packed, as it often was. There was no way I could trawl the aisles in search of a deformed pinkie. Perversely, the scale of the task gave me hope that Sebastian would turn up. The huge crowds and frequent chaotic brawls in the stone bleachers meant he might feel comfortable popping in without any watchers laying eyes on him.

There was one place where I had a decent chance of catching sight of him—the narrow hall where the gamblers congregated to lay their bets. I hung around the bookie windows, scanning the punters' hands. I saw a few tall, handsome Latinos, but they all appeared to be in full possession of their digits. An hour or so in, I got the strong impression I wasn't the only one doing the watching. When you've spent as long creeping around as I have, you develop a sense for when somebody else is creeping around you. My neck kept prickling, but every time I turned, nobody was obviously looking in my direction. After two hours,

Flo's boys started to take an interest in me—they probably thought I was trying to spot big bets and catch a whiff of a fixed fight—so I called it a night before they started asking questions.

I spent the next day pondering who might have been spying on me in the Colosseum. The men who'd tried to strong-arm Alexis could have spotted me when I visited her and put two and two together. Perhaps they figured I was their best hope of pinpointing Sebastian and were tailing me. Alexis could have decided to look for him in the Colosseum; my lurking presence would have alerted her I'd been dishonest in our meeting. It was also possible Laureen was keeping tabs on my movements, though I doubted it. She hadn't answered my calls, so I'd sent her a note via courier in the morning to let her know I was following a lead. I'd found the best way to stop anxious customers from bugging me was to keep them informed. I chalked her silence up to her efforts not to draw attention to my investigation.

I knew she hadn't abandoned me; my nightly visits were still suspended. Before my fruitless visit to the Colosseum, I'd stayed home, acclimatizing to the heavy vibe of the citywide torture. But hiding away meant I was squandering a golden opportunity to snoop around. If I was the sole human in the city free of the Torments, I had a four-hour window to go where I pleased. I intended to use the time to rifle Alexis's dressing room, in case she'd been as economical with the truth as I'd been, and then see what I could see around town.

When I reached the studio, twenty minutes after the Torments had taken control, the doors were locked. I'd never gotten around to mastering the delicate art of lock picking, so I smashed a glass panel with the butt of my gun and undid the catch. It wasn't like there was anybody compos mentis enough to hear me. Low moans and mutters filled the unlit corridors. Even though I knew I was the only one awake, I jumped every time a voice was raised or a flailing fist hit wall or floor. The beam from my flashlight flickered and wavered as I made my way to the dressing room, stepping over the bodyguard I'd bribed the day before.

The door was ajar. I nudged it open and stepped inside. My light crawled across the shining black eyes of Alexis sprawled in her chair. Her robe had fallen open to reveal her naked body. I folded the lapels over her breasts, which burned with a feverish heat, tuning out the words flickering across her lips. I rifled her drawers and turned up the picture she'd supposedly burned. I could see why she hadn't destroyed it despite her professed loathing for Sebastian. Charm oozed out of the photograph. He had the kind of face even women who knew better could fall for. With ruggedly handsome men, women got what they paid for. With guys like Sebastian, all soulful eyes and delicate features, a girl could kid herself his dick wasn't hardwired to his brain. I didn't have to meet him to know he traded on this misconception to get laid. I committed his features to memory, returned the picture, and searched the rest of the room. I found nothing of use.

When I emerged from the dressing room, a door clicked open behind me. Footsteps dragged along the concrete. My heart skipped a beat, and I ducked back inside, extinguishing my flashlight as I did so. The steps echoed my way. No other humans could be up and around; it had to be an Administrator—possibly the inside guy having come to the studio with the same idea as me of turning over Alexis's dressing room. There was nowhere to hide. The wardrobe was too small. Ditto the space beneath the dressing table. All I could do was squeeze behind the door and hope for the best. I drew my gun and held it flat against my side. I doubted the weapon would do much good against a demon, but it was the only talisman I had. The steps were close now, and I could hear the wheeze of laboring lungs. I tensed, ready to fire and run for the hills if discovered, but the feet trudged past. I waited for a count of thirty and chanced a look outside. I thought I saw a stoop-shouldered figure turn left, heading for the exit. I slipped off my shoes and tied a hasty knot in the laces. I slung them around my neck and followed in stockinged feet.

By the time I reached the door, it was flapping open. The figure was moving away, illuminated by the streetlights. The pillow that served as his hunchback stuck out from a pair of grubby dungarees. This wasn't the same guy Alexis had killed, but he was clearly playing the role of one of the axe-wielding clowns of the movie title. My first thought was that Laureen had made a deal with another sinner, but something about the way he walked gave me pause. His legs were barely lifting off the ground, and his arms hung limp by his sides. His hip bumped off the purple fender of Hrag's pimpmobile parked inside the studio compound. He looked like a sleepwalker.

I could have left it alone and gone home to rest up before spending another night combing the Colosseum. That morning, I'd returned to the apartment at five AM and snatched a few hours' sleep before the heat of the day woke me sweating. Fatigue was calling me bedward, but curiosity tugged me into the actor's wake. This nighttime stroll was new to me. I'd always returned to myself in the park, with no indication I'd moved during my sojourn to the Nimrod. Even though the actor was clearly unaware of his actions, he—or the Torment controlling him—appeared to be headed somewhere in particular. He turned left at the end of the street, traveling north along Plastic Avenue, where the surgeons who sculpted the sex workers into more marketable commodities plied their trade. They were the only doctors working in Lost Angeles. If you broke your back in a fight or contracted a weeping disease of the nether regions, all you had to do was kill yourself and wake up good as new. Death lost its power when you knew it wasn't permanent, and suicide was a better solution than paying some quack for treatment or waiting months for your body to heal. It also meant the plastic surgeons did a roaring trade. Any time one of the modified sex workers had a deadly mishap, they had to get their surgery done again.

Deciding there was no further need for stealth, I popped my shoes back on and caught up with the actor. His face was slack—eyes sheathed in black tar, lips mumbling. I trailed him north, out of Astghik and into the outskirts of the Seven Gates. The full moon that always lit the Lost Angeles skies at night rode high above the multistory superstores, shining off the metal signs bearing images of automatic weapons. He carried on at the same shuffling rhythm, paying no attention to his surroundings. Something stirred in an alleyway, sending me sprinting for the cover of a doorway. Another sleepwalker emerged, a bum with a tangled beard and grime caked under his eyes. He didn't exactly fall in behind the actor. Rather, I got the feeling that they happened to be meandering in the same direction. We picked up more along the way, jerky marionettes spilling out of houses, shops, and side streets. By the time we crossed the river in Diyu, more than two dozen drifted along in loose formation—all shambling, black eyed, and muttering. I could see no unifying factor to the crowd beyond their somnambulism: they were men and women, young and old, some of them in the uniforms of the Trustee gangs, some of them in civvies.

When the macabre parade reached Arcadia Road, they veered right. The silhouettes of many more walkers dappled the silver asphalt, swaying and slapping their feet on the ground. My skin crawled. This was no normal evening for them. The Torments were puppeteers, twanging on ligaments and muscles to herd their human vehicles toward an unknown destination. My nerves screamed at me to return home and pull the covers over my head. I had a horrible feeling I was about to receive confirmation of something I'd long suspected. I wasn't sure I wanted this knowledge. I'd never been brave. My wiring just made my curiosity stronger than my fear. So I followed, tucking myself in amongst the pack and giving it my best shamble in case any Administrators were watching from the looming walls of Avici Rise.

About a hundred feet before the road began winding up toward the demon compound, the sleepwalkers cut left. Here, countless feet had tramped the scrubby grass flat. The path curved through a defile between the steep hill sloping up to Avici Rise on the right and the sheer brick walls of the warehouses of Il Terzo Livello on the left, until it terminated at the fringes of the desert. I halted as the procession continued out into the blasted landscape. The sucking sand slowed their progress, but still they slugged on. I was pondering whether to follow—a brief flower of hope let me imagine they were being led to the mountain range, where some secret pass led them out of the city—when the first of them stopped before the folded ridges of a dune. The others followed until they stood in a loose knot perhaps a few hundred strong. I noticed then that the area they stood in was flat. They had passed through an opening in a low wall almost the same color as the sand. The words "holding pen" came unbidden to my mind.

The wind picked up, and dust began to swirl around the sleepwalkers, who as one raised their heads toward Avici Rise. The tornado, contained to the area bounded by the wall, built in speed and height until it obscured the crowd. I heard the squeak of rusty hinges and looked up. The hill leading to the gated community was at its steepest here, a hard scrabble for even the most committed intruder, who would then have to find a way over the high wall at the peak. At the base of the white stone fortification, I could make out a shadowy recess. As I narrowed my eyes, peering into the gloom to search for a gate, a dark shape darted out. My first instinct was to run, but I knew the movement could draw attention to my presence. Instead, I hunkered down, doing my best impression of a boulder. Whatever it was, it moved with frightening, liquid speed—too fast for me to make out details. I could tell the creature was big—at least the height of a man and three times as long. It bounded over the rocks on four legs, launched itself into the air, and sailed into the dust storm.

A few moments of silence followed; even the murmuring voices propelled outward by the whirlwind stilled. Only the hiss of shifting sands continued, fizzing in my ears like a detuned radio. Then a long moan rose across the desert, as if somebody had snapped the channel onto a station. Another followed, and another, and another, until hundreds of throats sang out a dipping and soaring wail. It echoed back from the hills, delayed and amplified so that the eerie chorus thrummed through the air. Every hair on my body stood on end, sparking chills along my hands, neck, and scalp. I forced my way into a bush, burrowing so deep that thorns dug into my flesh. I barely felt them. Through the jagged lattice of leafless branches, I stared at the vortex. There was movement within: dark figures writhing, threshing, and fading as a hulking shadow stalked back and forth. It took a long time, but slowly the wail decreased in intensity, the voices seeming to grow more distant rather than quieter. The shadow pantomime grew ever less frantic until silence returned.

I jumped when, from the top of the cloud, Torments burst out in a shadowy swirl, framed for an instant against the backdrop of the moon. They flew fast and low, passing so close overhead that I could see their blank faces and make out the creases on their wings. I'd never known a Torment to give off a scent, but my nostrils tried to seal up as a jumble of odors assailed them: burnt hair and gunpowder, dried shit and perfume, blood and lollipops, fear sweat and laundry soap—and beneath it all something so corrupt that vomit rose in my throat. When they were gone, I spat until my mouth was parched and the foul taste had receded.

I raised my head in time to see the creature pad out from the cloud. It moved slowly now, sated, giving me a clear view. The thing was black like the Torments, but otherwise it looked nothing like them. It had the head of a crocodile. The body of a lion. The fat haunches of some other beast. It was the monster Laureen kept penned up in the minitower. Like Hrag's boys in their farcical uniforms, it should have looked nonsensical, even pitiful. Yet something about the remorseless way it moved, about the pitiless stare and black razor teeth revealed when it yawned, froze my blood.

Motionless, I held my breath as it clambered up the slope. As soon as the gate creaked shut, the cloud spiraled outward and unfurled into a fuzzy column of dust. The wind whipped my hair as the sand blew past, dancing with the molten faces of hundreds of dust devils. I held my crouch until they had gusted along Arcadia Road and got to my feet. Where the sleepwalkers had been was now an empty clearing.

Now I knew for sure what happened to the disappeared. Now I had confirmation of my nasty suspicion about where the dust devils came from, although I could never have guessed at the gruesome nature of the transformation. They were the shattered remnants of the residents of Lost Angeles, condemned to drift through the streets, plucking desperately at the flesh they'd once known. I didn't know what those souls had done to deserve this next level of punishment, but I did know who was responsible: the Administrators. And I was working for one of them. I stared up at Avici Rise, my hands curling into fists.

I made my way back toward Cajetan on shaky legs, so lost in thought that I barely noticed the city waking up around me. There was so much I didn't get about Lost Angeles, and the more I probed, the less I understood. That was the problem with answers: they always led to more questions. One thing I was sure of, though: I was even more determined to work out what Laureen kept in the box. Everyone thought the Torments were punishment enough for their sins. Well, there was something worse. And what was there beyond what I'd seen? What other retribution did the Administrators hold in reserve? Kept, for example, in an innocuous wooden box?

It bothered me that Laureen was allowing me to roam the city and peel back its layers. She must have known I would wander once my evenings opened up, that I would chance upon the sleepwalkers and follow to witness their fate. Maybe she wanted me to see the scene as a further warning: do your job and don't ask too many questions or you'll join the procession of the damned into the desert. More likely I was already destined to end up the same way one day—we all were—and she figured it didn't matter if I knew what was coming. There wasn't much I could do about it.

When I found myself back on Providence Avenue, the brightly lit Colosseum visible above the rows of gambling joints, I tried to put aside the wider questions and popped into Benny's. I was tempted to buy myself a nine-fingered Mexican and let the tequila broom sweep away the memories of what I'd witnessed. I restricted myself to a single Ward Eight. I still had a job to do, and doing that job was the best way to put the pieces of the puzzle together.

11

I resumed my vigil in the Colosseum, attempting to focus on the task at hand. It wasn't easy; I kept looking at the press of gamblers, wondering which among them would be next to take the one-way shamble into the desert and fearful that Sebastian had already bitten the dust, no pun intended. I needn't have worried. After ten minutes, a tall man in a wide-brimmed fedora, wearing thick glasses and sporting a squinty Fu Manchu moustache, joined a queue in the middle. I cozied up behind him, zeroing in on the left hand jammed into the pocket of his yellow sports jacket. He laid down fifty bucks on each of the ten scheduled fights without batting an eyelid. When he turned to leave, I got a close-up of his profile. I didn't need to see the missing finger to be sure I'd hit the jackpot.

I tossed a buck at the bookie to keep my cover. "Give me Filthy Jack in the first fight."

He picked up my dollar and held it between his thumb and forefinger like a snotty rag. "Big spender, eh? That'll land you exactly ten cents. Jack's a stick-on winner."

"Then you should be grateful I'm not laying down a grand," I said, keeping an eye on Sebastian as he bought some popcorn. "Write me the slip."

He did so with bad grace and tossed it under the grate. I strolled after Sebastian, who was fisting salty snacks into his face as if he didn't have a care in the world. Clearly he fancied himself a master of subterfuge as well as thievery. His confidence was misplaced. He looked like a walking advertisement for a mail-order disguise store. The only thing missing was the sandwich board. If I'd made him so easily, other interested parties could do the same. I hoped his double-crossed employer didn't think he'd be dumb enough to show his face here.

He headed for the turnstiles, which along with the concession stands detracted from the period feel. I doubted the real Colosseum had sold two-dollar rubber death masks, "severed hand" foam gloves, and "buckets of blood"—normal sodas jazzed up with a dash of red food coloring. I'd always found the period setting tacky, the kind of themed nonsense a casino owner with more money than taste would build in Las Vegas, but the customers lapped it up. Sebastian clicked through into the ringside seats. He'd obviously been well remunerated for his treachery: tickets for that area started at one hundred bucks a pop, way too rich for my thin blood. I elected to keep an eye on him from the cheaper seats and follow him once the fights were over. I took note of the section he was sitting in and made my way to the turnstile that would take me into the area overlooking his position.

As I did so, my radar blipped again. This time I whipped around and caught sight of a slender figure ducking behind a hot dog stand. I took a circuit out wide and saw who'd been following me: Franklin. He hadn't been in Benny's the last two nights. I thought he'd taken the hint and gone off to pester somebody else. He'd clearly managed to get his hands on some cash, for he was decked out in new duds. They looked exactly like mine. He was pretending to conduct a forensic examination of the wilted buns, overcooked sausages, and crusted bottles of ketchup and mustard. I wandered over and tapped him on the shoulder.

"So, what you having?" I said. "Hot dog, hot dog, or hot dog?"

He rigged his bookish features into a look of surprise that wouldn't have been out of place on the mug of one of Hrag's execrable actors. "Kat, what a surprise!"

"Cut the crap," I said, grabbing his ear and yanking him off to a quieter corner. "Why are you following me? Like the look of my rosy butt cheeks?"

"I'm not following you." I gave his ear a healthy twist. "Ow! Okay, okay! I'm observing you."

"Same difference," I said, letting go of his blushing earlobe.

He rubbed the side of his head. "I'm watching you work. Trying to pick up some tricks. I want to be a detective like you, remember?"

"How many times do you need me to tell you? You don't have it in you. You should be a librarian. Maybe a bellhop. You'd look sweet in one of those cute hats."

He pouted, managing to make himself look even more like a sullen teenage boy who'd been told he had wrist strain and should lay off any jerky movements. "I happen to know I'd make a top-notch detective. For example, you're obviously interested in the man in the hat and glasses." He forked his fingers and pointed them at his eyes. "See? Powers of observation."

I poked him in one of his keen peepers. "How are those powers now? Listen, Franklin. I'm working a case and don't need you screwing it up. Disappear now before I poke you somewhere more tender."

I walked away, expecting him to wander off with his tail between his legs. He had more balls than I gave him credit for. "You can't make me," he shouted. "I'll keep following you. Maybe I'll even solve the mystery first. Then you'll look stupid. I bet that guy's cheating on his girl. He's probably in there right now, meeting his mistress. And you're missing it."

People were looking in our direction, attention I didn't need on this job. The leads were too frail and the stakes too high. I let him catch up before leaning in and speaking quietly. "Fine. You want to be a glamorous PI? I'll give you some pointers. But not now. If I agree to meet you in Benny's tomorrow afternoon at three, will you get out of here and let me work?"

He nodded his head the way a spaniel wags its tail, a big shit-eating grin plastered over his face. Meeting him would be a waste of my time, but at least the promise would get him out of my hair without creating a scene. I would feed him a few clichéd lines, try to scare him off by sharing a few tales of torture and downright nastiness, and then hopefully be free of the pest. I turned him around, ready to give him a shove toward the exit, when I saw some more familiar faces amid the crowd: the monobrowed muscle and his two pals from Benny's. I pulled Franklin into a corner, putting my finger to my lips when he started to protest, and pointed to the goons. His eyelid twitched, and he shrank behind my shoulder.

"See why it's not a good idea to play in Mom's office?" I said. "Sneak out before they see you. And for God's sake, get yourself some new clothes."

I left him cowering in the corner and sidled to the turnstiles, keeping my gaze on the bully boys. They didn't glance over, instead going straight to the same ringside seat turnstile Sebastian had entered. I frowned. That didn't scan at all. Where did a couple of low-level dunderheads like those three get the cash to rub shoulders with the big boys?

I grudgingly paid twenty bucks for the next level up from the high rollers. I would have preferred the ten-buck nosebleed seats, where there was no chance of a stray eyeball whizzing out of the ring to plop into your beverage, but it would have been too easy to lose Sebastian sitting up there. I pushed through the turnstile into my section and entered the Colosseum proper. Glaring flood-lights studded the high wall that rose from ring level to the first row of seats. In the real Colosseum, the wall's main purpose had been to stop competitors trying to flee; here the aim was to stop fights spilling over into the VIP section. The big spenders paid for a close-up of the action, not to have their heads bashed in by an errant mace. Even with a night breeze circulating, the Colosseum stank of caramel popcorn and beer. The arena would smell a whole lot worse when guts began spilling. The oval roof was open, and the moon hung in the middle like the silver pupil of some great black eye. I wondered if God was up there, watching and disapproving of the savagery being carried out in the name of entertainment. If so, it seemed a bit rich. If humankind truly was made in his image, then all this was his damn fault.

I edged along the busy row and squeezed into a spot directly above and behind Sebastian, sandwiched between a lanky guy in a Filthy Jack T-shirt and an elderly woman waving a Colosseum-branded foam axe. Monobrow and chums were sitting in the row behind Sebastian, about forty feet to his right. They weren't perving on the scantily clad cheerleaders who flipped and tumbled around the ring, instead scrutinizing the faces of the spectators. They were looking for somebody too, although surely not Sebastian. At one point, they seemed to look straight at him, and even that triumvirate of twits could have seen through his disguise. When Monobrow swiveled his neck in my direction, I sank farther into my seat.

With nothing better to do for the moment, I checked out the reserved Trustees' sections to see who was in. Hrag wasn't there, presumably still directing his masterpiece, but Yama sat ram-rod straight, surrounded by bodyguards. The drug lord looked deceptively harmless. He wore a sober black suit, and his graying hair was sculpted into a tidy side-parting. Yama was a diminutive man, and the wire-frame glasses he wore gave him the look of an accountant. I knew the only thing he liked counting was the number of enemies chained in his dungeons. Yama was a man I'd made a big effort not to cross. Sure, he couldn't kill you and make it stick, but languishing in a cell at the mercy of his torturers was a damn sight worse.

The other Trustee present was Adnan al Kassar. He lounged on the red cushioned chair set aside for him, one chubby arm around a voluptuous blonde, the other around a tall woman with a sculpted afro and a dress that plunged to the curve of her lower back. He was slurping a jumbo soda through a curly blue straw, pausing every now and then to let the blonde feed him peanuts. His saggy jowls wobbled as he crunched. He walked his hairy-knuckled fingers down the spine of the woman in the skimpy dress. She snuggled closer. Although not handsome—his nose resembled a squashed tomato, and his skin was as pockmarked as the predesert scrublands—Adnan was a ladies' man of the highest order. It wasn't power that made him attractive, though it helped. He had more charisma than a Hollywood leading man and, according to the rumors, enjoyed nothing more than employing his vast repertoire of sexual techniques to bring about screaming multiple orgasms in his belles of the hour.

I knew Adnan well. He'd offered me a full-time job when I'd helped him track down a gang that was ripping off his weapons. I believe he ripped off their arms in return. Repeatedly. When I declined his proposal, he didn't hold it against me. He respected a woman who knew her own mind. I was about to get up and invite myself to join him—his section was closer to Sebastian—when a fanfare trilled and the cheerleaders cartwheeled to the side of the ring. A short, bald man in a toga and laurel wreath bounded to the center of the arena, waving his hands over his head and egging on the applause.

"Friends, Lost Angelenos, countrymen. Welcome to the Colosseum," he bellowed into a microphone. "Are you ready for blood?" The crowd roared in the affirmative, tossing popcorn into the air like confetti. My neighbor bopped me on the head with the axe in her enthusiasm. "Then blood you shall have, by the bucket! To the mayhem!"

He ran through the program quickly: ten fights over two hours involving weapons ranging from knuckle-dusters to swords to chainsaws—with a short intermission to allow replenishment of snacks and the purchase of more merchandise. Tonight appeared to be single combat. On other evenings, they ran Roman-era battles, teams of gladiators hacking each other into bloody chunks; old West–style gunfights; death races (the cars were packed with explosives, which detonated in the losing vehicles when the winner crossed the line); and even an amateur night—when the loudmouths who fancied themselves better than the pros could sign up and watch their flying teeth glitter in the floodlights.

When the mob was suitably inflamed, the compere climbed to his position in the main tribune. Then the festivities began. Filthy Jack, a rangy brawler with unkempt red hair, lived up to both his name and his short odds—biting, gouging, and, when he was done messing around to please his fans, snapping the neck of his opponent. Even if I got nothing out of Sebastian, at least I was ten cents up. The next fight was between two women in bikinis carrying flick knives. I was glad of the extra distance my seat afforded as they set about each other at close quarters until one of them succumbed to multiple stab wounds. The weapons grew larger as the bouts went on; soon the ring was piebald with patches of bloody mud. I watched Sebastian as the fights continued. Filthy Jack's victory aside, he didn't seem to be doing well. His shoulders slumped ever lower, and by the time we reached the final fight, a pile of crumpled betting slips sat on the wall in front of him.

The chainsaw duel was the big finale, and it looked to be a horrendous mismatch. The competitors were dressed in brown leather loincloths and gloves. The first one in the ring stood nearly seven feet tall and introduced himself by juggling the whirring weapon—at one point lying on his back and catching it with his feet as the blade buzzed inches from his nose. The other guy was a midget by comparison; he looked like a dweeby drone dressed up as Tarzan for the office Christmas party. He dragged his chainsaw as he came into the ring, leaving a furrow of sand in his wake.

As the compere dropped his arm to signal the start of the bout, the little guy was still yanking on the pull cord. The big lout rushed in, holding the chainsaw aloft in one hand as if it were a novelty balloon. He swung, and the little guy ducked at the last minute, losing a lock of hair. He took advantage of his opponent's slow recovery to back off, finally getting his chainsaw going. They circled each other, saws spitting out a stuttering buzz.

"Stick it up his scrawny ass!" my neighbor bawled, again getting too frisky with her axe.

I leaned to the right to avoid the foamy swish, keeping half an eye on Sebastian. He was leaning forward, right hand splayed across his forehead, watching the fight through his fingers. It looked like he'd taken what must have been long odds on the little guy, who was darting glances left and right in a futile search for escape routes. Once the fighters were in the ring, the gates slammed down on the tunnels, and he was too small to leap up and get a handhold on the perimeter wall. His one way out was to get sawn up.

Minigladiator seemed to realize he was on to a loser, for his shoulders slumped, and the tip of his blade dipped. The beast spotted his chance and gunned his saw as it honed in on the smaller combatant's stomach. The crowd, sensing the fight was about to reach a gory conclusion, thrummed. At the last possible instant, the little guy spun counterclockwise with a grace he'd clearly been concealing. The thrust sailed harmlessly past as he swung his own weapon in a downward diagonal arc. The chainsaw whined as blade met flesh in the back of the big man's thigh. A roar went up, drowning out the screams of pain, and the spectators jumped to their feet. I followed suit reluctantly, not wanting to lose sight of Sebastian. I rose in time to see gobs of meat splatter off the whirring saw as the hustler finished the job.

Sebastian was jigging in a circle, hands held aloft in triumph. His fake moustache was swinging from one side of his lip like a hairy spider leg. The missing finger was clearly visible. I wasn't the only one who'd noticed. Monobrow was pushing his way through the throng, sidekicks coasting in his wake. His gaze was trained on the thief. We were looking for the same man after all. Monobrow was more stupid than I thought; it had taken him almost two hours to identify a guy in the world's worst disguise sitting damn near on top of him. The revelation raised questions about what they'd been doing in Benny's the other night, but I didn't have time to consider them right now. I couldn't let them get to Sebastian first. The cocky thief hadn't even noticed he was in peril. My plan to follow him was ruined, but maybe I could work this wrinkle in my favor by playing the savior.

I was much farther away, but I got lucky when Monobrow grew too liberal with the shoulder. The offended party delivered a roundhouse punch that caught the goon on the side of the head. Monobrow's boys retaliated. Within seconds, a good half dozen people were flailing at each other. I snatched the foam axe from the woman's hand and ran down the aisle to the wall dropping into the ringside area. The axe had enough heft that it flew more or less in a straight line and bounced off the thief's shoulder. He looked around and saw me waving my arms at him. I jabbed my finger to the right. His gaze followed, and the moustache fell off as his mouth dropped. Monobrow had clubbed his way through the brawl and was closing in. I couldn't fault the thief's decision making. He calculated that he would get snarled up if he tried to flee along the aisle and vaulted over the wall into the ring. He sprinted toward one of the gates, which had opened at the end of the fight.

Monobrow changed direction to follow, fumbling for his gun. I weaved back to the turnstile. I'd never outpace the athletic thief in a footrace, but he'd have to take a long circuit back around to reach the competitors' exit. I had a shot at heading him off, particularly as the crowds had yet to start filing out. When I emerged onto the street, I made a beeline for the closest parked car and smashed the window to the disinterest of the hookers waiting outside to proposition those successful gamblers with money to burn. I hot-wired the car in less than thirty seconds and screeched off in the direction of the exit I expected Sebastian to use. I pulled up to the curb as he flew out, timing it so well that he had to put his hands out to stop himself from slamming into the bodywork.

"Alexis sent me," I said out of the broken window, the lie slipping instinctively off my tongue.

He glared at me. For a moment, I thought he was going to trust his legs to get him out of trouble, no doubt weighing up whether he'd sooner face a savage and imprecise beating from three large thugs or a forensic thumping from Alexis. The bullet that pinged off the car roof made up his mind. He hauled open the back door and dove in. I was halfway up the street and around the corner before he managed to pull his legs in.

12

I drove erratically—taking random turns, weaving through lanes, accelerating and braking like a highly strung teenager in driver's ed—until I cut off five of Hrag's boys in an electric pink Pontiac Chieftain with a picture of their boss stenciled on the bonnet. They loosed off a few badly aimed shots but didn't give chase. Sure we weren't being followed and keen not to attract the attention of any more road warriors, I took the on-ramp to Route 666 and cruised in the slow lane.

I didn't think the goons had spotted me. Sebastian's body would have obscured their view of my face, and I'd burned more rubber than a week-long swingers' convention before they hit the street. But it wasn't worth taking the risk of going to Benny's or my apartment in case they'd seen me. A less suspicious woman might have chalked up their appearance at Benny's to coincidence. Not me. There were good odds the inside guy had discovered that Laureen was planning to hire me and that he'd instructed his pet humans to keep tabs on me. Not having enough brains to rub together to create even the tiniest spark, they'd arrived early and passed the time getting stabby on Franklin. They were on the hunt for Laureen's trinket too; at least now I knew who to look out for along the way.

Having Sebastian put me one step ahead of the competition, but I didn't want to start straight in with the questions. That would make it too obvious that I had a hidden agenda. I looked at the betting slip still clutched in his fist. "How'd you do in the last fight?"

Like all gambling addicts, he couldn't resist boasting about his good judgment, conveniently glossing over the preceding losing bets. "They gave me twenty-five to one on the midget."

"Good move. Always bet on the little guy. Just ask Goliath. I think I saw him in the deli queue the other week."

"Yeah. It's like dogs. It's always the tiny one's gonna bite your ankles. I put fifty bucks down on him."

Too late, he twigged he'd informed me he was holding a chit for over a thousand dollars. He pocketed the slip in a hurry, like I hadn't already seen it.

"Don't worry. I'm not after your winnings," I said.

"I guess that means Alexis is tossing plenty *fetti* your way to find me."

"You think she's paying me in cheese?"

"It means money, dumbass. What gave me away? The finger? It's always the fucking finger."

He got that look I'd seen a million times around town: a thousand-yard stare back to the moment of his death. His light fingers must have stolen something, and being light one finger must have gotten him recognized and rubbed out. It seemed he had a habit of stealing from the wrong people.

"That and the pubic hair you glued to your face," I said. "When you go back to pick up your winnings, get yourself a better disguise."

"Who are you? Pistachio Disguisey?"

His cultural reference sailed over my head. That was the thing I hated most about talking to people who'd lived after I died. It reminded me the world had gone on without me.

"Try going in drag," I said.

He curled his lip. "You serious?"

"The more flamboyant a disguise, the better it works. When you're a big man in suspenders and a basque, nobody looks closely at your face."

For once, I wasn't being a smartass. In LA, Danny had once gone undercover to get close to a transvestite who was blackmailing those upstanding gentlemen availing themselves of his erotic services. The disguise even fooled me. I remembered the day he walked into my office in full drag, talking in a camp voice and pretending to be interested in hiring me. I only caught on because he was wearing one of my few dresses, a cute little red number I wore when we went dancing. I locked the door and made him take it off. I lost myself in the memory, recalling the way I'd had to wrestle the frilly panties down his erection (he was an all-or-nothing kind of guy) and the sweaty, giggling wrestle that had followed.

"What you grinning at?" Sebastian said.

I snapped back to the present, for a moment unsure where I was. Then it hit me. I'd remembered Danny as my lover, not as my victim. I felt an unfamiliar warmth swell in my chest. It could have been hope; it could have been happiness; it could have been relief. It had been so long since I'd felt any real positive emotion that I couldn't tell the difference. I wanted more.

"I remembered something," I said.

I got onto the off-ramp near Il Terzo Livello to double back down Route 666, the unblemished memory tucked away in my skull for replaying later. Now that I'd broken the ice, I could tease out what I needed to know on the move—it was safer that way. Sebastian, who'd been fidgeting the whole time, struck me as the kind of guy who needed to fill silences, so I decided to shut up for a while. Things would go smoother if he seemed to be leading the conversation.

"Alexis isn't mad at me?" he said after a minute of my best stony-faced taciturnity.

"Oh, she's madder than a hatful of hornets. I wouldn't want to be in your shoes when she gets hold of you. Although I suppose the makeup sex would be spectacular."

"She likes to stab a fork into my *cojones* when she comes. She's a fucking psycho. Drop me off downtown. Tell her you couldn't find me."

"Can't do that. She wants me to bring you in. I guess she's feeling horny. And stabby."

I'd hoped to avoid resorting to threats, but Sebastian tensed. His hand sneaked toward the door handle. If he was prepared to dive onto a highway from a car traveling at seventy rather than face Alexis, he wasn't joking about her preference for violent sex. No wonder he'd vanished without telling her. I whipped out my gun, abandoning all plans to tease out the information.

"I'll shoot your other fingers off if you make a move for the latch." I could sense him calculating the odds as he looked at my hand. "You might be fast enough to grab the gun before I fire, but then we're going to have ourselves a jolly little crash when I yank the wheel. That's going to hurt. Besides, there's no need for unpleasantness when we can cut a deal."

His gaze never left my gun as he responded. "Alexis didn't send you, did she?"

"You got me. She didn't think you were worth my day rate. Doesn't matter; I'm sure she'll still whip out the cutlery when we get to her place. Maybe it doesn't have to go that way, though. If you tell me what I need to know, I'll let you slink off."

"What'd you wanna know?"

"I want to talk about your job up at Avici Rise."

His eyes narrowed. "How'd you know about that?"

"I know a lot of things I shouldn't. Whereas you don't know a lot of things you should. Like who you stole from and what a bad idea it was."

"I'm not a *pendejo*. I checked it wasn't Yama, Hrag, or Adnan."

"You stole from somebody much worse. You stole from the Administrators."

"You're just trying to scare me," he said, but his voice wobbled.

"Even the Trustees don't have enough money or power to live up on Avici Rise. If not them, who?"

Again, it was a question I should have asked myself a long time ago. Laureen and her pals must have projected some kind of collective mental blind spot onto the general populace to keep themselves hidden. That was a smart move. The city seethed with resentment against the Administrators, and it wasn't like we had much to lose. If they stayed out in the open, let everybody know they were lording it over us from a position of luxury, we'd have been over the walls waving pitchforks and burning torches long ago. The Jedi mind trick wasn't working on me any longer.

Sebastian leaned to his right, but instead of going for the door handle, he beat his head against the window. "I knew something wasn't right. You working for them?"

"I am, which means you're in a world of trouble. You think the Torments are bad? They've got far worse up their sleeves." Even though I was laying it on thick to spook Sebastian into talking, I thought of the cloud of newly born dust devils and shivered. "The good news is they don't care about you. They just want what's theirs. Answer my questions, and I can make it go away. Let's start with who hired you."

One of the negatives about working alone had always been the limitations it brought to my scare factor. If you were in a mob, intimidating people into talking was easy; all you had to was drop the name of whichever sadistic loon you worked for and hint that said maniac would be displeased if he didn't get what he wanted. All I'd ever had were a big mouth and a small gun, the former useless without the threat of the latter. When I was alive, my marks knew I couldn't shoot them despite any threats I made, since I was a licensed investigator. In Lost Angeles, I could shoot as many people as I liked, but the threat didn't carry the same impact. So it was remarkably gratifying to raise the specter of the demons and watch Sebastian's defiance crumble.

"Those three machos you saw," he said in a flat voice, "they came to see me a week ago. The big one called himself Jake. The others didn't say much."

"You never met anybody else?"

"No. But I could tell they were hired help. They gave me plans of Avici Rise and told me when and how to get in."

"And how did you get in?"

"I climbed up from the desert. Somebody left a gate open."

The gate through which the creature had descended upon its prey. It was definitely an inside job. "Did you see anybody, anything, inside? No big guard dogs, for example?"

"Place was deserted, like they told me it would be."

"And did Jake give you the combination for the safe?"

"He didn't know it. I cracked it myself."

"Then what?"

"I was to meet Jake at a bar in Eleutherios, give him the goods."

"But you didn't."

"No. I ran into some middleman looking for high-end shit after Jake gave me the job. I don't know how he found out I'd been hired to break in to Avici, but he offered me four times what I was being paid for whatever I got out, no questions asked. So I sold him the box. Then I hid out."

Sebastian's explanation of the chain of events fit with what I'd suspected. If it had been a straight ransom job from the beginning, the thief would have left the note in the safe. Instead, the note had been delivered later, once Sebastian had sold the box on. I understood what the person who now had the box wanted, but I still had nothing other than guesses as to why Sebastian had been hired to steal it in the first place. That worried me. In my experience, it was the unknowns in a case that usually bit you on the ass.

"Who was the middleman?" I asked.

"I don't know his name. He never told me."

"What's he look like?"

"Fat. Goatee beard. Wears three-piece suits. Big flappy ears like an elephant."

There were plenty of other brokers and middlemen operating in town apart from Enitan. I knew a lot of them, but Sebastian's description didn't ring any bells. "Do you know who he sells to?"

"The money he deals in, the things he's looking for—has to be a Trustee. I don't know which one."

I slapped the wheel, almost sending the car swerving into a truck. I'd had a feeling the Trustees would end up involved, but I'd been hoping I was wrong. If one of them had the box, that complicated matters. I briefly considered using my freedom of movement during the early evening to search for the box but discounted the option. I had eight Trustees to get through, and they owned hundreds of premises between them. The box could have been stashed in any of these locations. I would need months to comb them all. One week remained on Laureen's deadline. I needed to narrow the field. Then I would have a chance of stealing it back, which would be easy enough considering I could carry out my break-in while everybody was with their Torment.

Even so, I was nervous. Once the box went missing, the guilty Trustee would try to find out who took it. They would question Sebastian, which would lead to me. I hoped Yama didn't have the damn thing. I didn't fancy having one torture canceled only to be consigned to another involving electrodes and my nipples. I'd have to be very smart and very, very careful. My mind was turning to how to track down the broker, something I hoped Enitan could help with, when I remembered something Sebastian had said.

"You mentioned there was a hinky element to the job. What exactly?"

"Jake gave me a bag to carry the box in. He told me to wear gloves, not to touch it. But I took the gloves off to break the safe and forgot to put them back on."

"And?"

"It was some freaky shit. The box was small but crazy heavy. When I touched it, I heard this whisper in my head. It was my own voice. But not."

He paused, getting the distant stare on again and hugging himself.

"What did the voice say?"

"It told me humanity is drowning in sin. I can't be saved. Nobody can. It told me it would end my suffering, give me peace. I wanted to open it. I never wanted anything more."

"I'm assuming you didn't."

He shook his head, more to clear it than to answer in the negative. "I couldn't. There was no catch, no lid, *nada*. I put it down to get a knife and force it open. The moment I let go, the voice disappeared. I put my gloves on, stuffed it in the bag, and ran."

I looked at him incredulously—not because I didn't believe his story. This was Lost Angeles, and it had already become clear that this was no ordinary box. I was amazed at how dumb he'd been. "And you still sold it on. Didn't you stop to wonder who might own a psychic talking box? Didn't you think you were in over your head?"

He shrugged. "Four times the price. I told myself I'd imagined it. Who hasn't thought we'd be better off with nothing than this place? If there was a way to end it all, wouldn't you take it?"

I didn't answer. I'd already tried to end it all, which had turned out to be a mistake. But if there was a way out, some means to escape into the void, would I take it? Four days before, the answer might have been yes. If the box really did contain canned suicide, a final extinction for the opener, I could see how it would seem desirable to many—a reward more than a punishment. Now, with my Torment held at bay and Danny slowly coming back to me, I felt different. Besides, the questions I'd somehow never asked myself were crowding in, demanding to be answered. The scales had fallen from my eyes when Laureen had revealed herself, and I intended to find out as much as I could about the keepers of this zoo.

13

Franklin was waiting at Benny's when I straggled in bleary-eyed and fifteen minutes late for our appointment the next day. It had been almost four AM when I dropped off Sebastian. I'd returned the car to where I'd stolen it, popping fifty bucks in the glove compartment for the gas and broken window. There was a chance another thief would whisk away the car, and the money with it, before the owner reclaimed the vehicle, but I'd long ago decided not to live my life in relative terms. Many times, above and below, I'd witnessed the tendency of humans to excuse their own bad behavior by pointing to somebody who was a bigger shit than they were. I followed my own code of conduct, not one set by the lowest common denominator.

Once I'd made amends, I strolled home and lurked in a doorway across from my apartment for a while. I wanted to make sure Jake and his buddies weren't around. I saw no sign of them and hit the hay. I attempted to trawl up the happy memory of Danny, hoping it would follow me into my dreams. This time, perhaps because I was trying to remember rather than letting it happen, I saw his dead face again. The soft whisper of guilt told me I had no right to be happy, no right to remember the good times. It wouldn't listen when I wheeled out the arguments for the defense and tried to persuade it that I'd suffered enough. My crime hadn't been erased; it was only being allowed to fade into the background.

I lay awake, doing the Torment's job for it, until I drifted into an uneasy sleep as dawn blushed the curtains.

I didn't get out of bed until two PM, still struggling to shake off the images of Danny's last hitching breaths. The first thing I did after making myself a strong coffee was call Enitan, hoping he could give me a lead on the other broker—thus giving me a valid excuse to call off on Franklin. Enitan didn't answer, which meant I was stuck giving the kid a lesson. I supposed it was for the best. The sooner I got him—and his pesky enthusiasm—out of my hair, the better.

"How did the case go?" Franklin asked as I sat down.

"Oh, the usual. Stole a car, got shot at, saved a guy, threatened him, and, for my troubles, came out with nothing more than another slim lead. That's the first thing you've got to know, Franklin: a PI is like a dog chasing its own tail. You spend your time running after something that never seems to get any closer and often end up back where you started. And what exactly are you doing?"

Franklin was hunched over the counter, scribbling in a notebook he'd produced from a scarred satchel that looked like it had done serious dumpster time. "I'm taking notes. Look." He showed me the cover of the notebook, upon which he'd written in fancy, curling letters: *The Murphy Guide to Being a Dick.*

"Is that supposed to be funny?"

A giggle answered my question. I sighed and ordered myself a soda water. It was too early to start drinking, but I had a feeling I was going to need to very soon. I consoled myself with a cigarette.

"What was the lead you got?" Franklin said.

"None of your business."

"You're supposed to be teaching me. How can I learn if you won't tell me things? Can't we make your investigation a case study?"

"Didn't you go to school? We start with theory and then move on to practical. Tell me, what would you say is the golden rule of being a private investigator?"

Franklin scrunched up his brow. "Keep your gun handy and never miss?"

"No. A gun's your last resort. If you have to use it, you've made a mistake somewhere down the line."

I thought again of Danny. If only I'd not taken Bruno's anger so lightly, tried to smooth things over. Even if I'd gone to him and he'd killed me himself, Danny wouldn't have had to die for my stupidity. My second fatal shot was a mistake too, if mainly one of timing. I'd looked out for Bruno down the years, sure he would end up in Lost Angeles one day, dreaming up agonizing ways to rectify my error of failing to make him pay. He never pitched up. After a while, I became convinced he never would; he was the kind of slippery customer who would die old and gray in his own bed, his sins confessed and wiped clean by the family priest. I told myself it was probably for the best; the slimy bastard would fit right in around these parts and have himself a whale of a time.

I realized Franklin was looking at me expectantly. He must have come up with another suggestion while I was busy flagellating myself. "Sorry, I drifted off for a minute."

"I said, never take your eyes off your enemy?"

"You should be making sure your enemy never lays eyes on you." Again, another rule I'd broken with Bruno.

"Always stick to the facts?"

I forced myself to concentrate on the conversation, knowing that if I kept returning to the old wounds, I'd be useless for the rest of the day. "In this line of work, there's no such thing as fact. There's only what people tell you."

117

"God, I don't know. Be rude and obtuse to everyone you meet? Ask lots and lots of questions but never answer any yourself? Never wear pink braces on a stakeout?"

"Always assume everybody is lying."

"That seems a bit cynical. People tell the truth most of the time, don't they?"

"Maybe, but look at it this way: somebody's going to lie to you at some point. If you believe whatever you're told, that's when you get caught with your pants down. If you don't believe anything, you're always prepared."

Franklin sniffed. "Doesn't sound like an optimistic way to live your life."

"Life? Optimistic? You're in Hell. It applies double down here. This place is full of liars and cheats who'd screw you over in a heartbeat. If you don't want to stay in Desert Heights for a very long time, never mind become an investigator, you're going to have to wise up."

"Okay, but if I assume everyone is lying, that means you're lying to me about having to assume everyone is lying, which means I shouldn't listen to you."

"There's room in this bar for one smartass, and that's me. Do you want me to teach you or not?"

His guileless face crinkled up in consternation. "Of course I do. I'm not trying to be smart. I'm confused."

"Tell you what," I said, "assume everyone is a liar apart from me, and you'll be fine."

Franklin made a note in black ink and circled it with red pen. He also had blue and green pens and a short wooden ruler lined up alongside the notebook. This was going to be a slog. A few basic rules couldn't replace gut instinct, and he didn't have it.

The phone rang, and Benny answered. "It's for you."

"Kat!" Enitan said when I gratefully picked up the receiver. "How are you, my dear?"

I glowered at Franklin, who was further embellishing key points in green ink. "I've been better. I called you earlier."

"I thought that might be you. I was busy reading. I have uncovered something about your monster. Can you come over?"

"Love to. I've got something else to ask you about anyway."

"Most excellent. I will see you soon."

I hung up and headed to the exit. "I need to go," I told Franklin. "Important business."

"What? We've been here five minutes."

"And I've already given you the sum of my knowledge. This isn't rocket science."

His shoulders hunched, and he looked at me with puppy dog eyes. "But you promised you would teach me. Or was that a lie?"

I rubbed my forehead and looked longingly at the bottles stocked behind the bar. I didn't have time to schedule another session, as I'd be too busy trying to run down Sebastian's broker and figuring out how to bypass the army of whichever Trustee the trail led to. But Franklin was right: I'd made him a promise. And I was only going to see Enitan; it wasn't as if we would run into any situations the kid could mess up. "Fine. You can come, but keep your mouth shut, don't touch anything, and don't tell anybody I'm your teacher. You can say you're my manservant."

Franklin bundled his stationery into the satchel and skipped after me as I stomped to the door. At least one of us was happy.

14

Enitan dished out the customary hug when I entered his shop and looked at the kid with frank curiosity. I'd considered asking Franklin to watch the car, pitching it as stakeout practice, but decided I'd probably end up having to rescue him from a mugger. My new plan involved passing him off as a babysitting job for a client, hinting he was soft in the head and prone to getting into trouble—which was close enough to the truth to be convincing.

"And who is this fine young man?" Enitan said.

I opened my mouth, but Franklin beat me to it. "I'm Kat's apprentice."

The fence laughed at the thunderous look on my face, clutching his jiggling belly. "So the venerable master has taken on a pupil. It is long past time. Knowledge should be passed on, not hoarded."

"He's not my apprentice," I said. "He's a monumental pain in the ass."

"Now, now. Do not speak this way in front of your student. You will teach him bad habits."

"You're one to talk about bad habits. Started wearing underwear yet?"

"Some beasts were not meant to be tamed by the inventions of man. My manhood longs to soar on the breeze like a proud eagle, not cower in a cotton cave like a timorous mouse."

Franklin shot me a questioning look, which I ignored. "Speaking of real beasts, you've got something to show me?"

"Yes, yes. Follow me."

Enitan led us into the back room, which smelled even fustier than the front shop. There may have been a window somewhere, but if so, the stacks of paper teetering along every wall obscured it. Stray manuscripts carpeted the floor, making the surface treacherous to walk on. The paper towers, leaning against each other like drunks, vibrated in sync with Enitan's heavy footfalls. I worried he might start an avalanche and bury us.

"Looks like you're the one who needs an apprentice to sort this mess out for you," I said. "Ever heard of a filing system?"

"I do have a system," Enitan said, seating himself at an elegant carved wooden table upon which a manuscript shone white in the small pool of light cast by a cockerel-shaped lamp. "Your brain is merely too miniscule to comprehend its complexity."

Franklin was gazing around the room, mouth hanging open. "Are these all books?"

"Yes," Enitan said. "The combined knowledge and wisdom of the sinners who have passed through this realm. Feel free to browse. Two dollars for one, five dollars for three."

"Wow," Franklin said and began peering at the titles of the bound books on the closest stack.

He probably would have been less impressed had he read half of the tomes. I hadn't started *War and Peace*, mainly because I'd yet to get over the travesty of *Moby Dick*—which the reauthor had somehow morphed into a salty sea dog tale of pirates, high-seas battles, and sexual congress with attractive mermaids.

"How is your Egyptian mythology?" Enitan said.

"About as good as my knitting."

"Then let me enlighten you." He spun the manuscript and slapped a finger on the open page. "I knew I had seen your creature somewhere before."

I leaned over the page to view a well-executed drawing of the monster I'd seen emerge from the dust cloud. The text itself was scrawled and difficult to read, particularly as Enitan's arm partially blocked the light. "What is it?"

"That is the Ammit, the devourer of the dead. As you can see, she has the head of a crocodile, the torso of some kind of wild cat, possibly a lion, and the hind legs of a hippopotamus."

"Ah, a hippo. I would have guessed cow. What does this Ammit do?"

"According to ancient Egyptian religion, the Ammit was a female demon who resided by the scales of justice in the underworld. When the dead came to be judged, their hearts were placed upon a scale to be weighed against the feather of *Ma'at*, or truth. If the scales balanced, the sinner would continue on to the afterlife and blissful immortality."

"And if they didn't balance?"

"The Ammit would devour the heart of the unfortunate sinner, making them suffer the 'second death' and condemning them to an eternity as a restless spirit."

"No offense, Enitan, but do you believe this particular copy is accurate?"

"Oh, it's accurate," said Franklin. He brushed past me and looked down at the drawing. "Not a bad likeness, actually."

I grabbed his shoulder, my heart beating faster. "How do you know about this?"

Franklin flinched at the vehemence in my voice. "Religious historian, remember? I've studied every major world religion, including those from ancient times. I didn't go too deeply into the Egyptian side of things, but I know the Ammit."

I released him and grasped the edge of the desk. Not only was the physical description accurate—the mythology ran close to what I'd seen: the Ammit devouring lines of sinners and consigning them to their second death as dust devils.

Enitan was looking at me, one eyebrow kinked up. "Tell me again where you saw this drawing."

"I didn't see the drawing. I saw the real deal."

He stepped so close that our noses almost touched. "Where?"

"In the desert, by Avici Rise."

"What were you doing out there?"

Franklin was staring at me as intently, and it was this attentiveness that stopped me from spilling the whole story. Had we been alone, I would have told Enitan all about Laureen's problem, my Torment being called off, and the dreadful scene I'd witnessed. I didn't know Franklin well enough to trust him not to blab and draw attention to what I was up to. As it was, I'd already slipped up in my flustered state by revealing that I'd seen the Ammit in the flesh.

"Making castles in the sand," I said, flicking my eyes toward Franklin.

Franklin's gaze was fixed on the drawing. He had the look Enitan sometimes got when he was engrossed in one of his manuscripts. It occurred to me then that maybe Franklin wasn't a dead loss after all. I wasn't going to give him any details, but if he really was an expert on religions, he might have some insight on Lost Angeles. "Franklin, tell me what you think of this place."

"This room? It's marvelous. A touch untidy but all the same."

"I mean Lost Angeles. Hell. You studied human visions of the afterlife. Were you surprised when you arrived here? By what it was like, I mean?"

"I should say so. Pretty much every imagining of Hell depicts constant torture, vicious supernatural beings punishing sinners in gruesome ways. Lost Angeles is probably closest to Swedenborg's vision of Hell as a decaying city where the inhabitants brutalize each other. But the fit isn't exact, because we also have the Torments. And then there's the fact that people are allowed to sin and sin again without any apparent further penalty. Plus the names of the districts are unusual."

"What do you mean?"

"Well, take Avici. In Buddhism, Avici is the lowest level of Hell. Lots of graphic torture, multiple deaths and rebirths, and more torture for millions of years. Then you have the Seven Gates, named after the seven gates of Hell in Islam. Or Il Terzo Livello, the Third Level. In Dante's *Inferno*, a vision based on Christianity, that's where the gluttonous were damned. Plus you saw an Ammit, which is Egyptian."

"The Trustees named most of the districts," I said.

"I didn't know that. Makes it more fascinating. As far as I can tell from preliminary observations, this place is a mishmash of different beliefs. The real question, though, is one of chicken and egg. Do different human religions reflect certain aspects of this place, or does this place reflect certain aspects of human religions?"

"How long have you been here?" Enitan asked.

"A week."

"You seem to know a lot about the city already," I said.

Franklin blushed. "I was always a quick study. I'm trying to treat it like a research project, to take my mind off all the nastiness."

Enitan, never shy, stood up and gave Franklin his first hug. "I like you, young man. How would you feel about writing a book on this city? We have some books that go back down the years, mainly biographies, which you could use as source materials. What we do not have is a definitive history. With your keen mind, you could create a masterpiece that would sell by the tens of thousands. I could give you, say, a fifteen percent royalty."

"I could do that," Franklin said.

My mood picked up as I saw an opportunity to get shot of him. "Looks like you're the one with an apprentice now, Enitan."

"I'd still like to learn to investigate," Franklin said.

"Nonsense," Enitan said, the dollar signs almost visible in his eyes. "Why would you want to get involved in all that sordid business when you can become a best-selling author? Stick with me, young fellow, and you will go far. Allow me to find one of my standard contracts, and you can sign at this very moment."

Enitan rummaged in his desk, tossing pieces of paper out to join the mess on the floor. Franklin looked at me uncertainly. I shrugged. "Don't try to fight it. Once the juggernaut is in motion, you either jump on board or get mown down."

"I am a force of nature!" Enitan yelled, standing up to wave a fountain pen and a contract. "Sign here." As Franklin put his name on the dotted line, Enitan raised a finger in the air. "It occurs to me that perhaps Franklin can also help on the matter of the box. I was unable to turn up anything, but he seems to be far more knowledgeable."

Franklin finished signing, taking great care over his handwriting, before looking up. "I'm happy to help. What box are you talking about?"

I glared at Enitan. Asking Franklin about the city in general was one thing, but the box was part of a case, and an important one at that. I never talked about cases to external parties, mainly due to the fear of getting the job whipped out from under my nose by an enterprising rival—a thought that again brought an unsullied memory of Danny. Still, it had been mentioned now. Maybe Franklin would know something useful. I didn't have to reveal any significant details.

"There's a box I heard about," I said. "Very old, carved into the shape of a globe. It seems to have some sort of power, most likely not benign. It may be of significance to Hell."

"Hmm. Can I see it?"

"I don't have it."

"Shame. Offhand, the one thought that comes to mind is Pandora's box."

"Of course," Enitan said. "A classic tale."

"Indeed," said Franklin. "It's a complicated Greek myth, dating from around 700 BC. According to the tale, Zeus gave Pandora, the first woman, to Prometheus's brother, Epimetheus, as a bride. As a wedding gift, he gave them a box—well, actually a jar, according to early versions of the story, which became perverted in translation—and warned them never to open it. But this was an elaborate revenge plot against Prometheus, who had annoyed Zeus by stealing fire from Heaven. Zeus knew Pandora's curiosity would get the better of her. She opened it, and all the evils of the world came pouring out."

"But it was actually a jar," I said.

"Yes, but we can't take it too literally. It was a story, after all. The older a story, the more significance it accumulates. Perhaps some of today's works of fiction will form the basis of belief systems in the future. Anyway, stories come from somewhere—some divine inspiration or muse, if you believe writers. And if our myths and religions were somehow influenced by the real afterlife, it's possible the story was based on this box. This is all a hypothesis, of course. I'd need to know more. I'd need to see the thing."

I didn't like the sound of a box containing all the evils of the world, one that spoke to the bearer and tried to seduce them into opening it. Then again, in the myth, the box had already been opened. And you only had to take a stroll around Lost Angeles to see that all the evils of the world had been unleashed a long time ago. If this was Pandora's box, it was empty and therefore worthless, which didn't tie in with Laureen's desire to get it back. No, there was definitely something inside, something Sebastian thought would bring him oblivion. Franklin was barking up the wrong tree.

"Thanks for the theory, but I can't tell you much more. It's something I came across and was curious about."

Franklin gave me an appraising look. I was beginning to wonder if he wasn't as gullible as he seemed. "It does sound intriguing. I can keep an eye out for more in Enitan's library while I research the book."

"You do that," I said, grateful for anything that would keep him from dogging my footsteps. "Why don't you get started now? Enitan and I are going outside for a smoke. It's a fire risk in here."

Enitan looked as though he was going to protest that he didn't smoke, but he read my glance and nodded. We left Franklin running his fingers along the stacks and stepped out onto the street.

"So," Enitan said, "you seem to have gotten yourself wrapped up in something more tantalizing than the normal parade of human filth you wade through. Tell me everything."

I spilled the story from start to finish. He stroked his stomach ever faster as the details emerged. When I was finished, he squeezed my arm. "You must be cautious. I have never seen an Administrator, but I know they are dangerous. You must assume this box you seek on their behalf is the same. There is good news, though, in your tale. Your Torment has been called off, so punishment is not irrevocable. And what you saw in the desert . . . there was no scale, no feather, but if the reality is close to the mythology, the sinners were being judged again."

"And they all died the second death. I can't say I'm brimming with excitement at the prospect."

"On this occasion, yes. But in the mythology, some passed the test. Perhaps you were unlucky in what you saw. Perhaps some are judged to be worthy." He paused, eyes glittering. "And if that is true, there is a way out of this place after all."

15

I left Franklin browsing the shelves and headed home with that strange swelling back in my chest. This time, I recognized it as hope. I'd never imagined any of us had a chance at something better than this pit. But what if Enitan was right about there being a path to redemption? I wanted to believe him. The problem was that I didn't see much redemptive behavior from my fellow Lost Angelenos.

When I got home, I flopped into my armchair and switched my thoughts to less theologically convoluted issues. I had a case to pursue that, if successfully concluded, would definitely improve my situation. It was then I realized that, amidst the excitement, I'd forgotten to ask about Sebastian's middleman. I gave Enitan a quick call, but he was equally clueless. I had to find the middleman somehow and persuade him to tell me what I needed to know or narrow down my list of suspects some other way.

The phone rang, dragging me out of my thoughts. Laureen barked down the line at me. "We need to talk."

"Nice to hear from you too. Want me to come over?"

"No. There's an Italian restaurant in Il Terzo Livello called Osteria del Chianti. None of my people go there, mainly because it's a smelly dive. It should suit you nicely. Be there at two AM."

She hung up. I checked my watch and realized the evening's carnival of torture was almost upon the city. It was amazing how quickly the mind adapted. A week ago, sick dread would have already been bubbling up in my stomach. I wouldn't have had to look at the time. I considered venturing out again to the Ammit's desert courtroom to see if some of the convicts got lucky. But waves of tiredness were washing over my brain. Anyway, I didn't know what I was looking for. For all I knew, the Ammit had spared some of the sinners and sent them on elsewhere through some mystical means. I didn't carry out a before-and-after headcount, after all. Instead, I lay down on the sofa and sank into a much-needed sleep.

*   *   *

There were countless eateries in Il Terzo Livello, from fast food joints to high-end restaurants, many of them clustered around the central square. I enjoyed coming to Sofia's district. It was the closest you got to a normal life in the city. She kept the streets orderly as best she could, and since the main business revolved around food, the area felt less sordid. Even Hrag's hookers and Yama's dealers didn't come here. People with bursting stomachs were usually more interested in sleep than sex or any other kind of drug. You could get your lips around any cuisine you wanted: Italian, Indian, Lebanese, Moroccan, Mexican, Russian, French, and dozens of others. All the restaurants, markets, and delis were stocked with the finest ingredients the Administrators could ship in, which meant the food was delicious. As ever, the district was blanketed in a seductive fog of smells that waxed and waned as I searched for the meeting place: sage, coriander, roasted chicken, chili peppers, garlic, sizzling beef, fresh pastries, aromatic coffee, and many more I couldn't identify.

And there was the one sour note of Il Terzo Livello: it was nearly impossible not to eat to the bursting point. The Romans would gorge at feasts and orgies until their stomachs were distended, then, with the application of feather to tonsils, vomit it up to make room for more. Gluttons here used a shotgun instead of a feather. People would eat for months, until they swelled up like the Michelin Man, and hit the reset button. Then they would go all over again. Dozens of morbidly obese people tromped the pavements, some of them so large that others had to step onto the road to pass. These were at the end of the cycle—unless some of them had arrived in Hell that way, making it their default state.

I located Osteria del Chianti in a basement up a winding alleyway. It wasn't so much a dive as an uncoordinated plummet from a dizzying height. The gray linoleum undulated as though the premises had once served as the epicenter of an earthquake, and half the light fittings ended in open wires. The few lightbulbs gave off a sluggish glow, which allowed me to pretend I couldn't see the overflowing trash can parked outside the kitchen entrance. Laureen was the sole customer. She sat at a wobbly table in the far corner, in front of a mural depicting Tuscany or some such idyllic countryside. The grass looked bright green, but as I approached, I realized it was spongy mold. Laureen looked out of place, dressed as she was in a pristine white dress and matching straw hat.

"Lovely ambience," I said, sitting across from her.

She pursed her lips and glowered at me from under the brim of her hat. "Order. I'm not touching the food, but we need to eat something or they'll kick us out."

She was clearly in a foul mood, so I ordered a penne arrabiata from the hovering waiter and waited for her to get to the point.

"I received another note this morning," she said once the waiter had disappeared. She didn't elaborate, instead staring at me as though searching for a reaction.

"Want me to read your mind? What did it say?"

"It was a list of the people whose sins I'm supposed to forgive. Sixteen in total. All eight of the Trustees, plus seven of the next wealthiest and most influential businessmen and women in the city."

I whistled softly. "Smart. I doubt they're all involved, but this way, you don't know which one of them has the box. I can . . ."

I was about to tell her I could reduce the list to eight, but she cut across me. "You don't count well, do you? I said sixteen names. Eight plus seven equals fifteen. There was one other name, somebody neither wealthy nor influential."

She pushed a piece of paper toward me. As I scanned down the list, I recognized all the city's well-known figures. When I reached the last name, I did a double take. "That can't be right."

"Oh, it's right. Got anything to tell me?"

I looked down again, just to be certain. "Kat Murphy" was indeed appended to the bottom of the roll call of the affluent and powerful. "I have no idea why I'm on that list."

"Allow me to throw a thesis at you. Let's say, hypothetically speaking, I hire someone to find something for me, and this person gets the idea in her tiny mind that there's more to be gained than the generous payment I offered. She finds the person who stole my item and makes a pact with them. She agrees not to mention she's found my possession in exchange for a slice of the action. Sound about right?"

Even without eating what would probably be a very dubious bowl of pasta, I began to feel sick. Laureen looked like she was ready to set the Torment back on me or, even worse, feed me to her pet Egyptian deity.

"I don't blame you for thinking that. The same thing would have occurred to me. But I know you can't forgive my sins. You told me yourself when you hired me, and I don't think you had any reason to lie. If you could have quietly let the thief off the hook and gotten the box back without your boss finding out, you'd have done it. So there's no percentage in throwing my hat in with the ransomer. Even if I thought you could forgive my sins, do you think I'd do something so obvious? I'm not the sharpest knife in the drawer, but I'm not dull enough to mess with somebody who has the power to hand me back to the Torments."

She gave me a hard stare, and for a moment, I wondered if she could read minds. I still didn't really know what powers the Administrators possessed. My answer seemed to satisfy her, for she relaxed her shoulders and held out her hand for the note. "Any other theories as to why you're on there?"

I stared up at the ceiling and thought out loud. "None of those people owe me enough to do me that big a favor. The one thing I can think of is that the holder of your box knows you've hired me and threw my name into the mix, hoping you'd get rid of me."

"How do you suppose they found out I hired you?"

That was obvious. Sebastian was the one person who'd had contact with the middleman. He must have lied about not being able to get in touch. The money-hungry turd probably sold the nugget about me being on the case to his contact, who passed on the information to his employer. I should have given him to Alexis after all. The sole flaw in this theory was the question of why the ransomer had taken the route of dumping me in the shit with Laureen. Every Trustee had the resources to snatch me and keep me safely out of the way.

I laid out the progress in my investigation to Laureen, telling her my theory about Sebastian, my discovery that it was definitely an inside job, and the fact that one of the Trustees was likely now in possession of her loot.

"That's something, I suppose," she said. "What's your next step?"

"Find the middleman and extract the name of the buyer from him. After that, figure out where it's hidden, steal it back, and hand it over."

"That doesn't sound at all difficult."

"Is that sarcasm? It would be a lot easier if you grabbed the Trustees and got them to 'fess up."

I was thinking specifically about dangling them one by one in front of the Ammit until the culprit's tongue loosened, but I couldn't say that. I didn't want Laureen to know how much I'd found out.

"I can't do that. We're here to keep the city running, not to interfere with the system."

"You called off my Torment. Seems like interfering to me."

"We have discretionary powers, but we're not supposed to use them unless absolutely necessary. Messing with a Torment or two is small potatoes, not likely to be noticed. If I yank all the Trustees out at once, it'll cause upheaval. My boss will want to know why I did it."

"And then what? You'll get sacked?"

"That's about the size of it. I need you to pull your finger out and get the box back. You've got six days left."

"It could take longer."

"No, it can't." She fell silent, twiddling her hair, and then seemed to come to a decision. "My boss is coming into town for a meeting in seven days. An inspection, rather. That replica won't fool him. When he finds out the box is gone, he'll take over. And that, Kat, will mean our deal is off. I tell you this so you understand there can be no delays."

I looked down at the grubby tablecloth so she couldn't see the worry thrumming across my face. Six days was going to be tight. Still, I had to project confidence. I swallowed hard and met her gaze. "I'll get it back."

"You'd better."

The conversation lapsed, the only sound the buzzing of the lightbulb overhead. I wanted to probe more about the contents of the box, but she would give me the brush-off. Still, I figured I might as well try to extract some other information.

"So what's Satan like?"

"Nobody calls him Satan. That's more of an unofficial job title. The current incumbent is called Mr. Stanton."

"Is he really scary?"

"Not at all. He's underwhelming, in fact: a small man, short-sighted, smells of boiled cabbage. He is an excellent administrator, though, and doesn't suffer fools gladly. Which is why you should be getting on with what I've hired you to do. As in now."

"What about my pasta?"

"You're better off without it. Last time I ate here, I found a cockroach in my salad. I'd ordered beetle. Before you go, let me be clear about something. Your priority is to get the box back. But if you get the chance to find out who hired the three individuals you seem to think are so inept, take it. Now go do what you do."

Laureen fumbled in her bag and produced a pack of cigarettes as I rose to go. The flame shook as she lit her smoke. She was scared. I didn't have much sympathy. She didn't have a Torment hanging over her head and the more distant fear of a one-way trip into the guts of the Ammit. The meeting had left me feeling ten times worse. If Sebastian had spilled the beans, then the ransomer knew I was coming. The middleman would go to ground, and I would be left with no leads. Even if I did somehow get the box back, the guilty Trustee would know I was responsible and want revenge. Either way, I was screwed.

16

The next forty-eight hours confirmed my worst fears. I burned through my savings like a socialite on a spending spree as I gadded about town, visiting all the places you might expect to run into a middleman with close ties to a Trustee.

I tossed a few token bets on the roulette wheel at the Lucky Deal and stopped in at the Colosseum again. I dodged lewd propositions at Hrag's main brothel, the Palace of Perversions, until asked to leave for not sampling the merchandise. I pretended to smoke a pipe at Yama's highest-end opium den, peeking out through my curtain at the passing customers. I cracked open a spiny lobster at Fusion, Sofia's flagship restaurant, and inspected the earlobes of the other diners for excessive size. I popped in to Adnan's firing range and slammed slugs into a target while watching the comings and goings. I drank at the fanciest bars in Eleutherios, where Jean-Paul and his associates sipped cognac. I spent a few hours hanging around outside Wayne Beat's financial stronghold, named Walled Street in honor of its very large walls topped with armed guards. There was no sign of the middleman.

All the while, I was expecting a posse of armed henchmen to bundle me into a van. To anybody watching my wanderings, it would be clear I was still investigating. If one of the Trustees had put my name on the list in the interests of sabotage, they would know the ruse had failed. But nobody seemed interested in what

I was up to. Maybe I'd made it onto the amnesty list for another reason, which I couldn't begin to guess at.

I made a similar lack of progress working out if any sinners had survived the attentions of the Ammit. I visited the desert clearing the following two nights. On the first occasion, around two dozen people turned up. They all seemed to go the way of the previous batch. The second night, nobody showed face. I also saw nothing of Franklin. Enitan told me he was spending all his time in the back room, leafing through manuscripts.

At five AM on the second night, grinding my teeth at the lack of progress, I hit the sack and lunged into a vivid dream about Danny. It wasn't a memory this time; it felt like a vision of the future. We lay naked between soft cotton sheets in a dazzling white hotel room. A cool breeze whispered through open bay windows that revealed a glittering azure ocean, which dwindled until it met the cloud-fluffed sky in a hazy kiss. Soft jazz drifted over the gentle swish of the waves. I could see the dilated pores on Danny's nose as he leaned in to brush his lips across mine. He smelled of soap and warm skin. Tranquility suffused my body. Words were unnecessary. There was no sin, no pain—just a perfect moment that rendered the past and future irrelevant.

When I woke up, the sun streaming in through the windows, I could almost still feel the weight of his body pressed against mine, and I had the wild idea that I'd conjured him into solidity. But the space next to me was empty. Even so, he felt closer than ever, as if any moment he would walk out of the kitchen holding two mugs of coffee and clamber back into bed. I stared at a peeling corner of wallpaper through misty eyes and realized what my sleeping mind was trying to do. It wanted me to believe there was a chance of winning entry to Heaven, where Danny would be waiting to forgive me. But as a car engine roared and gunfire crackled, I knew this was an unattainable dream. Any acts of kindness I carried out in Lost Angeles were pebbles tossed on the other side of a scale weighted down by a mountain of sin. Enitan was wrong. If there were a second judgment, the Administrators wouldn't have created a place where the pigs could do nothing but wallow in their own filth. I was doomed to be consumed by the Ammit. The best I could hope for was to stay Torment-free and live with the dream Danny rather than the real one. To do that, I needed to satisfy Laureen.

I swung my legs out of bed and made myself the coffee I'd longed for Danny to bring. The middleman was a dead end. I needed to narrow the field down fast some other way to give myself a fighting chance. There was a time for beating around the bush and a time for setting fire to the forest to see what scurries out. With the clock ticking down, the time had come to pull out the metaphorical can of kerosene and strike a match.

One Trustee had already worked out how much leverage Laureen's trinket offered. On that basis, the others would want it as badly for their own ends: not necessarily to have their sins forgiven but to expand their power and influence. Yama, for example, would probably seek to use the box to take over the city, so he was at the bottom of my list of suspects. Everything I'd heard about him suggested remorse wasn't his strong suit, and he seemed at home here. The others were harder to judge. I would have expected Adnan to view it as another weapon to sell on. Hrag lacked imagination in anything other than the arena of sexual deviancy, but he would probably want to possess the box because it made him seem important. Sofia, Jean-Paul, and Tyrell seemed content with what they had, but the fact that they were in power at all suggested ambition of some sort. Wayne already had more money and influence than he could possibly need, but that had never stopped any bigwig I knew from pursuing more. Flo was the biggest mystery, but I had to assume there were things he wanted. In the end, there was no way of knowing for sure how each individual would use the box, so I couldn't discount any of them—which was why I needed a filter.

I intended to spread the word that I would soon come into possession of an item from Avici Rise, working on the assumption that the Trustees at least must have always known where the Administrators lived, as they dealt with them. I would hint that the item in question would bring great advantage to the highest bidder. I would have to be deliberately vague about the item. The details were irrelevant anyway. The fact that it belonged to an Administrator who was desperate to get it back would be enough to pique interest. The Trustees would come running, hopefully all except the one who already had the box—unless that party was smart enough to figure out my ploy and pretend he or she wanted in on the action. Even in that scenario, I hoped to make an educated guess. If all eight responded, the last to arrive would become my chief suspect, as they would probably think over their best strategy before acting.

The play was weak, but it was all I had.

There was risk involved. If Sebastian hadn't talked after all, and the Trustee in possession of the box hadn't noticed I was on the trail, they would know for sure something was up. Maybe the guilty party would simply scoop me up and subject me to some recreational torture until they nailed a deal with Laureen. That would not play well for me, since Laureen had no intention of making a deal. On the plus side, knowing the way the Trustees' minds worked, I was confident they would provide unintentional insurance over the next few days. If I did get the box back, I would deal with the consequences of not actually handing it over to one of the Trustees later.

I called Enitan to clue him in on my plan and rope him into getting the word out. He thought I was insane, pointing out that

Yama was the kind of charming individual who would take the box from me by force rather than wait for the chance to pay lots of money and possibly lose it to one of his enemies.

"He would if he could, but he won't have the chance," I said.

"Why not?"

"You know the Trustees: they don't trust themselves, never mind each other. You're right—the first thing Yama and a few others will think of is how to get their hands on the loot early. The second thing they'll think of is how the others will be thinking about getting their hands on the loot early. The third thing they'll think of is how to stop that from happening. I'll be followed night and day the minute we announce this. If one of them makes a move, the others will step in. It'll be like having my own personal bodyguard."

"Do you really think it wise to set these people against each other? You could start another war and make the most vicious people in this city extremely cross with you."

"You worry too much. They're all sweethearts really."

Enitan—who knew that once I'd made up my mind, it couldn't be changed—stopped arguing. He offered to front the fake sale without revealing my identity. I refused. If he did that, all the heat would come his way. He didn't deserve to run my risks for me. He agreed to notify his contacts with every Trustee, asking them to register their interest for an auction that was supposed to take place two days after Laureen's deadline expired. Enitan was a born salesman. He would spin a convincing tale about the incredible opportunity the purchase of this rare prize would offer.

I didn't have to wait long for the first responses to come. Adnan himself called one hour after I spoke to Enitan and began playing on our personal relationship to weasel out an advantage.

"You've been a very naughty girl," he said when I answered.

"Wrong number. Phone sex is 244-2517, not 2571."

He laughed. "You know it's me, Kat. Why are you auctioning this allegedly marvelous piece when you know I will pay you a handsome price?"

"Your prices are as handsome as you are. I've got bills to pay."

"The ladies do not complain. Nor will you. Let's talk business and avoid the need for something so uncouth as an auction."

"No dice. The other Trustees are in the loop, and you know how grumpy Yama can get."

"Tell me, then, why I should come to your auction."

"I'm sure Enitan's given you the basics. This is a genuine Administrator artifact, one of a kind."

"And what exactly is the power this artifact holds? Enitan was unclear."

"Did I mention it belonged to an Administrator?"

"Administrators possess many ordinary objects. How do I know you're not trying to sell some old socks?"

I'd already drawn a satisfying red line through Adnan's name on my suspect list, so I didn't need to convince him to come to an event that would never happen. It would have seemed weird to be offhand, though, so I did my best to pretend I needed his fat wallet. "Do you really think I would invite such a mighty figure as yourself to an auction if this object wasn't extremely desirable? If I didn't know for a fact that the Administrator in question would pay a high price and give many concessions to get it back? If you don't want to come, that's your choice. I'm sure Yama or Hrag would be happy to take it off my hands."

"You are a sly one, raising the specter of my rivals. I will come," he said and hung up.

Hrag was next to eliminate himself through a brusque phone call from an underling. I fretted for another hour before a knock came on the door. I sidled up to it, my hand hovering near the holster. I looked out the peephole to see a slender woman whose woven hair hung over the shoulder of her tight black T-shirt. She had delicate features marred by a deep scar, slightly lighter than her dark skin, that ran from her right eye to the corner of her mouth. I knew her by repute: Yolanda, one of Yama's chief enforcers. She was renowned for knowing exactly how and where to apply various parts of her body for maximum agony—including her braids, which had razor blades embedded in the ends. The drug lord was taking this seriously. I opened up and waved her in. She didn't budge.

"You will sell the item to Lord Yama," she said, the formal tone indicating she was delivering a message verbatim. "You will bring it to him as soon as you have acquired it. He will tell you what he shall pay. If you do not do so and attempt to go ahead with an auction, he will be most displeased. If you attempt to double-cross him, he will be most displeased. If the item does not prove to be as significant as you claim—"

"He will be most displeased," I interrupted. "I get it."

Since I was stringing everyone along and needed the next few days to be as peaceful as possible, I decided to play nice. Yama was the one guy who might be crazy enough to try to seize the box and damn the other Trustees. "Tell Lord Yama his terms are acceptable."

Her face fell. "Really?"

"You seem disappointed."

"Lord Yama informed me you would probably rebuff his generous offer while making lots of smart remarks. You have a reputation. I was to persuade you to accept."

"By punching me around the head, I assume? Sorry to spoil your fun. Lord Yama also has a reputation, far more concerning than mine. I'd prefer not to end up on his shit list."

"Can't I slap you upside the head once?" she said, ditching the formality. "I spent five minutes downstairs warming up, and my knuckles are itching."

I looked at her closely and detected the hint of a smile.

"I'd rather you didn't," I said. "I've got a modeling assignment in an hour."

"Too bad. You've got a very punchable face."

"I've heard that. One thing before you disappear to vent your frustration on some other unfortunate: tell Yama not to worry if it seems like the auction is still on. I need to continue with the pretense so I don't raise the suspicions of the other Trustees. I'll contact him once I have the item."

She gave me an appraising look. I could tell my rapid folding under pressure had raised her suspicions. My reputation had indeed preceded me, and for the millionth time, I told myself I should try to be less of a smartass.

"Yama's not the kind of man you want to lie to," she said and left.

I crossed to the coffee table to strike out Yama's name. I was already three suspects down, which wasn't bad for a morning of sitting around the apartment. I'd achieved far less over the last few days despite expending much shoe leather. Admittedly, I'd also placed my neck firmly on Yama's chopping block. I'd think of something to appease him. If I didn't, there was always Plastic Avenue.

17

I mooched around the apartment, too restless to read, as I waited for more RSVPs. If none of the others got in touch, the field would be too wide to give me any hope of completing the job on time. Jean-Paul, Flo, Sofia, Wayne, and Tyrell owned more real estate among them than British royalty. As the afternoon dragged on, I lit one cigarette after the other until dirty gray smoke festooned the living room. Any time I heard footsteps in the hallway, I looked up expectantly only to hear no knock. When the phone finally shrilled, I leaped out of my seat and answered before the first ring had died away.

"How is it going?" Enitan said.

I disguised my disappointment at hearing his voice. "Not bad. Three down, five to go."

"Make it six down. Sofia's second-in-command popped in two hours ago on another matter and told me to tell you she was in. One of Wayne's bankers called me five minutes ago to say he would attend. And Tyrell sent a note."

Some of the tension left my neck as I scribbled the three names off my list. Now we were getting somewhere. "While I'm grateful for the news, couldn't you have called earlier? I don't have many cigarettes, or nails, left."

"I became distracted. I discovered a most interesting document about your mysterious box and wanted to read it fully. You had better come over."

I checked my watch. It was after five, close enough to the nightly penance to make it unlikely that I would get any further messages for the next seven hours. I grabbed my car keys and took the stairs two at a time. This was a major bonus, as I hadn't expected Enitan to find anything. The box seemed both too esoteric and too real an object to feature in any mythology. Everything else had elements of grandiosity or horror: the winged Torments, close to the Christian portrayal of demons and emanating from the occult symbol of the tower; the voracious Ammit from Egyptian lore; the endless cycle of punishments that featured in every carrot-and-stick world religion. From the somber tone of Enitan's voice, though, the innocent-looking box was as bad as all of those if not worse.

As I pulled into traffic, one of Hrag's pimpmobiles fell in a few cars back. The tailing had begun, but Hrag's boys, in their outlandish vehicles and absurd getups, were as discreet as a seven-month pregnancy bump at a shotgun wedding. I felt a warm flush of satisfaction at my instincts being proven correct. When I took the ramp from Providence onto Route 666, I spotted another car directly behind the pink monstrosity. This one was a black sedan with smoked-glass windows. That was bound to be Yama's. He had an unhealthy fondness for black. As far as I could tell, these were the only two tails so far, but Adnan would probably be planning a similar action. He did so hate to be left out.

Our procession glided across town, and I made sure to give my companions a poke by skewing into the turn for Diyu at the last second. They both managed to follow me, but I'd let them know I had their number. When I pulled up outside Enitan's, they made no effort to hide, parking a few dozen feet farther on. The rival groups clambered out of their vehicles. Hrag's boys flexed their muscles, while Yama's lot made sure their hands were close to their holsters.

"Talk amongst yourselves, folks," I shouted and entered Enitan's cave.

At the chime of the bell, the fence poked his head out of the back room like a cautious turtle from its shell and waved me up to join him. Once he'd closed and locked the door, I took in the room and whistled. The floor was empty of paper, displaying splintered floorboards, and one wall had been cleared to allow the installation of a bookshelf. Colored notes had been taped underneath neatly filed manuscripts.

"Your apprentice has been busy," I said.

"Indeed. I must thank you for bringing him to me. He has a most orderly mind."

"Don't mention it," I said, thinking I was simply happy to be shot of the pest. "So you hit pay dirt?"

"Yes," Enitan said, his voice dropping into a whisper.

"You got a sore throat, or are you trying to inject some drama into the moment?"

"I do not want anyone to overhear us," he said, although his voice gained volume.

"I'm hooked. Tell me."

"You are familiar with the concept of the apocalypse, Armageddon, or whatever you wish to call it, yes?"

"End of the world. Lights out and don't let the door hit your ass on the way out."

"Close. In the Bible, it refers to a final battle on Earth between the forces of good and evil, which will lead to the ultimate downfall of Satan."

"So a happy ending then. That's lovely."

"Not for the billions judged impure and cast into the pit with him. Anyway, as we know from bitter experience, the Bible is lacking somewhat in accuracy. Besides, there are many other apocalyptic myths and tales, most of them involving unpleasant phenomena such as plagues, floods, meteors, fireballs, and so on."

"What's that got to do with the box?"

"I found this," he said, sliding a slim volume across the desk. I picked it up, noting the fragments of ripped paper along the tape-bound spine that indicated missing pages.

"*Apocalypse Myths and Their Origins Throughout History*," I read out loud. "Sounds like a real page-turner."

I thumbed through the pages, glancing at the titles of the first three chapters: "Ragnarok," "The Mayan Apocalypse," and "The Zombie Apocalypse." On the title page of chapter four was a drawing—rough and ready but unmistakably an image of the replica I'd seen in Laureen's safe. The chapter was titled "The Oblivion Box." The rest of the book had been ripped away.

"That's it?"

"Yes," said Enitan. "I could not find the rest. But do you not see? You told me the box spoke to Sebastian, promised him eternal peace. It was not for him alone. This will wipe out everything if opened."

"Oh, please," I said, feeling distinctly underwhelmed. "Apocalypse in a box? That's taking the concept of convenience too far. How could something so small obliterate existence?"

"After all you have seen down here, you think it is not possible?"

"You've got a point, but look at the other chapters," I said, turning back and scanning the pages. "Norse gods springing out of the afterlife to bash each other over the head with big hammers. The dead returning to life with an insatiable appetite for human flesh. What makes you think the one about the box is any truer?"

He stabbed a plump finger onto the drawing. "Because we know this exists."

That pulled me up short. The box did indeed exist; I'd seen its replica and heard Sebastian's tale, both of which dovetailed neatly with the document. Too neatly, as a matter of fact. I flicked back through the document. The pages looked fresh, and from the quality of the prose, which was worse than Enitan's standard fare, the document seemed to have been written in a hurry. My eyes narrowed.

"Tell me," I said, "how did you come across this?"

"It was in Franklin's to-read pile. I flicked through to see how his research was going."

"Was he there at the time?"

"No, he said he had to go out."

"Did you buy this recently?"

"I do not believe so."

"Do you remember buying it at all?"

"No, but that is not so unusual. I buy a lot of books."

"Don't you think this one would have stuck in your mind, especially since it looks so new? At the rate the mold's spreading in here, you would have bought it in the last few months."

Enitan's brow knotted. "I imagine so."

"Did you mention anything else to Franklin about my case?"

"Of course. I told him all you told me."

"I didn't want to tell him anything. I thought you got that message."

"When did you tell me not to say anything?"

"The other day, when I brought him in. I didn't want to talk in front of him. I gave you the eye signal."

"I thought you had a twitch."

"Seriously? Everybody knows the eye signal. We went outside to talk."

"You said you wanted a cigarette."

"That was a pretext!"

Enitan crossed his arms. "How was I supposed to know that? You brought Franklin to me. Two pairs of eyes are better than one, and he has a sharp mind. I thought he could help. What are you saying now? You do not trust him?"

I considered what I was trying to say. The arrival of the three goons at Benny's on the night Laureen had shown up might not have been the only seemingly coincidental event that proved to have been deliberate. It was unusual for a total novice to wander into Benny's and strike up a conversation with me—a novice who just happened to want to be a PI, who followed me and asked lots of questions about my case, who turned out to be an expert on religious history at a moment when that was precisely what I needed. If my freshly flowered suspicions were correct, Franklin knew way more about this business than he was letting on and was trying to worm his way into my graces for a very specific reason.

"I'm saying I find it peculiar that, a few days after letting Franklin in here, you turn up a manuscript you have no memory of buying, one that miraculously gives us a name, an accurate drawing, and a purpose for a box nobody in human history had heard of until a few days ago. I think Franklin may have written this particular tome and planted it. He wanted you to read it and tell me what you found. I think our friend might not be who he says he is."

"I do not believe it. He looks so innocent. If he is not Franklin, then who is he?"

That was a good question. If he was the Administrator who'd paid Sebastian to steal the box, it would make sense for him to get close to me as I zeroed in on the current owner. But then why had the goons gone for him in the bar? And why, if he was their employer, would they still be blundering around after Sebastian? Surely he would have known those Neanderthals would get in my way. And then, if he was the dodgy Administrator or even a previously unknown third party, why go to the trouble of writing a document that gave me more information on the box—if what he'd written could be believed?

"I don't know," I said, "but I aim to find out. Do you know where he is?"

"No. He said he would be gone the rest of the day."

"Making himself scarce so it would seem like you were the one who uncovered the information. Do me a favor: don't tell him anything else, particularly about the auction. When he comes back, show him the manuscript and act like you don't suspect anything. See how he reacts. And call me."

"I will do as you ask, although I think you are being paranoid."

"A healthy dose of paranoia never hurt anybody."

It worried me that I might have gotten Franklin so badly wrong, that he might have fooled me. I needed to be on top of my game now more than ever, and if my antennae were malfunctioning, I would be blundering around in the dark.

Enitan cleared his throat. "It is almost time," he said. "For me, at least."

I patted my pocket for the car keys but realized leaving now wouldn't be my best move. If I set out across town minutes before Torment time, it would look suspicious to my tails, who were most likely preparing to suffer where they stood. Nor could I slip out when they were under the influence. Once they woke up, they would expect me to still be in Enitan's. If I wasn't, it would look odd. I didn't want them to suspect that I had the advantage of freedom of movement. I would need to use it later.

"I know this is a big ask," I said, "but do you mind if I stay here while . . . you know? I've got good reason; otherwise, I wouldn't ask."

Enitan didn't say anything for a while. He was already withdrawing into himself. When he spoke, his voice was hoarse. "It does not matter to me. I will be elsewhere."

"I'll sit next door," I said.

Before I left to wait in the front shop, I squeezed his shoulder. He didn't seem to notice.

I took a seat in a battered armchair by the front entrance, as far away from Enitan's bookish haven as possible. I didn't want to risk overhearing his muttering. A few grim-faced stragglers passed the window. When I glanced up the street, I saw that my companions had retreated into their vehicles—all except Yolanda, who stood with her head held high, staring in the direction of the tower. An old grandfather clock ticked in the corner, lulling me into a daze that I jumped out of when something rattled. I looked up to see the doorknob shaking. Black fluid appeared and spread until it covered most of the door. The fluid thickened into sludge, which expanded outward and began to take form as though flooding an invisible mold.

"Door wasn't locked," I said to the Torment. "Or do you like a big entrance?"

The weak joke did nothing to dispel the chills caused by the creature's proximity. It stalked forward, intent on one thing, and melted through the door leading to the back room. Enitan moaned. Even though I knew there was nothing I could do, his voice was so fear loaded that I felt the urge to kick the door in. Enitan began talking, his voice loud enough to hear through the closed door. I put my fingers in my ears and waited it out.

18

As soon as the Torment had finished its ugly business, I made myself scarce. Enitan didn't know we cried out while under the influence. If I'd waited until he emerged, still wrapped in the cocoon of his guilt, my face might have betrayed what I'd overheard. Several times, he'd shouted for his mother in anguish. Even when I went outside to hover on the deserted street for a smoke, I heard him when he screamed, so loud that his voice cracked, "I don't want the money anymore. Take it back, please, take it back!" I still couldn't bring myself to judge him. He was a good man—I could sense it in our every interaction; he was just a good man who'd done something bad in a moment of desperation. And who was I to judge? I was living in a glass house with a whole heap of jagged stones lying around outside.

I made sure to appear unsteady on my legs, holding on to the fender of my car as the Torments winged home overhead. Even though Laureen had told me they were mindless beasts, I felt an urge to whip out my gun and fire into the air. It would have been a waste of bullets. From my vantage point on the hill, I'd seen plenty of sinners empty their clips into a Torment to zero effect. My guard of honor was still there, huddled inside their cars. I gave them a few minutes to recover before I climbed behind the wheel and made my way across town. I wanted to drive fast, eager both to distance myself from my unintentional violation of Enitan's privacy and to see if any more messages had arrived during my absence. I reined in my impatience and drove at the funereal pace befitting a woman still suffering from shell shock.

As I pulled up outside the apartment, I noted two men leaning against a lamppost and apparently engaging in casual conversation. Adnan's watchers had joined the party. I wasn't the only one to spot them. Yolanda unfurled her legs from the car and glared daggers at the newcomers. They didn't appear intimidated, although it was gloomy enough outside the circles of light cast by the streetlamps that they probably couldn't see how ferocious she looked. If they made the mistake of messing with her, they'd find out. I left them to their standoff and took the stairs. I had no way of knowing if I'd missed any calls, but I was hoping that if one of the last two Trustees had tried and failed to ring, they would have dropped off a note.

I was slack. With the ever-accumulating clump of henchmen outside, I'd assumed I would be safe. I hadn't accounted for the stupidity of Jake and his double shadow. The first I knew of their presence was when I shouldered open the door and clicked on the light, my eyes on the carpet for some sign of communication, and heard an intake of breath. Jake had squeezed his bulk into the armchair facing the door and was pointing a gun at me. They must have sneaked into the apartment earlier on, when I'd taken my tails over to Enitan's.

"Surprise!" Jake said.

The pistol cracked. I had a millisecond to register the impact before everything went black. When I came back, heaving the first rasping breath into my lungs and grabbing at the phantom hole in my forehead, I was splayed on the sofa.

"I owed you one," Jake said. "Where's the box?"

I groaned, pretending to be suffering from the aftermath of my resurrection, and rolled to the floor. I used the opportunity to mark the location of his two pals, stationed on either side of the door like extremely ugly gargoyles. I reached for my holster. It was empty.

"Looking for this?" Jake said, waggling my gun. "I'll ask you again. Where's the box?"

I said nothing for a moment, trying to parse this new development. Their appearance didn't make sense if they were working for Franklin. He'd gone to the trouble of setting up the book ploy with the likely intention of making me confide details of the investigation. Maybe I was missing something, but setting the hounds on me didn't strike me as a smart play.

"I don't keep my money box here," I said. "Bit of a rough area. Can't trust the neighbors. We'll need to go down to the bank."

Jake didn't have much variety in the way of facial expressions and so gave me the lopsided snarl again. "Don't get smart. I heard about your auction. Strikes me you might be selling something that belongs to us."

Although I'd expected the Trustees to try to keep the auction quiet to fend off other interested parties, I knew there were enough curious ears pricked up around their enterprises to overhear the information. Still, I hadn't expected the news to spread so quickly, which was partly why I'd let these idiots take me by surprise. That was no excuse. First, there was my possible misjudgment of Franklin, and now this. I was definitely slipping. "I would say possession is nine-tenths of the law, but there is no law here. Plus I don't have it."

"So what you selling, hot air? You got enough of that to be a millionaire, I guess."

"You're trying to make jokes now? I thought you didn't like funny. Maybe you should beat yourself up. Let me know if you need any help."

"The only person who's going to get beaten around here is you, unless you start talking."

"I'll talk, but not to you. Let's go meet your boss."

"My boss likes his privacy." He lowered the barrel of the gun and pointed it at my leg. "Last chance. Where's the box?"

"You don't want to fire again," I said.

"I think I do," he said and pulled the trigger.

The bullet thudded into my thigh. Sure it stung, but I'd been shot enough times to absorb the pain in silence. On this occasion, taking my punishment stoically wasn't the smart play. I screamed at the top of my lungs and got onto my hands and knees. I crawled over to the window overlooking the street below, as if searching for an escape route, and slapped my hand against the glass.

"Please don't shoot me again!" I screeched.

Jake grinned. "Ha! I knew you were a phony. Acting all tough. You're just a typical whiny woman. I'm going to keep shooting until you give it up. A bullet in each limb, then I start on the tender areas."

His single eyebrow dropped in the middle, like a cheap mattress sagging under the weight of a big ass, as I returned his grin with interest. Footsteps were pounding the stairs.

"And you're just a typical blustering man," I said, "with a hair trigger and a brain too soaked in testosterone to think about the consequences of shooting your load."

Jake swung his arm toward the door as Yolanda scorched into the room. He got one shot off, but she was already diving for the floor. The bullet caught one of his buddies in the shoulder, sending him reeling against the wall. Yolanda turned the dive into a roll, curled up onto the balls of her feet, and leaned every ounce of her momentum into a ferocious punch that walloped Jake square in the balls. He let out so much air, I thought he was going to deflate completely. While Jake fought for enough breath to fend off the savage follow-up blows Yolanda was raining on his head, his uninjured pal clawed for his piece. He managed to get it out of his jacket in time for one of Hrag's boys to arrive and hack a machete into the rising gun arm.

There were four people, including me, bleeding profusely onto my carpet. As the room filled with the remaining henchmen, all I could think of was how difficult it would be to get the stains out. I started to laugh hysterically, light-headed from blood loss. That was when I realized the bullet must have nicked my femoral artery. I raised a hand, trying to find my voice and ask everyone to stop pounding Jake and his chums into tenderized steak. Now that they were subdued and more likely to be malleable, I wanted to grill them about who'd hired them. Yolanda, however, continued to purge her pent-up aggression on Jake's now decidedly misshapen face. His two chums were faring just as badly. I tried to get up, which proved the last straw for my body. I faded into unconsciousness; the last thing I saw was Yolanda snapping Jake's fingers.

I must have been out for a good ten minutes or so before I died, because when I did my second Lazarus act of the night, the apartment was empty. I rose woozily and looked out of the window to see Yolanda sitting on the curbside, licking her knuckles. Of Jake's cohort and the rest of Yama's crew, there was no sign. Too tired to walk downstairs, I opened the window.

"Feeling better now you've smacked somebody around?" I called down.

"Absolutely," Yolanda said. "Thanks for the opportunity."

"You're welcome. I don't suppose you can tell me where they've gone?"

"Your pals? For some reeducation. You're welcome, by the way."

I cursed under my breath. My shot at interrogating Jake had gone. If they were released after the next few hours of unpleasantness

GARY PUBLIC LIBRARY

in Yama's dungeons, they surely wouldn't be so stupid as to come back for me now that they knew I had protection.

"You have my undying gratitude," I said, not wanting to seem ungrateful to a woman who could rip my head off without breaking a sweat.

"You know how to repay me," she said and went back to nursing her grazed knuckles.

I headed for the kitchen, intending to grab a bucket and cloth and sponge up the worst of the blood before it dried—the way my funds were diminishing on this gig, I wouldn't be able to replace the carpet. I stopped when I saw a folded piece of paper, kicked into the corner behind the front door. I unfolded it, smiling as I realized the night wasn't a total write-off. The note was from Jean-Paul, expressing his interest in the auction. We had a winner for chief suspect: Flo.

GARY PUBLIC LIBRARY

19

I spent the next morning preparing to breach Flo's apartments, which seemed the most likely place for him to keep his valuables. Even though he would likely know I was on the trail of the box, I hadn't heard a peep from him. Maybe he thought I was bluffing; maybe he was just odd, as his hermit behavior suggested; maybe he put a lot of faith in his security measures. All guests had to check their weapons upon entry to the casino, and a steel door, guarded around the clock, sealed his private quarters. The casino rose so far above the surrounding constructions that there was no way to get onto the roof from adjoining buildings other than grabbing onto a Torment's legs and jumping as it passed over.

Unbeknownst to Flo, I retained the advantage of being able to stroll through the casino unmolested as everyone suffered. I only had to get through the door to his apartment. If I was lucky, one of the guards would have the key in his pocket. To be safe, I laid out a hammer, a crowbar, a flashlight, and a heavy-duty drill and then ventured out to the Seven Gates—with all my buddies plus a couple of extras from Jean-Paul and Wayne in tow—to purchase some plastic explosives. There remained the possibility that Flo wasn't interested, that one of the others was in possession of the prize and had been smart enough to throw me off the scent by joining the auction. This was my best shot, however, and I had to take it.

I toyed with the idea of giving Laureen a status update but decided against it. She would ask how I'd narrowed down the list of suspects, and my chosen method didn't fit her desire for a low-key investigation. She would hear about the auction soon enough. By that point, I would hopefully be in a position to return the box and soothe her fevered brow. I was hoping she would be relieved enough to accede to my request for a bonus. After the melee in my apartment, I'd concluded that I would never be able to untangle the mess I'd created. The Trustees were giddy at the prospect of getting their mitts on something from Avici Rise; their disappointment when it didn't materialize would manifest itself in a desire to exact revenge on my sorry hide. I was going to ask her to inform the Trustees that I was off-limits. I didn't know if she would agree or if the Trustees were scared enough of her to comply if she did, but it was the one chance I had of remaining unscathed in the coming weeks and months.

I'd just finished packing all the necessaries into my kit bag when the phone rang. It was Enitan again.

"Franklin has returned," he said in a whisper. "He is next door looking at the manuscript."

"How'd he react when you showed it to him?"

"He came across as genuine. Surprised, excited, and a little scared."

"We already know he's a good actor."

"Or you are a bad judge of character."

In a way, I hoped I'd gotten it wrong. I'd been so sure I had Franklin down when I met him that I hadn't questioned his appearance at Benny's on a night of such significance. If he really wasn't who he said he was, I'd been duped too easily. Still, I had time to rectify my mistake and confirm whether Franklin had written the manuscript. For that, I needed Enitan's assistance. "Tell me, during all this research, has he been taking notes?"

"Yes. I gave him a very nice notebook and a satchel to keep it in so he could write the first draft as he goes along."

"Bring him to Benny's in an hour. Make sure he has the notebook on him. And bring the manuscript too."

When I arrived at Benny's at the appointed time, the bar was deserted save for Enitan and Franklin—and, of course, Benny, who sighed when I interrupted his attempts to build a house out of playing cards to order a Ward Eight. The bored gang members clustered outside as I settled into a booth next to the fence, drink in hand, and nodded at Franklin.

"Enitan told you about the manuscript?" Franklin said, his voice hurried.

I examined him, searching for tics that would indicate whether he was genuinely excited at this academic discovery or keen to see if I'd swallowed the story. "Seems we got lucky."

"There's nothing lucky about it," he said. "Enitan owns nearly every book in the city."

"What's your take from a religious history perspective?"

"It's certainly fascinating. I've never heard anything like this before. Then again, there've been so many belief systems down the ages that even a lifetime's research would barely scratch the surface. It's a shame the rest of the manuscript was missing. It would help if we knew which culture the box came from and had more information on exactly what it's supposed to do and when. These myths usually have some specific time frame associated with them. I don't suppose we could find the author?"

"As I told you, I do not remember buying this," Enitan said. "And the name of the writer does not sound familiar."

That's because it's made up, I thought. Franklin's words seemed too measured, his body language too controlled. He lavished eye contact on me, his face sat unnaturally still, and his hands were folded in his lap—to stop them from jerking into the nose tugs and ear pulls that gave away lies, I suspected.

"So we agree we don't know a lot, as usual," I said. "Given what we do know, does it sound feasible?"

"If I didn't know the box was real, I'd dismiss it as another myth, and not a very convincing one. But what's in the document ties up with what you've found out. I'd say there's a strong possibility the box is what the manuscript says it is."

"And what is that exactly? All we know is that it's called the Oblivion Box. Maybe it has a bottle of gin and a handful of Quaaludes inside."

Franklin leaned forward, talking ever faster. "Would they list somebody's stash in a book about apocalypses? Would you keep alcohol and pills in a box that talks to anybody who touches it? I think we can assume it's a doomsday weapon."

Now I could see the angle for planting the manuscript. He wanted me to believe that the box was incredibly dangerous. Before too long, he would suggest I give it to him for safekeeping. "You think I shouldn't give it back?"

He didn't bite right away. "I think you should ask yourself to what use a demon would put such a device."

"She's had the box for a long time and done nothing. Why use it now?"

"Like I said, every religion and myth has a specific moment set aside for Armageddon—certain events or portents, a certain era. The time could be approaching."

"So you're saying if I give the box back, I could bring about the end of the world?"

"I'd say that sums it up."

I was now nearly certain that Franklin was playing me, but I had one more check to carry out before accusing him.

"Shit!" I shouted, banging the table hard. As my left fist came down, drawing Franklin's gaze, my other hand flicked over my untouched cocktail. The liquid sloshed over the table and poured into Franklin's lap. He jumped up and tugged at his sopping wet trousers.

"Sorry," I said. "Got a bit carried away."

"It's understandable," he said.

"There's paper towels in the gents," Benny said. "On the house."

"You're too kind, but I'll let it dry."

I hadn't given Benny the full picture, but I'd clued him in on my suspicions over Franklin and that I needed him out of the way for a few minutes. I gave Benny an encouraging nod as Franklin peered at his soggy groin.

"This is a classy establishment," Benny said, rounding the bar and grabbing Franklin's shoulder. "Think I want it to look like my customers piss themselves and sit in the mess? Clean yourself up."

For a moment, Franklin clutched at the table, something close to anger flaring in his eyes. Then he gave in and let Benny usher him toward the toilet, walking like a bandy-legged cowboy. As soon as the toilet door closed, I delved into the satchel, which contained two pens and the notebook.

"Get the manuscript out," I told Enitan, who obliged.

There wasn't much in the notebook: a few lines on books to read, a few doodles, and an appallingly phrased first paragraph that told me Franklin was no writer. It was enough. I placed the notebook and the manuscript side by side.

"What do you see?" I asked Enitan.

He flipped through the pages of the notebook and frowned. "I see enough to make me glad I did not give him an advance. He has done nothing the last few days."

"Not true. He wrote *Apocalypse Myths and Their Origins*. Look at the handwriting."

Enitan looked from one document to the other, and a light came on in his eyes. "They are the same. You were right."

"My favorite words."

I left the documents on the table where Franklin could see them and drew my gun. At least I knew one more thing about the Administrators. Franklin had died when Jake had stabbed him in the eye—a murder I now knew to be a smokescreen. The same rules that governed us applied to them, which meant a bullet would put him down for a while. I crossed my legs, leaned my wrist on my knee, and waited for him to finish toweling himself down. He came out, giving himself one last scrub, and looked up to see my gun pointing in his direction. His eyes flicked to the notebook and manuscript, then back to the weapon. I thought he was going to stick to his story even though I had him dead to rights. He surprised me by not trying.

"Crap," he said. "You figured it out."

"It's an annoying habit of mine. The book turning up so soon after you got access to Enitan's library was too convenient. You should have waited a few more days before planting it or hired somebody to sell it to Enitan. Shame really—you were doing so well."

"We don't have a few more days," he said, his voice shifting from reedy and halting to a deeper, more confident tone.

"Why not? You going on holiday? I suppose you would get the chance to do that, seeing as how you're an Administrator. The one who had Jake hire Sebastian to steal the box."

"I made the mistake of engaging Jake's services, yes. But I'm not a filthy demon."

"Really? Then explain how you knew the box was there and how you were able to tip off Sebastian to the right time to steal it. Not to mention how you stopped the Ammit from munching him up."

Franklin strolled over to the bar and leaped up onto a stool. He was no longer hunched as though trying to present a smaller target to the world, and his eyes were narrower. He sat with his legs open, one arm draped over the counter like a world-weary barfly. I almost didn't recognize him. "I'm going to sit here so you don't get nervous, okay? I need to explain something. You're going to want to listen carefully."

"I'm all ears, but first tell me your real name."

"Franklin will do fine. You're right—I've been living up at Avici Rise. But I'm not one of them. I am, to put it in human terms, a double agent."

I glanced at Enitan, looking for some reflection of the cynicism I was feeling. He looked like he was enjoying the scene. "Oh, this is going to be good. Who're you with, the CIA's special supernatural unit?"

"Similar agency, different employer. Think of Hell as the KGB. In that case, who would be the CIA?"

"You are an angel?" Enitan asked, his eyes wide.

Franklin touched his left index finger to the tip of his nose. I had to give him credit. Caught out in one fake persona, he'd slipped seamlessly into another. Still, I was curious to hear where he was going, and keeping him talking would buy me time to work out what to do next. "You don't look much like an angel to me."

"Does Laureen look like a demon?" He had me there, so I said nothing and let him continue. "I've been in deep cover for a long time, posing as an Administrator, as you euphemistically refer to the demons. My job was to keep an eye on what they were up to, in particular with regard to a certain box. Recent developments required I take a more active approach and steal it. Unfortunately, I was unable to gain access to Laureen's safe."

"Couldn't you have used your laser eyes to melt it open?" I said, making no effort to hide my skepticism.

"You're mixing me up with Superman. We don't have as many powers as you'd imagine, and I've always been dreadful with technology. Don't let this unwrinkled face deceive you. I'm very old. When you get to my age, it's hard to keep up. So I hired somebody."

"You didn't choose very well, did you?"

"I didn't have many contacts in the field of robbery," he said, shrugging, "so I hired the first insalubrious braggarts I came across. They found Sebastian for me—who, as you are aware, turned out to be a very good thief but also extremely dishonest."

"A dishonest thief? Whatever next? A corrupt politician?"

He ignored my jibe. "When Sebastian went missing, I remained keen to get the box. I needed to be sure it stayed out of Hell's hands. So I sent Jake and friends out looking, although I had little hope of success. As you pointed out, they're useless. But I knew Laureen would be pursuing her own avenues of research. I kept tabs on her and discovered she was planning to hire you."

"So you decided to increase your chances of success by cozying up to me."

Franklin spread his hands. "People spoke highly of you. It appeared you were the best hope. And when I asked a few questions myself, I heard that beneath your tough shell lurked a soft core, so I decided to play the ingenue in need of rescue. Jake did get carried away. He was supposed to beat me up and let you pile in to the rescue. I didn't appreciate being stabbed in the eye, although it worked out okay in the end. It got me out of the bar faster, which meant I didn't bump into Laureen. Oh, and I must apologize for their behavior last night. I didn't order that. They were intended as a diversion to keep you from looking too closely at me. They got carried away again, as they appear wont to do."

"Very kind of you to tell me all this," I said. "What was your plan? Wait until I found the box and then take it yourself?"

"I merely intended to nudge you in the right direction. Feed you information about the true nature of the object, hence the manuscript, until you decided to do the right thing."

"Which is?"

"Don't give it back to Hell, obviously. All the myths about Armageddon are wrong. God doesn't want to punish all sinners or destroy the world to build a new one. Noah and the flood was fiction. God wants humanity to flourish and work through its problems. Satan, jealous and bitter, seeks to destroy God's work. This box is his doing alone. Inside truly is the end of the world. A lasting end, souls and all. And the time has come for Hell to open it."

"How exactly will this end the world? Seems to me it's too small to hold a bunch of nukes."

"Size isn't everything. There are dimensions within dimensions, worlds within worlds. What you see as a simple box could contain a whole universe. But the truth is, we don't know exactly what is inside. It's their invention. We only know it will wipe out the Earth."

"Why now, though?"

"They have all their portents. We're well into the new millennium, and the world's in shambles. All the planet's little wars are joining hands. Radical Islamists are rampaging through the Middle East, carving out a new caliphate, while the West drops bombs willy-nilly to no effect. You've got terrorists gunning down infidels in shopping malls, restaurants, churches, and offices across Europe and the US. Russia's flexing its muscles again. Genocide and ethnic cleansing have become so common that a maniac has to kill at least a million to get noticed. Droughts, floods, earthquakes, and tsunamis wipe out tens of thousands every year. You've got all kinds of nasty diseases cropping up. There are ever more people and ever fewer resources to go around. And that's just the big stuff: War, Famine, Pestilence, and Death. The Four

Horsemen have ridden out and brought a few friends. So Satan has given the go-ahead to open the box. That's why Laureen wants it back in a hurry. He's coming in a few days, and they plan to take it upstairs for the closing ceremony. I'm trying to stop them."

I ran a finger under my collar and signaled Benny, who was listening with a look of consternation on his face, to bring me a drink. I'd hardly paid attention to the list of woes. Franklin had said we were well into the new millennium, but how far? Ten years? Twenty? If I'd had to guess at how long I'd been in Lost Angeles, I would have settled on two decades maximum. I didn't want to know how much longer it was in reality.

Franklin said nothing for a while, giving me time to swallow half of my drink. The booze hit my stomach and rebounded into my head. I took a deep breath and tried to focus on the matter at hand rather than the length of my internment. Franklin was starting to sound increasingly convincing. His tale made a twisted kind of sense, but I'd already been taken in once before and wasn't about to make the same mistake again.

"So you want me to give you the box?"

"That would be ideal. Primarily, I don't want you to give it to them."

I looked down and noticed the rest of my drink had disappeared. I retained no memory of drinking it—just as half my miserable existence down here had disappeared in the mists of time. "I hate to rain on your parade here, but if they created it, couldn't they make another one?"

"Maybe. But they'd need time, and that would give us a chance to intervene. The forces are assembling as we speak."

"How do I know this isn't another story you're telling?"

"You don't. But if I'm telling the truth, and you return the box, the end of the world will be on you. Yes, you'll face no further Torments, and bully for you, but you'll have seven billion other deaths on your conscience. And not just deaths. Their souls will be destroyed, which means no afterlife for them. Could you live with that?"

I lit a cigarette, inhaled the calming smoke deep into my lungs, and ignored his thorny question. "You're asking for a big leap of faith here, and you haven't exactly distinguished yourself in the field of honesty. Prove you're an angel. Turn some water into whisky."

Franklin walked across the room in measured steps, his gaze never leaving mine, until he stood over me. "No. Like you said, Kat, this is about faith. Do you put your faith in Hell, the regime that slathers vile sin on this city, that sends the Torments each evening, that unleashes a beast to condemn every soul to an eternity as a tortured wisp of sand? Or do you put your faith in God, your creator, who stands against them?"

I could see nothing now but his eyes. They seemed to tunnel deep inside me, seeking out the dark crevices of my soul.

"I believe you're a good woman, Kat, even if you're working for the wrong side. I choose to put my faith in you, as God puts his faith in humanity. I'm not going to try to persuade you any further. I'm going to call off Jake, if I can find him. What happens next is up to you." He wrote down a number in the notebook and pushed it across the table. "Once you've made up your mind, call me."

The gun lay slack in my fingers as he turned his back on me and walked out the door. A shocked silence blanketed the bar—broken when Benny clicked his tongue.

"I knew he was a wrong 'un," he said. "You can't trust a man who never buys a drink."

"This is very bad news," Enitan said, snapping the notebook shut. "I will not be getting my best seller."

When I didn't react to his attempt at levity, Enitan rested his hand on mine. I was glad of the contact, which brought me back to the moment: to this seedy bar, where the only two people I could call friends were looking worried. It was strange. In the context of my existence, surrounded by the supernatural, Franklin's story should have been perfectly believable. But Lost Angeles had become normality, its bizarreness and cruelty part of my everyday life. I'd swallowed my discovery of the Ammit, as I'd seen it with my own eyes. This revelation, however, remained words. I had Franklin's say-so as evidence, and the end of the world was so vast a concept that I couldn't begin to imagine it. Plus some of Laureen's behavior didn't make sense in his telling of events. If this was about putting a full stop on humanity, Laureen surely wouldn't have entrusted the retrieval of the doomsday device to me. If Satan was prepared to obliterate an entire planet, what would it matter if his lackeys first tore Lost Angeles apart to get what he needed?

The problem was that even though I no longer trusted Franklin and his story appeared farfetched, I couldn't discount his version of events. Laureen had given no motive for the theft of the box. Franklin's explanation provided a compelling motivation. Finally, his willingness to walk away and put his faith in me challenged my skepticism the most. Deep down, though, I knew that the reason I didn't want to believe him was rooted in selfishness. If he was telling the truth, I wouldn't be able to give the box to Laureen. That meant I would be once more condemned to murdering the man I loved every night of my life.

"Do you believe him?" I asked Enitan.

"That is not the question we should be asking."

"What question should we ask?"

Enitan squeezed my fingers. "Can we afford to run the risk of not believing him? As far as I know, I still have family in the world. My children. My grandchildren. I wish them to die fat and old in their beds, a lifetime of happiness and good deeds behind them."

I had no family to think of. I was an only child, my parents had died in the sixties, and Danny and I didn't have any kids. It didn't matter. Enitan, my friend, had people he cared about. If I made the wrong decision, I would be killing them along with everyone else. My own desire for peace meant nothing weighed against all those lives.

"What will you do now?" he asked.

I stared at the smoke swirling over my head and thought over my options. If Franklin was lying, I could give the box back to Laureen with a clear conscience. If he was telling the truth, it was too dangerous to leave floating around. If I didn't act, I would be as good as handing it back. Laureen would take drastic action and get it one way or another. One certainty remained: I needed to get my hands on the box.

"I'm going to break into Flo's and get the damn thing," I said, stubbing out my half-smoked cigarette and getting to my feet. "Then we can decide what to do with it."

20

At eight on the dot, as the sun blinked out behind the hills and the Torments sallied forth, I picked up my clinking bag of tools and left the apartment. Even though I was on the clock—I needed to be out of Flo's by eleven thirty to ensure I had enough time to return home and look like I'd never left—I took the stairs slowly. I wanted the Torments snuggled up inside their human hosts before I emerged. I lingered inside the street-level exit until the flapping of wings and entreaties for mercy had subsided. I opened the door and stepped over the legs of a prostitute slumped against the doorway, his eyes bulging like eight balls.

I stayed alert as I drove the short distance to the Lucky Deal. Franklin had said he would leave me in peace, but I couldn't be sure it wasn't a ploy to make me relax. Working in my favor was the fact that anybody doing anything livelier than lying on the ground drooling would stand out. Nonetheless, I kept snapping my head around at twitches of movement, which all turned out to be the spasmodic jerks of dreaming sinners rather than Franklin dogging my steps. I parked outside the casino, walked past the prone Sid, and tested the double doors. They gave slightly but remained closed. By the rattling sound as I shook the doorknob, I guessed that a hefty chain secured them from the inside. I took out the hammer and sidestepped to the plate-glass window. It took three blows before the tempered glass caved in. Shards tinkled to the pavement. I listened for movement, from either within or without, but heard nothing. I knocked away the remaining slivers and climbed in.

The silence was oppressive where normally all was chaos: the chatter of coins cycling through hungry slot machines, the click of chips shuttling through nervous fingers, the rattle of balls on spinning wheels—above it all, the burble of voices calling for drinks and, more often than not, bemoaning their bad luck. Rows of empty baize tables flanked the carpeted central aisle, which bore an elaborate pattern of asymmetrical purple-and-green swoops. When the plastic chandeliers bristling with overly bright bulbs were on, the carpet was so eye-popping that it was hard to concentrate—which, along with free drinks for players, was a tactic to swing the odds further in favor of the house. I'd never understood the draw of gambling in casinos, unlike Danny. At least at the fights or the races, you could enjoy the spectacle while you threw your money away. In a casino, all you had to look at was a ricocheting ball or a slew of cards. Still the gamblers came to try to float on that elusive current of good fortune—a commodity in short supply in Lost Angeles.

Tonight, muted side lights embedded low in the walls provided the sole illumination. They were bright enough to provide a small circle of decent visibility, but any farther than ten feet ahead of me, the room dissolved into gloom. It created the nagging worry that somebody, or something, was waiting to pounce from the shadows. I passed four insensible security guys on my way to the staircase, each one sitting in an armchair, weapons perched between splayed legs. They were there to ensure nobody could stage a lightning raid on the casino in the fuzzy-headed minutes after the city woke up. They were also another reason to make sure I was long gone before midnight. I'd already eaten more than my fair share of lead over the last few days. I wasn't hungry for more.

I jogged through the casino, taking the stairs past the private rooms on the first floor, where the big spenders threw down obscene amounts of cash on Texas Hold'em, and the second floor, where the bar, stage, and dance floor occupied most of the real estate. Another two floors—which held the counting rooms and recreational spaces for the staff—passed before I reached the final set of stairs ascending to Flo's haven. Two guards lay on the floor at the top. I frisked them for a key, avoiding any contact with their skin in case the Torments sensed my presence. I came up blank. I was going to have to resort to a big bang.

I'd never blasted a door off before, but I didn't have to be an engineer to guess that the weakest point would be the hinges. I patted down a healthy dollop of explosive putty on each, pushed in the contacts as per the instructions the salesman had doled out, and unspooled the connecting wires down the stairs and around the corner to the detonator. As I was about to turn the switch, I remembered the guards and returned to drag them down the stairs. I didn't know what would happen if I blew them apart while the Torments were inside and felt that was one unanswered question I could live with. Once they were safely stowed, I detonated. The blast pummeled my ears, and fragments of plaster and metal blew out of the stairwell to ricochet off the walls. While the dust was still settling, I crunched through the rubble and inspected my handiwork. The door hung on its hinges, held in place by the lock. I jammed a crowbar into the gap between twisted metal and doorjamb and heaved. The door squealed in protest but capitulated enough for me to slip through.

I emerged into darkness so deep that it seemed textured. Rather than rummage in the bag for my flashlight, I patted the wall until I chanced upon a light switch. Pale-blue lamps flickered into life along a long hallway, off of which half a dozen unmarked doors led. There were no paintings or decorations of any kind. The first room I tried proved to be a spacious and empty cupboard. I poked around for a fake wall. All seemed kosher. The second door led to a kitchen coated almost entirely in plain white tiles. Again I rummaged around to be thorough. Simple fare filled the cupboards and fridge, the kind of inexpensive staples the poorest of the city subsisted on. There was no alcohol. The next room proved to be a large and austere living room. There were no paintings on the walls behind which a safe could nestle. The few items of furniture clustered in the middle of the room—a functional gray sofa, a white wooden table—looked forlorn amidst all the space. I tapped every square inch of the floor, listening for the hollow echo that would indicate a hidden compartment. I heard nothing. The bathroom, next up, was even less interesting: a toothbrush, a bar of soap, and an old tub that, from the few flakes of paint still clinging to it, I suspected had once been purple.

Flo's den unsettled me. Considering he spent so much time in this space, I'd expected it to be a luxurious haven. Yet the man who raked in hundreds of thousands of dollars a day through his many concerns lived like a monk. There had to be a reason for such unusual behavior, but I couldn't figure it out. I shrugged it off; Flo's idiosyncrasies weren't my concern. As long as he had what I'd come for, he could flush his fortune down the toilet as far as I cared.

There were two doors left, and the first one didn't budge when I pushed. I gave it a few experimental kicks to test its solidity. It didn't seem like it would cave easily. I wasn't as adept as Sebastian at safecracking and so needed to conserve my remaining explosives just in case. I tried the last door in the hope that I would find either the box or a key for the locked room inside. It opened into a bedroom. A four-poster bed, similar to Laureen's, butted up against the far wall. White netting enclosed the bed, and the light from the lamp on the far side diffused through the gauzy material to cast gossamer patterns on the ceiling. Flo lay on his side in jockey shorts, his back to me. Something about the sprawl of his body, the way one hand pillowed his head, sparked a strange burst of familiarity. I felt a strong desire to part the net and slip in beside him. I blinked hard to clear my head and put it down to the urge to take a look at the face of the city's most elusive Trustee. I would sneak a peek before I left; first, I wanted to get the most pressing task out of the way. Apart from the bed, which at least demonstrated that Flo wasn't completely immune to comfort, the room contained two walk-in wardrobes, a bedside table holding a framed photograph, a dresser, and a rocking chair by the open window that looked up the street toward Benny's. The positioning of the chair made me wonder how much time he spent there, staring out at the district over which he exercised so much control but had withdrawn from.

I made for the wardrobes first and slid the doors open. My nostrils flared as the scent, that indescribable odor of a specific human being, hit me and plummeted straight to my gut. I knew that smell, had greedily sucked it in so many times that the memory had lodged in my mind for all eternity. I hung onto the clothes rail to stop myself from falling, not to the ground but back into years of old memories. I failed. Images of Danny engulfed me: the first time I'd seen him, berating the judge from the witness box; his face filling my vision as we whirled around the dance floor in some half-remembered club; our last proper night together, his chest rising and falling in a post-coital daze as I traced patterns in the sweat on his stomach.

I backed out of the wardrobe, not ready to look at the prone form on the bed, unable to believe what my senses were telling me. My gaze fell on the photograph. I picked it up with trembling fingers. It was a picture of me, taken by a long lens as I emerged from Benny's. Taken from that very window. I walked around the bed as though in a dream. The hand that pulled back the net seemed to belong to somebody else. I looked in and confirmed with my eyes what my nose had already told me: Flo was Danny.

21

I stumbled backward, my vision dimming as the net swished back into place. The backs of my knees butted up against the chair. I sat down hard, setting the rocker in motion. My head lolled back and forth as the chair seesawed and the room spun. I felt like I'd spiraled down a whirlpool into yet another alternate world where nothing made sense. I stamped my feet on the ground to still the rocking motion and slapped myself hard in the face. The room swam partly back into focus, but it seemed to have shifted subtly—the edges blurry, every molecule charged with unreality. Everything was the same. Everything was different.

I told myself the man on the bed couldn't be Danny. I'd killed him all those years ago, and he'd done nothing to earn a place in this shithole—even if a hanging judge had sentenced him for some minor crime, we would have arrived at the same time. Our paths would surely have crossed during those confused early days in Desert Heights. Flo simply looked like Danny. But I didn't believe my mind's reflexive attempt to recoil from the truth. This explained everything: why Flo had overlooked any indiscretions on my part down the years, why he hadn't come down hard on me when he realized I was after the box. Above all, the scent lingered in my nostrils, prompting a primal response I couldn't ignore. Somehow, Danny had ended up in Lost Angeles, had assumed a new identity, and had risen to power without the slightest inkling on my part. The tiny selfish part of me rejoiced; the rest of me recoiled at the knowledge that he was suffering here instead of bathing in the peace I'd imagined.

I fell to my knees and shuffled to the bed. I pulled back the net once more. His body seemed lifeless, and for a disorienting moment, I thought I was back in the motel. My hands plunged to his chest, searching for the wound so I could plug it and save him. When I found no hole, no blood—only warm flesh—I came back to myself. I didn't want to look at his face again, not with the Torment still inside him, rendering his eyes curdled, black, and cold. I wrapped my fingers through his, not caring if his Torment reached out to suck me in. I rested my head on his chest and, entranced by the tremors of his heart, forgot where we were, what I'd done, all the things that would have to be said when he woke up. Time, already a loose concept in this city, lost all meaning. Finally, blissfully, I was with him again.

The spell broke when he moaned and yanked his hand from mine. The pins and needles thrumming in my legs told me I'd been kneeling for hours; my head was slower to return to the actuality of the room.

"It wasn't supposed to be you," he said.

It all rushed back at me in a bitter wave. I knew then that he was in the Nimrod Motel, his life leaking out onto the grubby carpet. All those years, we'd been a few hundred feet apart, both living the same nightmare. But that didn't make sense. He hadn't sinned in that motel room. I had.

The liquid gushed from his eyes like a geyser of freshly struck oil. The jet of black tar arced and formed a gravity-defying, swiftly expanding blob in the air. I retreated to the corner of the room as the Torment's sleek body, blank face, and ribbed wings coalesced from the primordial soup. Springs squeaked as it put its weight on the bed and stepped over Danny, who groaned as its shadow blocked the light. Without a glance in my direction, the Torment leaped through the window and sailed off into the night. Danny raised his hands to his face and began to weep. I wanted to fold him in my arms but couldn't move. How could I go to him when all he would see was the face of the woman who'd killed him moments before?

"I'm sorry," I said, my voice crushed with the weight of the years I'd longed to ask him to forgive the sin I couldn't forgive myself for.

"No, I'm sorry," he said.

His words were slurred, his movements sluggish. He was still halfway between the recurring nightmare and the real world and hadn't realized I was actually here. He was talking to the dream Kat, not the real one. All the same, his words thawed my limbs, and I clambered to my feet. He heard the rustle of movement and sat up. His gaze fell on me, a shadowy figure in the recesses of the room.

"What are you doing in here!" he yelled. "Nobody comes in here. Get out!"

Heavy boots ran up the hallway, voices raised in alarm. The guards had noticed my dramatic entrance and heard him yell, but I didn't care.

"It's me, Danny," I said, stepping into the circle of light around the bed, my hands raised. "It's Kat."

He grew still. Our gazes locked, and I read the shock in his dilated pupils. "No," he said, shaking his head. "I'm not ready."

"I didn't know it was you," I said, words I'd said before, which now had a double meaning: I didn't know it was you when I fired; I didn't know you were Flo, or I would have come sooner. I now understood why he hadn't come to me. He wasn't ready to forgive me. But I couldn't leave, even though I was sure he wanted me to. I had one chance to make him understand the grief, sorrow, and regret that the twitch of my finger on the trigger had brought into my life. I had to let him know I would do anything to take it back.

"I never would have—"

That was as far as I got. The door hammered against the wall as the two guards burst into the room. I didn't reach for my weapon, didn't even look at them. All I saw was Danny lifting his hand, the word "no" framed on his lips, before their bullets slammed into me, and I fell to the ground.

When I opened my eyes, I lay on the floor with my head in his lap. A single tear dropped into my open mouth, the salt mingling with the iron taste of blood in the back of my throat. The guards were gone.

"Danny," I said, "I . . ."

This time, an unexpected kiss stopped the words. It was like all the years of anguish had been erased. I wanted it to never end and craned my neck upward as he broke the kiss and pulled back to look at me. Then I saw his face, distorted with pain. I curled up like a withered leaf and buried my face in his stomach.

"I'm so sorry," I said, my voice muffled. "I didn't know. You understand, don't you? I didn't know."

"You shouldn't be here," he said quietly, even as his warm hand pressed the nape of my neck. "It wasn't supposed to be like this."

"Please, don't ask me to leave. I need to explain."

He said nothing for a long time but didn't let go. I let the silence stretch out. All I wanted to do was bury my nose into his flesh and drink in his scent, feel his stomach—so much smaller than it had been—swell against my face with the warm breath of his existence. Finally, he pushed me off his lap and got to his feet. I would have grabbed at his ankles, but he walked to the window.

"You shouldn't be here, not yet. But you are, and you need to know," he said, almost talking to himself.

"I'm so sorry. I killed you, Danny. I deserve to be here. I deserve every ounce of punishment they've given me, and more. I have no right to ask you to forgive me."

His head dropped, and his voice grew so soft that I could barely hear it. "Oh, Kat. You mean you don't know? I thought you'd have figured it out by now. All these years, you've been blaming yourself. I need to ask for *your* forgiveness, not the other way around."

My head was buzzing with the conflicting emotions, like a boxer pummeled left, right, and center by dozens of invisible opponents. I couldn't make sense of his behavior, of what he was trying to tell me. "I don't understand."

"What do you think I was doing in the motel that night?"

"Hiding."

"And why do you think I shot as soon as the door opened?"

"You were protecting yourself."

He looked over his shoulder. The ghost of a smile brushed his lips, although it contained little humor. "Some tough nut you are. Most people hold others to higher standards of behavior than they do themselves. You're the other way around. You cut everybody else slack, but not yourself. You always did. You saw the best in me, and it blinded you."

I opened my mouth to speak. He held up a hand. "For once, and I know this is going to be damn near impossible, I want you to keep your mouth zipped." His voice was still soft, but it now contained a hint of the old drawl. "I've got a story to tell, and you need to be quiet until it's over, no matter what I say, no matter how it makes you feel. If you understand, nod your head. It'll give you some practice for shutting the hell up."

I nodded my assent, and he turned back to the window. His shoulder blades rose to points, making me long to dart across the room and kiss them. He held the deep breath for several long seconds and charged into his story.

"About six months before the Nimrod, I hit money troubles," he said. "Business was slow. I needed to make the rent on the office, pay my bills, all that jazz." Without looking around, he held up a hand to forestall the comment swelling in my throat. Even after all this time, he knew me too well. "No, I couldn't have asked you for money. One, you weren't exactly rolling in it, and two, I couldn't be your kept man. You wouldn't have respected me, and I wouldn't have respected myself.

"So I hid it from you. I was fine when you were around. I could hide it from myself then too. There was a week, though, when you were working almost every night. I hardly saw you, and that meant I had to face my failure. I got maudlin and one night got stupid drunk. Stupid enough to go to Bruno's casino, hoping to win enough money to tide me over for a month. Stupid enough to keep going past my limit and take out an IOU, which Bruno was happy to extend."

I clenched my fists. Bruno was always happy to extend IOUs, at least to those people he knew could repay him one way or another.

"When I sobered up the next day," he continued, "I found the slip in my bag. I was over ten grand in hock to him. So I went to see him, to explain I didn't have the money and ask if I could work it off—meaning doing some free investigating, rousing bad debts, and sniffing out any enemies that might be plotting to encase him in the foundations of a new skyscraper. He wasn't interested, said private investigators were ten-a-penny in LA. He gave me three options. The first involved you working off my debt on your back, with him humping sweaty on top."

"Why? I mean, it's not like he was short of better options."

"Because he was a bastard and didn't want me to take that option. I declined vociferously, of course. The second was for Bruno to shoot me, and you, as an example to other welchers. I didn't take much of a shine to that one. So I took the third option."

He stopped for so long that I thought he wasn't going to continue. Finally, after bending double and heaving his shoulders as if he was trying to hack up a nugget of vomit, he forced out the words. "I agreed to do two hits for him."

As hard as he had to fight to get the words out, I had to fight to keep mine in. They weren't words of censure for him. They were for me. I couldn't believe I'd been so dumb, so self-absorbed, to have missed all this.

"The first was some rival of his, a real lowlife," he said. "He was trying to muscle in on the casino operations, so Bruno wanted him in the ground. The thing was, I knew the guy. He'd raped an old friend of mine back in New York, but he'd bought off the cops. He needed to pay for his crime, and I needed to pay for my stupidity. So I killed him. Shot him when he went trawling for hookers and turned up a blind alley. I didn't feel bad. He got what was coming to him, and I spared other women more of what my friend got.

"Bruno waited a while before asking for the second payment. He was smart. He knew about the rape. He knew how angry it made me. He told me the second hit was another pervert, some businessman who'd lured his cousin back to his condo and forced her to go down on him. He told me he'd arranged a meeting with the guy. All I had to do was lie in wait and shoot him when he came in the door." He paused, and when the final words came, they rode out on a single tortured breath. "Bruno sent me to the Nimrod Motel. I was sent to kill you, Kat. And even though I missed, I succeeded. I put you here. And I'm sorry."

The moon hung bloated outside the window. He stood silhouetted against it, hands clutching his elbows. He was so thin now, so fragile. He looked like he would shatter if I touched him. I searched for some anger, some sense of betrayal; instead, I found pity for him and blame for myself. Yes, he'd hidden his troubles instead of coming to me, but I'd still noticed he wasn't himself and had done nothing. And I'd made the sorry mess worse by not telling him I was on Bruno's shit list. If he'd known, maybe he would have put two and two together and worked out the real target that night. Even with the realization that I'd failed him at this crucial juncture, I felt lighter than I had in years. This could be fixed. I'd spent my whole time in Lost Angeles castigating myself for killing him, believing I deserved everything Hell threw at me. But it was they, not he, who'd judged me. Only his opinion mattered.

He'd said I saw the best in him, and that was true. Lovers were the ultimate cherry pickers, grabbing the succulent fruit and letting the rest wither unseen on the vine. I didn't see any reason to change now. Circumstance had made him a killer, as it had me. I didn't care what he'd done under duress. He was still my Danny. Now we could be together again. We'd lost so much time already, and I didn't know how long remained before we faced the Ammit. Even if it was one day, it could still be the best day of my life. I didn't intend to waste a second of it.

I walked across the room and slid my hands around his waist. His entire body was trembling from the effort of holding his muscles locked. "You did what you had to do," I said. "If it hadn't been you, it would have been somebody else. Bruno was the real killer, not you. And technically, you killed one person. You missed me, remember? I shot you and then myself. That's two to one. Makes me way worse than you."

"You'll forgive me, just like that?" he said, his voice hoarse.

"Just like that," I said. "Nothing you could do would make me stop loving you."

For a moment, I thought he was going to relax and turn into my arms, but he pulled away. "There's one more thing I need to show you."

He crossed to the bedside table, pulled a key from the drawer, and left the room without a word. I followed him into the hallway at the end of which the two guards were poking around the remnants of the door. They looked at me with frank curiosity. I guessed Danny didn't have many lady callers, particularly ones who made such a dramatic entrance. He unlocked the door I'd been unable to open and flicked on the light switch. I stepped into one man's private Hell.

22

The room was bare except for a folding chair set up in front of a cylindrical glass tank full of dark-green water. Inside, a naked man drifted, his toes dragging the bottom. Gray hair streamed out like seaweed from his bowed head, and the tip of his stubby penis poked out from under a fat gut like a limpet on a rock. I hadn't believed the legend of the previous gambling kingpin kept at Flo's pleasure. But here he was all the same, dead in the water.

I blinked as the wave of reset hit me; when I looked again, the captive's head lifted, his features hard to discern in the murky liquid. He began thudding his fists and feet against the walls of his watery grave. Not a sound escaped the thick glass. I wondered what he'd done to make Danny vengeful enough to subject him to this punishment. When his jerking limbs propelled him forward and his face mashed against the side of the tank, I got my answer. The legend was only partly true. I knew that face, and it wasn't the former head of this gambling business. It was the former head of another. He looked decades older than when I'd known him, and madness had added further eons, but there was no mistaking his ugly mug.

"Holy shit," I said. "Bruno."

Danny took up a position over my shoulder. He spoke in a matter-of-fact manner, as if discussing a fascinating piece of interior decor or a pet, which in a way Bruno was. "He marched into the casino one day, asking who ran the place, telling everyone who would listen that he was a gambling guru and wanted a meeting. My people were going to throw him out, until I spotted him. I gave him his private appointment. He came at me with a sharpened piece of plastic he'd smuggled in. He hadn't gotten the message that assassination didn't work and thought if he killed Flo, he could be the new boss. I broke both his arms. Then I let him have a good look at my face. He was a touch surprised."

"I know that feeling," I said.

I approached until my nose was almost brushing the tank. Finally, I was face-to-face with the man who'd taken away everything that mattered to me, the man I'd so often fantasized about wreaking just such a brutal revenge upon. He was now too busy straining against the tightly sealed lid to apprehend the significance of the moment, so I tapped the glass. His gaze snapped to mine, and recognition flared in his bulging eyes. Astonishingly, he leered and gave me the double finger. He mouthed, "Fuck you." Then he died again.

"How long has he been in the tank?" I said as his lifeless body turned.

"Long enough to get wet," Danny said. "As you can see, not long enough to be sorry."

"Did he tell you why he did it before you dunked him?"

"I kept him dry for a while so we could have a chat. He wanted you dead because you pointed a gun at him and stopped his fun, which was a dumb move, by the way. He thought it would be sweeter to get me to do it."

"He always was a petty asshole."

I watched Bruno in silence until the next blink started the cycle again. I wondered how many times he'd died and been reborn—if each time he woke up, he enjoyed a few seconds of peace before he remembered what was about to happen. I turned my back on the thrashing form and looked at Danny. How many hours had he spent in that chair, letting Bruno see his face as he died in silent agony? This was my revenge, our revenge. But now that I had it, I didn't want it. This was too grotesque, too cruel. Don't get me wrong: I didn't give a shit about Bruno. Sure, his Hell was more extreme than most people's—he probably looked forward to the visit of his Torment for some respite from the tank—but his behavior had been more extreme. He'd no doubt tortured and killed dozens of people in his lifetime in ways similar to this or worse and made many more miserable in countless other ways. He'd gotten what was coming to him. No, I felt nauseated because of what the torture told me about Danny, what death and decades in Lost Angeles had done to him. The Danny I'd known would never have been so callous. I barely recognized him, his face congealed into a mask of loathing as he stared at our nemesis.

It was easy for me, standing there with Danny back and looking at Bruno through fresh eyes. If I'd been there when he'd arrived, aflame with righteous anger, maybe I'd have left him to soak. Or maybe not. Even by Yama's standards, this was a cruel and unusual punishment. What I really needed to know was how far down the rabbit hole Danny had tunneled and if he could be brought back to the light. I hoped the real Danny was still in there. I had to remind him who he was, not who Bruno had made him. I stepped in front of him, blocking the view of the tank.

"You don't need to do this," I said. "It's over. We can be together."

"It's not over, Kat. We're still going to have to relive each other's deaths every night, thanks to that soggy fuck. How do you think that's going to feel when we wake up next to each other?"

I didn't feel like making any jokes, but I had to try. It was the one chance I saw of reminding him of the way we'd been—when every night was a verbal duel, winner goes on top—and so showing him this life could be possible again. "Kinky? Death and sex go together—that's what they say. We'll screw our way out of it."

He didn't come back with a witty rejoinder. "Fine, say we can screw our way out of it. But we're still here in this godforsaken city. I want out, Kat. I want us both out."

"Then why didn't you come to me sooner? We could have tried to find a way together. We could have been with each other, made this existence more bearable."

"I couldn't. I saw you the first day, you know, tripping through the alleys of Desert Heights. You looked broken. I'd never seen you so weak and fragile. I knew what you'd done straightaway, and I knew it was my fault. So I hid from you."

I forgot Bruno as his words sank in. Hours after our deaths, he'd been within touching distance. He'd laid eyes on me in my anguish and done nothing. All those years of agony could have been avoided, or at least tempered, if he'd had the balls to face me. His mistakes upstairs, I could understand. But not this. My temples began to throb.

"What was it, your fucking pride?" I said. "All you had to do was show your face. I'd have fallen down and kissed your feet."

"I thought you'd have figured out how it happened and would blame me. How was I to know you'd be such a dumbass?"

Our voices were growing in volume, each feeding off the anger at the injustices we'd suffered. "Because you lived with me for years. You saw me light cigarettes at the wrong end, put my socks in the fridge and the milk in the laundry basket."

"That's not stupid. That's preoccupied. You could have worked it out if you'd been objective."

"How could I be objective about murdering the only man I ever loved, the only man I'd have taken a bullet for?" I shouted. "I blamed myself, like you, but if I'd caught even a glimpse of you down here, I'd have chased you around the city until my feet were bloody! You let me go."

"I didn't let you go!" he screamed back, stepping in so our faces were inches apart. "Everything I've done in Lost Angeles has been about you. Every last fucking thing. Every waking minute, I've thought about you, how to make you forgive me, how to get you back." He leaned closer and spoke in a fierce whisper. "Every waking minute, I've thought about what I was going to do to you when I got you back."

As his breath hissed in my ear, the fire in my belly dropped a foot and turned into an inferno. I hooked my leg around the back of his and shoved. He toppled backward, and I followed. His mouth closed over mine, and for a few moments, I was aware of nothing but his probing tongue and fingers working at my belt. He broke off to nibble my neck. I arched my back to press my groin against his even harder and threw my head back to allow better access to my throat. I let out a yelp when my gaze fell upon the tank. Danny took my vocalization as encouragement to bite harder.

I forced his chin up. "Bruno," I said.

In our burst of pent-up passion, I'd forgotten about him. He'd momentarily stopped drowning to bob in the tank, staring at us with a hungry look. I didn't look down to see if he was showing his interest in other ways. I couldn't get it on with an audience, particularly one so macabre; more important, I realized this was a chance to press my point.

"Let him out," I said.

"Now? You want a threesome?"

I knew then that Danny was coming back, emerging tentatively from the years of hurt. I could have expended a million words trying to convince him, trying to heal the wounds, and gotten nowhere. There was no need for declarations of forgiveness. This, the language of our bodies, couldn't be mistranslated or misinterpreted. It wasn't about sex. Well, it was about sex—glorious, messy, sloppy, passionate sex—but it was so much more. There was fucking, and there was making love, that connection created in the mind and spirit and forged by the roaring heat of blood. Our bodies hadn't forgotten we belonged together, that there was no barrier the simple act of letting go couldn't overcome.

"Not unless you've got a better-looking specimen in another jar. I meant release him. Throw him onto the street and let him rot. He can't hurt us—he's mad, weak, and alone. If you keep him in there, he can hurt us. He's a link to the past, a reminder of how plain fucking dumb we both were. Revenge does as much damage to the one who carries it out. We have to let go. We have to let him go."

He gave Bruno a lingering look, doubt clouding his eyes. I put my hand on his cheek and turned his face back to mine. "I know it's hard. He's a real hunk of man love and a joy to look at. But you don't need him anymore. You've got me."

For the first time, he smiled. It was like an old lightbulb turned on in an abandoned cabin, weak and faltering but enough to dispel the worst of the darkness.

"Let's talk about it later," he said. "We have more important things to take care of first."

I didn't push it, mainly because my thoughts were turning fuzzy as the less-sentient parts of my body took over. My torso followed his as he sat up; I held on as he rose to his feet. He staggered out into the hallway, my legs wrapped around his back, and took me into the bedroom.

23

I'd never had sex as a dead person, despite the many temptations on offer. I was delighted to discover that kicking the bucket didn't seem to have made any difference to the sensitivity of my nerve endings or the euphoric postcoital mental drift. We lay on Danny's bed in a daze, a happy one this time, entwined in a knot I never wanted to break again. If his leg hadn't been hooked over my body, I might have floated up to the ceiling.

"Just like riding a bike," he said sleepily.

I slapped his chest. "Excuse me?"

"I meant you never forget. It's been a long time."

"That would explain why it was over so quickly."

Now it was his turn to slap me, choosing my ass as his target.

"I've been such an idiot," he said.

"I agree completely." He shot me a dirty look as I grinned dopily. "Ah, was I supposed to disagree?"

"Yes, you were."

"Fine. You couldn't have known I'd be such a pushover. Look on the bright side: we've got a lifetime of hanky-panky to catch up on."

"Give me ten minutes to get my breath back, and we can get going again."

"I think you're overestimating your recovery capabilities. Make it twenty. And since we have time to kill, why don't you tell me about Flo?"

He said nothing for a while, and I cursed my rampant curiosity, which even now couldn't take a few minutes off. I worried I'd ruined the moment by asking him to recount the years of heartache. When he spoke, though, his voice was relaxed. "I said I had to make it right before I saw you again. To do that, I needed knowledge, power, and influence. So I started looking for opportunities. I found a way in at the casino."

"How? Did you storm the place single-handed?"

"Give me some credit. I'm more subtle than that. The guy who ran it then needed people. I persuaded him that I had experience in casinos."

"By subtle, you mean dishonest. You lied."

"No, I fudged. I've spent plenty of time in casinos. On the other side of the table. Anyway, it wasn't hard to make a difference. He was an amateur. I professionalized the operation so he made more money and did deals with the other Trustees so we could all prosper. When he realized I was on the ball, he made me his right-hand man. He'd tried to rule by fear and force. It wasn't working well. I gave the crew respect, kept them sweet by persuading him to pump some of the increased profits into raises. I knew one day his management style would get him the chop. I wanted to be sure I was the one the gang would turn to. Then one night, he disappeared during his Torment session. I took over."

I knew where the old boss had gone but didn't think now was the moment to tell Danny. It would shift the onus of conversation to me and cast a dark cloud over our reunion. I could have lain there and listened to his deep voice forever. "How come I didn't see you while you were doing all this? You must have been out in the open then."

"A couple of times, you almost ran into me, but I managed to dodge you. It wasn't hard. You were blind drunk most of the time at first. Once, I thought you did see me, but I slipped into the crowd."

I nodded. I'd seen Danny everywhere at first, in the face of every man who looked even the slightest bit like him, in the body of anybody with a protruding gut. I'd never pursued any of them, writing it off as my imagination conjuring up something I could never have. If I'd been sober, it might have been different, but there was no point crying over spilled whisky.

"When you started to dry out," he continued, "I knew I couldn't let you see me. So I locked myself away most of the time, only really going out to meet the other Trustees and the Administrators. Every now and then, I'd put on a disguise just to torture myself by getting closer to you. You have no idea how hard it was, watching you pass by on the street within arm's length or sitting up here, watching you come out of Benny's every night and knowing you were going to have to kill me all over again. Every time I saw you, I wanted to tell you the truth and make it easier on you. But I couldn't face seeing the hurt in your eyes. I was a coward."

I could guess how hard it was. From the way he lived in austere conditions despite squatting atop a mountain of wealth, he'd clearly been flagellating himself the whole time. I sensed his mood was perched at the top of a long slide back into unhappiness; I squeezed him so tight that he grunted. "It doesn't matter now."

"It mattered then. Everything I did was designed to make amends, to find a way for us to be together. I sucked up to the Administrators, behaving like the model Trustee. I did everything they asked, and more, to keep them sweet."

"What did they ask?"

"They wanted more casinos, more fights, more money rolling through the tills. They never asked for a cut, though. They only wanted people to gamble. It's the same with all the other Trustees.

All that matters to the Administrators is to have every human vice on tap."

"Don't you find that strange? On one hand, they punish us; on the other, they let us indulge every sin that put us here in the first place without batting an eyelid."

"I didn't ask why. I didn't care. I only wanted to know if there was a way out. At first I figured there had to be an access point. All the food, booze, and fuel has to come from somewhere, right? And I know the Administrators go off on trips. I usually dealt with Laureen, but sometimes she would go walkies for a few weeks."

"You tried to drive out, I take it?"

"Of course. You know what happened. They can get in and out. We can't. And I never saw them deliver any goods; they appear when we're all under the influence. Sofia told me her warehouses fill up every night while she's away. Same with Jean-Paul."

"So they magic supplies in?"

"Could be."

I thought of the nights I'd spent watching the Ammit feast. The clearing was right next to Sofia's warehouses, but I hadn't seen or heard any activity. It wasn't too much of a stretch to imagine food could just appear, when nobody aged and every day thousands of people came back to life as easily as waking up after forty winks. Plus it wasn't much different from the world I'd left behind. Nobody raised and killed livestock or grew their vegetables any longer. Food appeared on supermarket shelves, slabs of shrink-wrapped pink flesh that made it easy to ignore the blood, fear, and screams of the animals butchered to create them.

"So you didn't find an escape route."

"No. I looked for another way to get at the Administrators. I looked at how they lived, what they did, and realized they're not too different from us. They have desires, feelings, needs, attachments. When somebody has those, they have weaknesses.

I figured the best bet was through a bit of old-fashioned leverage. I put the word out that I'd pay big money for valuables stolen from Avici Rise, on the off chance I could get my hands on something they'd be prepared to strike a bargain over to get back. I waited years, and nothing. Most people seemed to forget the place even existed."

He paused to lick his dry lips. I knew where he was going. The reason for my visit had slipped to the back of my mind amid the revelations, but I hadn't forgotten. Danny was about to tell me he had the box, which explained why my name was on the list of people to be forgiven. This was his way to make things right. I knew we had to deal with the issue that had brought me here, but part of me didn't want him to get to the crunch. Once we began talking about it, the conversation would turn to what would come next and end the all-too-brief moments of peace we'd enjoyed.

"Then Sebastian popped up. One of my guys heard him boasting in a bar one night about how he'd been hired to do some big job up at Avici," he said. "I had no idea what he was supposed to be stealing. It could have been worthless. But nobody had ever managed to get a thing out of the damn place. So I put on one of my disguises, met him to be sure he was legit, and threw money at him."

"Ah," I said, "you were the mysterious middleman. That explains why I couldn't find him."

He grinned. "An unsolved puzzle. That must have driven you crazy."

"You should have gone in drag. Then I'd have figured it out."

His eyes glittered. "Now that brings back some nice memories. Got any dresses I can squeeze into?"

"Focus, pervert," I said, slapping away his now-wandering hands. "There's plenty of time for that later."

He pouted but went on with the story. "When I saw the box, I thought he'd fobbed me off with some piece of crap. Then I touched it." He shivered, and his eyes lost focus. "I knew it had to be important to them. So I sent the ransom note. When they hired you, I knew they were desperate."

"Desperate? Am I that bad?"

"You know what I mean. They wanted it back bad enough to risk involving a human and exposing themselves. It means you're that good."

"How did you know they'd hired me?"

"I had Sebastian followed in case somebody started poking around. It turned out to be you. I didn't think you'd get this far, to be honest. I knew what you were up to but didn't see how you could get to me, even with your psycho play with the auction—which is going to bite you on the ass, by the way. I should have known better. Anyway, it doesn't matter. You're not going to turn me in."

And so arrived the point where I would have to burst his bubble. "It wouldn't matter if I did or not. Laureen won't give you what you want. She can't."

"How can you be sure?"

"She says she doesn't have the power to forgive sins. I believe her. She's scared. This box isn't hers. It belongs to the regime, and her boss—you know, Satan—is coming to town. When he discovers the box has gone missing, he isn't going to be jumping for joy. She wants it back quietly, and the best way to do that would have been to give in to your demands. If she could have, she would have." As I told the story, it again struck me that Laureen's approach wasn't consistent with somebody about to end the world. Franklin had told a compelling tale, but I'd misjudged him before. I couldn't shake the suspicion that he was trying to get the box from me for some other, possibly sinister, reason. "Instead, she hired me to get it back without a fuss. If I don't, she's going to have to give way to her boss. Apparently he won't take such a soft approach."

Danny had never been prone to histrionics, but on this occasion, I would have forgiven him a few minutes of wailing and gnashing of teeth. I'd told him his last shot at freeing us from Lost Angeles was doomed to failure. Maybe it was because he'd enjoyed a roll in the hay and so was in a more relaxed frame of mind, but his reaction was muted. He sucked his teeth and turned his gaze to the ceiling.

"I don't think I ever really believed the plan would work. But I was at my wits' end. Part of me wanted her to find out I'd stolen it. I thought she'd destroy me completely. Disappear me like the old boss." He put his hand on my stomach and began another journey south. "Suddenly, I don't feel so frantic. Guess we're going to have to stay here and screw our way out of the midnight funk."

"Maybe not," I said, again stopping his hand despite less-sentient parts of my body welcoming its progress. "She can't forgive sins, but she can do other things."

"Like what?"

"Didn't you wonder how I broke in?"

"You blew my door off, drama queen. I'm going to bill you for that."

"I mean how I managed to be here waiting when you woke up."

He frowned. "It didn't occur to me. I was too surprised to see you."

"I didn't tell you what Laureen was paying me for the job. She's called off my Torment. If I get the box back, it stays called off."

Danny sat up abruptly, hair mussed and eyes wide. "She can do that?"

"Yes. Which means you could still get something out of this. I could tell her your price has dropped: one extra Torment-free existence, to go with mine for getting her box back. I think she'll pay up."

"We could stay here together," Danny said. "Run the casino and wrestle in our spare time."

"I'd like nothing better. There is a wrinkle, though."

"Ah. There's always a wrinkle."

"I'm not sure we can give the box back."

I told him everything. I didn't want to snatch the hope away, but I couldn't conceal the truth. We'd both tried that with our respective Bruno problems, and look where it had brought us. At least I'd learned one valuable lesson. From here on in, I would tell him everything. Plus I needed his brains to figure out the next play. I knew I'd been right to be honest when he spoke after a few seconds of consideration. He didn't ask about the Ammit or if I thought that's where we would end up. He got his professional head on. "Do you think it really is what Franklin says it is? If so, we have a problem. If not, we can give it back guilt-free."

"I don't know for sure. I haven't seen it. What do you think?"

"It has power, that's for sure. I brushed my finger against it, and . . . well, you'd best find out for yourself. Follow me."

He disengaged himself. I felt a pang as he slid away from me but didn't try to hold him down on the bed. I followed him to the closet, where he reached behind the racks of clothes. Something clunked, and he delved in amongst the suits. I hadn't had time to search the wardrobe, as his smell had knocked me sideways, but there was clearly a hidey-hole back there. I followed and, sure enough, saw a door had opened in the wall.

"Are we going to Narnia?" I said.

"Not that impressive, I'm afraid."

We entered a small, windowless room. A telephone sat on the desk, from where Danny no doubt gave the orders. Filing cabinets lined the walls. He dialed a code into a wall safe and pulled out a purple bag, struggling with the weight as he set it on the table. "It's all yours."

I approached the bag and undid the string. The cloth fell away, and there, finally, was the box. It looked nearly identical to the replica: an old, carved hunk of wood that wouldn't look out of place amidst Enitan's junk. Looking at the innocuous object made Franklin's story seem like a bad joke. You could more easily imagine the shabby thing being full of paper clips than Armageddon.

"If I start trying to open it, hit me over the head with something," I said. "Just in case."

I placed my moist palms on the box and found out again how deceptive appearances could be. The moment the wood came into contact with my skin, the globe began to thrum. Cold raced up my arms and numbed my heart. The room faded as though reality were on a dimmer switch, until it was just me and the box floating in the void. I was vaguely aware of the real world beyond the veil, that my feet were still planted on a solid floor in Lost Angeles. I felt no fear. The absolute blackness was like a warm bath into which I could step and dissipate painlessly, molecule by molecule, thought by thought, until not a scrap of consciousness remained. A seductive voice began to speak in my head—my own, but somehow not.

Aren't you tired? You've endured so much pain, and there is so much more to come. There is always more pain, no matter what brief mercies the fates grant you. You know this to be true. You can end it all now. You need never suffer again. No one need suffer again. The abyss will erase all sin. It will save you from the Ammit, from an eternity floating as fragments of what you once were, lost and alone, torn apart and never to be whole again. You are beyond redemption. Humankind is beyond redemption. The abyss is the one true perfection, the one true release from the guilt and agony of your life.

And then it showed me its vision of the world: a Technicolor reel of violence and hatred and woe that opened up in the darkness like a cinema screen. Some scenes I recognized; others I did not. A mushroom cloud blossomed over Nagasaki; skeletal Jews stumbled to the gas chambers; a burned child ran down a long, dusty road; a row of dark-skinned bodies lay butchered in a forest clearing; a massive plane plunged into the side of a tower of glass and steel; a father undid his belt buckle and loomed over his daughter's bed; a silent crowd stood by as three men set about another with a machete; on and on and on until, in some other reality, I felt my knees buckle.

This is humanity, the voice said. *This is what you have always been and always will be. Open the box, Kat. Embrace the void and free the world.*

I was aware of the ghost of my left hand clutching the box, my right probing and prodding for a catch. I longed for the promised release. Somehow I clung to the thought of Danny: the memory of his skin against mine, his heady odor in my nostrils, his voice whispering in my ear. The images of violence grew faster and more intense, but I barely noticed them. My love for Danny swelled and pushed back against the void, which grew granulated, lighter. My disembodied hands loosened their hold on the box.

"I lo—" I said, but my profession of love was rudely interrupted when something crunched into the side of my head. The room snapped back into place around me as I dropped the box and sprawled on the floor. Danny stood over me, holding the heavy telephone he'd thumped me with.

"Ow!" I shouted.

"You said to hit you if you tried to open it."

"Not that hard. You could have killed me."

"And?"

My legs were trembling—whether from the horrors the box had shown me or the vicious blow, I didn't know. Danny hauled me to my feet and steadied me with a hand on the shoulder. I pulled him close, reveling in his solidity. Eternal blackness was all well and good if you had nothing to live for, and maybe even a few hours before, I wouldn't have been able to fight its spell. But now I had Danny, a buoy to cling to in an ocean of misery. I wasn't about to give him up.

"Jesus," I said, "I wanted to open it."

"I don't think you can, to be honest. But I thought it best to be safe. What do you think's in it?"

"The end of the world."

Silence shrouded the room. I thought of the hundreds of people on the floors beneath me, damned for sins such as those the box was so keen to show me. I wondered how many of them would choose nothing over this existence. Plenty, perhaps, but that wasn't the point. The box had been selective in its screening. There was a whole world upstairs full of love, sunshine, friendship, music, books, and laughter. Surely the good outweighed the savagery of which we were capable? And it was that world under threat—not our corrupted city where nobody was innocent.

"Then we have to destroy it somehow," Danny said.

I didn't think it could be destroyed, at least not by us. If Laureen really did plan to open it, we would have to hide it—drop it in the Styx or bury it deep in the desert. But I wasn't ready to give up on our chance of release.

"Just because Franklin told the truth about what's in the box, it doesn't mean the rest of his tale is true," I said, thinking out loud. "The best lies are weaved around a nugget of truth."

"We need to know for sure."

"My thoughts exactly. You hang onto the box for the moment."

"Any idea how you're going to confirm Franklin's story?"

"That, I don't know. But you know what would help me think?"

"Coffee? Cigarettes? A brain transplant?"

"Hot sex," I said and hauled him through to the bedroom in search of a sweeter, more temporary oblivion.

24

I left before dawn, feeling an ache build in certain areas I hadn't used for a very long time. In between our episodes of lovemaking, Danny and I had discussed our options. We concluded that there was no way to know for sure if Franklin's angelic credentials were legit—it wasn't as if I could call God and ask for a reference. I needed solid evidence of evil intent. There was one place I would find it: Avici Rise.

I'd wanted to stay at the Lucky Deal, but I needed to sleep before carrying out the plan we'd hatched together. There would have been little chance of that if I'd stayed. Besides, I didn't want to draw attention to our relationship; the other Trustees would assume I was plotting to sell Flo the box directly. That would lead to trouble neither of us needed.

I hurried through the casino, which was still half-full despite the impending daybreak, and, after a quick check for any prying eyes, dashed to my car. I drove past Bruno a hundred feet up the road. He was sitting on the curb, looking as wrinkled and soggy as a squid hauled from the ocean, taking deep breaths and staring at the lightening sky. At some point during the night, when I was dozing, Danny had risen and spoken to the guards. I'd heard the sloshing of water and hoarse shouting. I'd said nothing when he returned to bed, too keen to burrow back down into our cave of intimacy. Looking at Bruno now brought an uncomfortable knot to my stomach. It wasn't just how hard Danny had become to be capable of wreaking such a brutal revenge that worried me. It was how hard he might have been in the first place. I couldn't escape the fact that he'd murdered a man, something I would never have thought him capable of—even if the victim had raped his friend. I was also imagining what else the Torment showed him. Did it, for example, take him back to the day when he'd sliced off a philanderer's dick before bringing him to the motel? I'd never before considered that he might have been the one the wife had hired to do the deed. Now I wasn't so sure.

It occurred to me then that perhaps my real sin had been pride. I'd always been so reliant on my omniscient gut, always so damn sure that the great Kat Murphy could read anybody. But I'd royally fucked up with Bruno, dismissing the depth of his anger. He always was a sexist asshole, and I'd humiliated him in front of his employees. The whispers had probably run around the casino: a woman had gotten the better of the boss. He couldn't have let that slide. If I'd engaged my brain better, things could have turned out differently. Franklin had fooled me easily and may have continued to do so had he been more subtle. Maybe I'd also misjudged Danny. I tried to push the doubt to the back of my mind. I didn't want to poison our relationship before it got going again. Whatever he'd done, however life and death had warped him, we could deal with it.

I didn't want my shadows to know I'd been absent without leave, so I parked outside Benny's and knocked on his door until, bleary-eyed and stinking of stale booze, he opened up. He hadn't found time to put clothes on—he was wearing disturbingly skimpy and suspiciously yellow underwear—but he'd managed to grab the shotgun, which pointed waveringly at my guts.

"I need to use the back door," I said.

He said something incomprehensible, which I took as permission to proceed. The clunk of bolts followed me as I walked through the bar and out into the hallway that led to Benny's one-room apartment. I unlocked the back door and emerged into the alley running up to the rear of my apartment. I made the short journey at a jog, eyes peeled in case the watchers had twigged to the back route, and knocked on the ground-floor window. The tenant, a young transsexual prostitute, peeked through the curtains.

"Oh, it's you," she said, opening the window. "What's up?"

"Mind if I sneak in through your apartment? It's a bit crowded out front."

"They're out there for you, are they? Thanks for that. I picked up some customers. I owe you one, so feel free."

When I reached my apartment, I opened the blinds and stood by the window, stretching and yawning as if I'd recently woken up. The watchers were still there, although a new shift had taken over. They didn't appear to have noticed my car wasn't there. It was an understandable oversight, since they didn't know I was free to wander while they suffered and hadn't seen me leave the apartment. Now that I'd let them know I was home, I picked up the phone and called Laureen.

"Where the hell have you been?" she shouted the moment she realized it was me. "I've been trying to reach you since last night."

"Careful now," I said. "Somebody might overhear you. We're supposed to be keeping this discreet, remember?"

"Discreet? I turned up at your apartment a few hours ago and found half the thugs in the city parked outside, giving me the evil eye. There's a nasty rumor floating around that you're going to auction something valuable from Avici Rise. It had better not be what I think it is."

"It's exactly what you think it is, but I'm not really trying to sell it. I called the auction to draw out the Trustee who had the box."

"Did it work?" she said, her voice suddenly hopeful.

"I'll know by tonight. Come to my apartment at ten PM, when they're all busy with their Torments. We don't want any of them to see you. You know how people love to gossip."

I hung up abruptly so that she didn't have time to ask any further questions about the progress of the investigation. I didn't want her to start suspecting something was afoot, and I needed her to be tantalized enough to come see me. Not that I would be there. I would be busy breaking into her house.

25

I crouched behind the same bush in which I'd cowered when I'd first seen the Ammit, my car stowed out of sight in the car park of a burger joint on the edge of Il Terzo Livello. I kept my gaze on Arcadia Road, waiting for Laureen to zip past on the way to our meeting. I needed her to come soon. The evening's victims had been gathering for a while. The crowd was healthy tonight, which was good for me if not for them. I estimated it would take the Ammit a good hour or so to munch through the assembled delicacies, giving me enough time to get in through the gate, turn over Laureen's house, and make myself scarce before it began considering dessert—which would be me if I wasn't careful. I also needed some fortune on the timing. Laureen would be gone for about an hour, the time it would take her to reach my place and return when she saw I wasn't there. These windows needed to open at roughly the same time, or I had no chance of success.

I got lucky. At nine thirty PM, a black limousine drove by, heading in the direction of town, as the number of arrivals began to tail off. I caught a glimpse of a curly-haired woman in the back seat. A few minutes later, the gate scraped open, and down thumped the Ammit. I'd almost convinced myself that this wasn't an incredibly stupid course of action. After all, breaking in and sniffing around was an integral part of my job, nobody would be expecting a human intrusion during Torment time, and I had to discover Laureen's intentions. When I saw the creature, though—all teeth, muscle, and appetite—I felt an intense desire to vomit. If anything went wrong, the last thing I saw would be a close-up of its tonsils. The moment it disappeared into the dust cloud, I sprang from my hiding place. Screams pursued me across the open plain, raising goose bumps on my flesh. I sprinted for all I was worth to minimize my time in the open, the exertion doing nothing to settle my stomach. I didn't exactly blend in with the moonlit desert landscape. If anybody was looking, I would be easy to spot.

I reached the steep incline without any alarm being raised and climbed hand over hand, clutching at tufts of scrubby grass to haul myself up. The plants kept giving way under my clumsy grabs. I wasn't a cat burglar like Sebastian. The speed I was moving, I was more like a tortoise burglar. Near the top, my hands slick, I lost my grip. The firm and excruciating snagging of my crotch on a jagged rock arrested my descent. By the time I reached the top, I was sweating buckets, and my limbs trembled. When I glanced back at the desert through watery eyes, the Ammit was still busy chowing down. I looked at my watch and saw that I had forty minutes left. It was going to be tight.

I crawled through the gate, hugging the wall, and looked for signs of movement. Bright arc lights dyed the grass an artificial lime green, and figures moved around inside the houses closest to me, but there was no activity outside. At least I'd been right on that score. I'd expected security to be generally lax while the Torments were loose, and Laureen couldn't have ramped up patrols without warning the others that something was up. All the same, I had to be careful. It would take one Administrator to peek out the window at an inopportune moment, and the jig would be up. Luckily, there were gratuitous quantities of shrubbery to duck behind as I zigzagged toward Laureen's pad.

As I crouched behind a leafy peacock, about fifty feet from my target, a guard appeared around the corner of the neighboring house. I froze. The peacock was a touch on the thin side, yet whoever had crafted it had been so proud of their work that they'd decided to put a spotlight behind it. My and the bird's shadows were thrown twenty feet high onto the wall of the house the guard was approaching. Fortunately, he appeared to have other things on his mind. He ran his fingers through his hair, cupped his hands to sniff his breath, and knocked on the door. It opened, and a hand yanked him inside by his lapel. He was going to be busy for a while. With luck, they would both be screamers and mask any noise I made.

A few minutes later, I pitched up against Laureen's house, which was reassuringly dark inside. I was hoping she'd left something unlocked. My absence from the meeting I'd called would be suspicious enough. I was going to claim a mugger had left me unconscious for a few hours and hope Laureen bought the story. If she came home to a jimmied-open door, she'd think twice about my story. Fortunately, Laureen had learned nothing from the previous theft or thought lightning wouldn't strike twice—the patio doors were unlocked. I slipped through them and into her living room.

I turned on the flashlight and, careful to keep the beam pointing toward the floor, began searching the house. I wasn't sure what I was looking for. A file stamped "Hell's Evil Plan to Destroy the World" in screaming-red letters would be handy. There was nothing in the living room that looked like a likely repository of secret information, although I wasted a minute running the light over her book collection and salivating. It would have been easy to snaffle a few, but I never stole anything on such jobs unless it was related to the purpose of my visit. As I lingered by the groaning shelves, it struck me that for somebody who supposedly hated humanity, she showed a lot of interest in its culture. I always found the extent of a person's book and music collections a good way to judge character. I was finding it increasingly difficult to swallow that Laureen was as rotten as Franklin would have me believe.

I reluctantly left the books and headed for her bedroom. The floor safe had been empty save for the replica, which meant she didn't keep any important papers in there. It was just as well, since I had zero chance of opening the damn thing. The desk drawers contained the usual crap: old pens, half-used writing pads, and loose change. I already had a strong feeling I was holding a busted flush, but I continued my search all the same. Through bathrooms, spare bedrooms, and kitchen I prowled, letting the flashlight swing to and fro, hoping the beam would fall on some small snippet. The only item that stopped me in my tracks was a full-color photograph held to the fridge by a magnet. A dozen people stood on the lawn, jammed together for a group snap. Laureen was front and center, as befit her status as the top banana. Franklin stood behind, one hand on her shoulder, the other thrown around the blonde next to him. Everyone was pasting on a smile for the camera, but his was far wider than the scene seemed to warrant. It looked like he was trying too hard to fit in, but I could have been reading too much into the situation. For all I knew, the unseen hand of the blonde was doing something that was making him look so jolly.

This, ultimately, was why I was at Laureen's looking for hard evidence. Sure, I'd always set a lot of store by gut feeling, but my increasingly flawed record could mean that that flutter was only gas. The human mind was wired to find patterns where there were none: in the swirl of clouds or the flaking paint of a ceiling. When all you had was your instinct and somebody's story to go by, you could look at any situation or image and make it fit your favorite theory. In reality, all the picture told me was that Franklin was working as an Administrator—whether as an angelic spy or a member of the regime gone rogue was open to interpretation. The stakes were too high for me to proceed without knowing for sure that I was taking the right course of action.

I checked my watch and found that fifty minutes had elapsed. It was time to make myself scarce. I returned to the living room to slip out the patio door. Through the gaps in the buildings, I could see the gate was still up, which meant the Ammit had yet to return. The compound looked as quiet as it had when I'd arrived. My mind was already turning to what I would do next as I stepped onto the terrace. My lack of focus cost me. Too late, I sensed another presence. I caught the faint impression of a human figure in the corner of my eye before something hard came down on the back of my neck, and I knew no more.

26

I came to on Laureen's sofa, a throbbing pain at the base of my skull, and fought to focus on the two blurry figures watching me. One of them was the randy guard. He'd obviously finished the job in time to emerge and see my light moving through Laureen's house. He stood by the door, gun pointing in my direction—all puffed up at his success. The other person, sitting in the armchair across from me, was Laureen. She clearly wasn't handling the stress of the ticking clock well. Her hair was starting to frizz, her blouse was crumpled, and her skittish eyes were pink rimmed.

"Mind telling me what you're playing at?" she said as I rubbed my neck and sat up.

I cast around for a good reason to be rummaging through her house, but my head was too fuzzy to scrape up something facetious, never mind a convincing lie. All I had left was the truth and the leverage point of the box. I sincerely hoped the latter would save my ass.

"You're not going to like it," I said.

"Do you think you could piss me off any more? Talk."

My head was clearing fast, which was just as well since I was about to play a risky game. I took up a sprawled position, arm draped over the back of the sofa to disguise the tension jittering through my muscles. "You might want to send your minion outside first. Don't worry, I'm not going to try anything."

She gave me a hard look and nodded. He looked miffed but left.

"I know who has your box," I said. "I've seen it. I can get my hands on it anytime I want."

I detected the sag of relief in her face. "So stop playing silly buggers and give it to me already."

"I don't know if I can do that."

Her brow puckered. "Why? You know what'll happen if you don't cough it up."

"Too well. But I need to clear some things up first, which is why I came here. Before we get going, understand this: if I don't turn up to a prearranged appointment by one AM, my associate will bury the box so deep in this city that you'll need to dig up every square inch to find it. And you know what'll happen if you don't have it in the next few days."

I wasn't bluffing. Knowing there was a chance I would get caught, Danny and I had agreed he should encase the box in concrete and drop it in the river if I didn't return. I'd tried, and failed, to dissuade him from the follow-up plan, which was to launch a full-scale assault on Avici Rise to rescue me. If I didn't show, his crew would come in all guns blazing. I hoped it wouldn't come to that; no matter how many heavily armed men and women Danny sent, they'd all disappear down the Ammit's gullet.

"You're making a big mistake, Kat," Laureen said, her voice low and hard. "I can make life very unpleasant for you, way beyond the Torment."

"You mean you'll set the Ammit on me?"

Laureen didn't react at my use of the beast's name. She must have noticed my surprise at her lack of surprise, for she raised an eyebrow. "You think I didn't know you were poking around? If you saw anything, it's because I let you. I suppose you went to the clearing."

"That's right, and I didn't like what I saw."

"You'll like it even less when I introduce you to the Ammit up close and personal. Don't be a fool. Tell me where the box is."

"I'm not telling you a damn thing until you answer some questions."

"Brave words. Why don't we see how brave you really are?" She closed her eyes briefly, features set into grim lines. "It's coming."

Nothing happened for what felt like a long time. An arc light outside the patio buzzed, and the white curtains stirred lazily in the breeze. I gripped the edges of the cushion to anchor my rebellious body, which was demanding permission to run. But fleeing wouldn't do any good. I would never outpace the Ammit; I needed to face both it and Laureen down. I drew out a cigarette, concentrating on not letting my hands shake.

"Got an ashtray?"

"No need. You won't have time to smoke it."

I heard a heavy tread on the gravel outside, and that feeling of creeping, unfocused dread I'd encountered at the Ammit's kennel stole over me. The front door creaked open, and a long snout telescoped into the room. The rest of the beast followed, claws clicking on the polished floorboards. Hulking in the calm, polished interior of Laureen's house, its black fur glistening in the lamplight, the Ammit looked even more terrifying. Slabs of muscle rippled along its flanks as it stalked toward me, jaws parted to expose rows of sharp, curved teeth. The reptilian eyes were as black as the rest of it and utterly pitiless.

"Is that thing house-trained?" I said with the hint of a wobble in my voice as the Ammit halted beside Laureen. "I'd hate for it to take a dump on your nice white rug."

"I've figured you out, Kat," Laureen said. "You joke when you're scared. It's your tell. Right now, you're petrified. You should be. Tell me where the box is, or you're a bedtime snack."

I didn't think she would really do it. Not because she was squeamish but because she needed me. Still, I couldn't be sure, and the beast's malevolent presence sucked out my confidence. We were playing a high-stakes game of chicken, and such stand-offs always had the potential to go terribly wrong.

"Go ahead," I said. "You'll never see your box again."

She pointed at me, and the Ammit padded forward. Its jaws yawed open, sending ripples through its black mane. On its breath, I could smell a jumble of scents similar to those the Torments had given off on the first night at the clearing. I was breathing in the remnants of the sins of the devoured. I gagged but put the cigarette to my lips, concentrating on not letting it shake, and blew smoke down the beast's throat. It didn't flinch. Nor did I.

"Last chance," Laureen said, her voice tight.

Sitting and waiting it out was too passive, too much the act of a woman paralyzed by fear. I had to take the initiative and show her I wouldn't falter. "I've always wanted to be a lion tamer. This is only part lion, I suppose, but it's the best chance I'll get."

Straining against my fear-soaked muscles, I leaned forward and inserted my head into the Ammit's mouth. An incisor scraped against my cheek, opening the skin. Blood dropped onto its tongue. A rumble vibrated deep in its body. The back of its throat opened up with a glottal click. Air rushed past my ears as though a door had been opened onto a vacuum. My buttocks left the sofa as my head slid toward the blackness of its throat. I kept thinking Laureen would call it off, but she said nothing. Its tongue hooked under my chin, smooth and sickeningly ticklish. The creature was preparing to reel me in—its tongue the hook, me the helpless, flopping fish. My heart hammered against my ribs, trying to get as many beats in as possible before it was stilled forever. Still Laureen said nothing. It occurred to me that maybe she wasn't bluffing, that maybe my misfiring instinct had led me astray again. I thought of how, if this thing did swallow me, Danny would come charging in to the rescue and go the same way as me. In an instant, my resistance collapsed. My arms were already moving to grasp the side of the Ammit's head and fight its pull, my mouth opening to promise to give up the box, when the creature's throat closed. It spat me out like a half-chewed peanut.

I collapsed onto the sofa, every bone in my body turned to jelly. The Ammit stepped back, closing its jaws with a snap.

Laureen cocked her head and looked at me with something close to admiration. "You are one crazy bitch," she said.

She waved her hand, and the Ammit padded out of the room, showing no signs of resentment at having to give up its snack. The weight lifted from the air, and the room appeared brighter again.

"Fine, you're not going to cave," she said. "What do you want? Better pay? Were you here looking for something to hold over me? I assumed you were above that kind of cheap tactic."

I smoked the remainder of my cigarette through the misshapen filter in three long draws, brushed the ash from the armrest, and placed the butt tip up on the floor—buying myself time to gather my ragged composure. Yes, I wanted better pay, but now wasn't the time to ask. "I came here for information. The Oblivion Box. Tell me about it."

She tucked her chin in and frowned. "The what now?"

"Your box. The Oblivion Box."

"Have you been reading comic books? It doesn't have a name, let alone something so cheesy."

"Play it that way if you want. Let me tell you what I heard, and you can let me know if I'm getting warm. There's something very bad inside that box, something that will swallow the world the way your mutt swallows souls. Satan isn't coming to town to check up on you. He's coming because it's time to open it."

She stared at me, an incredulous smile on her lips. "Open it? Why would we do that?"

"Because you're a demon. You want to destroy God's creations."

"And put myself out of a job? I'm here because of the human world."

"Yes, and you hate it. Look at what you do to us down here, the way you delight in torture, the end you have in store for all of us. Forgive me for suspecting you may be a little evil."

Laureen sighed. "Ah, to not be misunderstood. You think I want to destroy the world? The world I visit on holiday every year to dip my toes in the warm Mediterranean, drink sumptuous red wine, indulge in the tweaking of luscious Italian waiter buttocks, and be pampered head to toe in luxurious spas? You think I'd like to destroy all that and instead squat down here in this grotty sandbox with you lot without a break?"

"That's right," I said. The already forced conviction faded from my voice in face of the list of happy pursuits she enjoyed upstairs and the memory of all the books she'd collected.

"But you're here anyway, trying to convince yourself otherwise, which means you have doubts about your theory. You're hoping you can still give the box back and get your payment."

I let silence answer for me. She had me pegged. I was being selfish, and I knew it. I shouldn't have taken the chance, should already have done whatever was necessary to keep the box out of any hands that might open it. Yet here I was, risking the lives of billions of people to chisel out a better life for Danny and me. The sad fact, though, was that most people would have done the same in my place. Grand gestures were for Hollywood, which shone a light on the best of humanity so we could goggle at the screen and pretend we were better than we really were. Hrag's flicks were a more accurate depiction of human existence.

"Well, since I'm so evil, I suppose I could torture you into giving it up," she said when it became apparent that I wasn't going to say anything. "I've got a lovely set of Victorinox kitchen knives. Great for chopping carrots—would do just as well for fingers. Would that work?"

"No," I said, even though she was clearly messing with me—which again didn't suggest she was a powerful force for evil whose plan to end the world had just been uncovered. "Convince me I'm wrong, and you'll get it back. That's the only way."

"Just as well. I hate torture. It's messy, noisy, and gets bodily fluids all over the rug, which you correctly surmised I'm very fond of." She tapped her teeth, then abruptly crossed to the drinks cabinet and filled two crystal glasses with what looked like very expensive brandy. She handed one to me and clinked the glasses together. "I don't normally bring out the good stuff for house-breakers, but you're going to need to fortify yourself. Bottoms up."

She gulped half the glass in one. I allowed a tiny splash of the nectar to caress my lips. She sat down beside me and poked me on the shin with the tip of her elegant leather boots.

"You, my misguided little cherub, have got the wrong end of an infinitely long and endlessly complicated stick," she said. "First things first, my pet peeve: we're not the bad guys. You are. Every single soul in Lost Angeles is here for one reason only. You all broke one of God's unbreakable laws—in plenty of cases many of them, on multiple occasions, with malice aforethought and gay abandon."

She paused. Perhaps she wanted to give me time to respond, to argue that we weren't all prime examples of assholery. More likely she wanted her barb to sting long enough for me to feel its truth.

"Tell me," she continued, "do you consider a police officer a bad guy? A prison warden? That's what we are, nothing more.

God created everything, including this place. There are no demons and angels, dark side and light side. We all work for the big cheese—whether we're stuck down here with you filthy lot, poncing around in Heaven having a jolly old time hillwalking and singing around campfires, or keeping an eye on things up on Earth. Even Satan is an employee, albeit a senior one. He does what he's told."

"You're telling me God created this place?"

"Like I said, he created everything, including the grotty bits. It's simple, but I'll say it slowly so your dim brain can grasp the concept. God gave people free will, so he also had to give them consequences for their actions. Hence Hell."

"What about the religious literature? The Fall, the antichrist, demons battling God and beavering away to corrupt humanity?"

She shrugged. "All stories. Some we told you, some you told yourselves. Yes, way back through the mists of time, Hell used to send up the beasts to frighten the humans. After a while, it wasn't necessary. Belief systems became entrenched and took on a life of their own, and you developed systems of governance and punishment to keep yourselves in line—up to a point. And your imaginations invented far worse depictions of the afterlife for bad people than we could manage. That isn't to say Hell wasn't more unpleasant in the past. There may have been some fire and brimstone and the occasional application of pitchfork to bum. But it didn't work. Constant punishment corrupted the souls even more. So we changed our approach, became more modern. We set up cities like this one."

"There's more than one city?"

"Of course. There are seven billion people up on Earth now, and plenty of them are naughty buggers. We couldn't fit all the sinners in here. There are dozens of other rehab facilities."

"Hold on a minute. You torment us every night. You feed people to your pet Egyptian monster. You let everybody run around killing each other, gambling, taking drugs, having perverted sex, and generally being unfettered assholes. How is that rehab?"

"If God had wanted humanity to be mindless, well-behaved automatons, he wouldn't have created sin in the first place. He wants you to choose to be good. Doing the right thing is easy, meaningless when it's the only option. Dump an alcoholic on a desert island, and he'll kick the booze all right. Stick him in a free bar at a wedding, and you'll soon see how strong his character is. That's what we do here. We give you every opportunity for depravity. At the same time, the Torment reminds you of the consequences of indulgence. We leave the rest up to you. The only way we can know a sinner is redeemed is when she does the right thing in the face of a thousand temptations."

"Have you looked around this city, or do you spend all your time up here sunbathing? I live my life on the streets. I don't see many people doing the right thing."

"You're not looking hard enough. Your line of work takes you amongst the worst of the worst. Plenty of people go quietly about their lives without wallowing in the muck. Plenty of people reform."

"Like the Penitents?"

"Hell, no. Sure, they run around being all charitable, but only because they think it'll get them off the hook. It doesn't count if you're doing it to get points in the credit column. Beside, they're a bunch of hypocrites. After the day's good works are done, most of them are down at the brothels, justifying the shagging by telling themselves it keeps the prostitutes in a job. But plenty of other souls have proved they're ready."

"Ready for what?"

"The next step."

"And that would be?"

"Reincarnation, for the most part."

The conversation had been getting increasingly more outland-ish, but suddenly I wanted to believe every word coming out of her mouth. If she were telling the truth, Enitan had been right. There was a way out of Lost Angeles. I blinked and shook my head, try-ing not to get sucked in. I'd seen the monster devouring sinners, which didn't sit comfortably with her explanation. "And what about the Ammit?"

She held out her hands, palms up. "A lot of souls can't be saved, no matter how long we give them. Consider it the death penalty."

"I've seen the dust devils. That's way worse than death."

"If it's any consolation, I don't think they're aware. The Ammit draws nourishment from the untainted parts of the souls. The rest is, if you'll forgive the crudity, shat out. The dust devils are the corrupted fragments of a devoured soul, nothing more."

"If you want to rehabilitate people, why don't you tell them there's a reward for behaving themselves? Or tell them the Ammit's waiting for them if they don't shape up? Apart from the Penitents, everybody thinks they're down here forever. Why do you think lifers upstairs go around shivving other prisoners for farting in the showers? They've got no motivation to behave."

"Every one of you had the carrot-and-stick model to follow up on Earth. You still ended up here. Actions have consequences, but people are expert at convincing themselves they don't. That's why smokers smoke, killers kill, and husbands and wives cheat; they genuinely believe they won't get lung cancer, end up in jail, or get caught with their pants down. Bad things only happen to other people until they happen to you, right?"

"So nobody believed it upstairs. But people here know. This whole place is one enormous awful consequence, for Christ's sake. At least give them some ground rules."

"Again, if we did that, they'd only be behaving themselves because they stood to profit. God wants people to be good for goodness's sake. He's basically Santa in a white robe. That's why he has such a soft spot for well-behaved atheists. They don't have damnation or salvation to egg them on. They do right by others because it's the moral way to live, not because they've got one eye on the eternal reward. You had your chance upstairs, when you had all the guidance you could wish for. You didn't take it."

"It still doesn't make any sense. You have everybody here locked into the day-to-day grind for survival. How can anybody aspire to be better when they have nothing to inspire them? No hope. No art. No development. Nothing to look forward to but another day in the thresher."

Laureen's face darkened. "Have you got a degree in sociology? It works. The sin's the thing. Nothing else matters. Anyway, I don't need to justify anything to you. I'm only telling you this so you understand how far off the mark you are and give me back my bloody box."

She returned to the bar and poured herself another drink. She didn't offer me one. Her tale was all fine and dandy, and like Franklin, she told it well, but it didn't address the elephant in the room. "Since you mentioned the box, how does that fit in with your story? I've touched it. It spoke to me. Are you going to deny what's in it?"

She kept her back to me, adding a splash of water to her drink. "No. It does indeed contain the end of the world. Mind, body, and soul. Nothing survives."

"How does it work?"

"That knowledge is above my pay grade. God created it. Maybe it contains what scientists these days call strange matter. Given the right conditions and charge, a tiny ball would eat up the whole world. Maybe it's a mini–black hole. Maybe it's a mind-bogglingly vast pan-dimensional hamster that will nibble the Earth to death. I haven't looked inside to find out since opening it would, you know, destroy everything. I'd rather that didn't happen."

"But why would God create something that would trash all his work?"

"Why would a writer throw out the draft of a book? A painter crumple up a canvas? It's a delete button, a cosmic bin. When God decides the human experiment is a washout, we'll open it."

"And isn't that now? The way I understand it, the world's an unholy mess."

She sat down again and rolled the glass over her forehead. "Do you ever run out of questions? The world's getting better, not worse. The Middle Ages were rancid. Black death, black teeth, and brutish rulers. And today's conflicts are nothing compared to the First or Second World Wars. Between them, those two babies killed almost a hundred million people. The Cold War's done, the threat of nuclear apocalypse has receded, living standards are rising, and people are generally a lot more pleasant to each other, even taking into account all the localized conflicts and terrorists running around. We've got a whole stats department tracking everything, you know. The difference now is the age of instant communication; everybody's hunched over their gadgets, drinking up every last slurp of bad news. Makes it seem like the world is falling apart."

My head was buzzing from the info dump. I was already way beyond the point where I could attempt to make sense of what she'd told me and come to a conclusion. I needed to distill it to the one point that really mattered. "So you're telling me everything's hunky-dory and you don't intend to open the box?"

"Maybe it'll happen one day, but it isn't my decision. As far as I'm aware, God has zero plans to do it now. I don't foresee that changing for a very long time."

"So why are you desperate to get it back?"

"Wouldn't you be pooping your pants if you'd lost something your boss had entrusted to your care? Mr. Stanton is coming in a few days, and if I don't have it, I'm buggered. I'd prefer not to spend the next few hundred years cleaning out the lavs." She drained her drink. "Seriously, where's this nonsense coming from?"

"I spoke to the Administrator who arranged for the box to be stolen. He says he's an angel, that he infiltrated Hell to steal the box and stop you from destroying the world."

This time she laughed out loud. "Spy angels? That's ridiculous."

"No more ridiculous than what you've told me. He spun a convincing yarn."

"He knitted the wool over your eyes, more like. What's his name? What does he look like?"

"I'm not ready to tell you."

Laureen curled her lip. "Remind me again why I hired you. You've been fed a healthy dose of bobbins so you'll give up the box. If I were you, I'd be more worried about what he's going to do with it."

We sat in blessed silence as I digested both my brandy and what I'd heard. There were so many other questions I wanted to ask about Lost Angeles itself—why it had frozen in the fifties, how everything regenerated, where all the goods came from, why it was such a mix-up of different religious beliefs, if the place itself was even real or some kind of collective nightmare. But my tiny brain was already spluttering. Further information would have caused it to detach itself from my spinal column, clamber out of my ear, and throw itself into the Ammit's mouth for a bit of peace and quiet. I took a deep breath and tried to filter out all the blah, to focus on the one thing that mattered: was Laureen telling the truth or not?

She seemed legit. She'd displayed none of the liar's body language: she didn't cover her mouth as she spoke, turn her body away from mine, fidget, or sit on her hands to stop them from betraying her. Every instinct told me she was being straight, but that didn't mean much. I'd been on jury duty and witnessed the advantage the lawyer who spoke second gained. Good liars could make anything seem plausible, and the last one to speak always seemed the most convincing. And I was all too aware that I wanted to believe Laureen over Franklin for my own selfish reasons. Finally, my ever-growing list of misjudgments meant I no longer trusted my instincts. I had two opposing stories and a choice to make—one that if I got wrong would end the world. I needed to know for sure who was telling the truth.

"I've told you everything you wanted to know," Laureen said when it became apparent I had exhausted my list of questions. "Now do what I'm paying you to do and go get me my blooming box. That replica isn't going to fool anybody."

I started, splashing some of my brandy on the sofa, as Laureen's words sparked an idea so obvious that I cursed myself for not coming up with it sooner. I'd been an idiot, running around in circles, listening to lots of blab, and trying to guess people's intentions. But there was a simple way to cut to the heart of the matter.

"Brilliant," Laureen said as I shook my head in disgust at myself. "First cigarette ash on the floor, now booze on the upholstery. Want to pee in the plant pot? Take a dump on my bed?"

"Thanks for the offer, but I'll pass. Listen, I know how to sort this out once and for all. But I'm going to need you to give me something first. Agree and, if you're telling the truth, you'll get your box tomorrow. Guaranteed."

I'd put her on the spot, and she knew it. I was the one person who could give her what she needed. If she refused to help me, it would seem like she was afraid of being caught out in a lie. Then she would get nothing and be forced to admit her mistake to Satan. She had to play ball.

"You'll give up the dodgy Administrator too?" she said, rubbing her eyes wearily.

"Of course."

"And you'll stop asking me so many bloody questions?"

"That I can't guarantee."

"Well, it's not like I have any other options. I'll give you whatever you want, within reason." She pointed her index finger at me. The curved, manicured nail looked worryingly like a talon. "Be warned, though: if you're trying to pull a fast one and I don't get the box back, I'll find you. Then you'll be Ammit shit before you know it."

27

All the way down from Avici Rise, I kept glancing in the rear-view mirror to see if Laureen, or one of her proxies, was following. She'd given me what I'd requested, not even asking what I intended to do with it. That made me wonder if she might be harboring intentions of having me followed as I prepared to carry out the freshly concocted final phase of my plan. Then again, she might just have been sick of the sorry saga. If so, I knew how she felt.

I normally loved this point of a case, when I only had a few threads left to twitch to bring the spider at the center of the web gamboling out for me to squish. This time, I wasn't feeling so energized. The threads I was twanging led to an ugly and poisonous tarantula, which would sink its dripping fangs into my ankle at the slightest wrong move. In fact, the threads led to too many potentially deadly spiders—including Yama, who would be lurking in the wings to gobble up whatever scraps Franklin or Laureen left behind. Having such an array of individuals possibly out for my blood made me as jumpy as a frog on a trampoline, but I saw nothing to suggest anybody was shadowing me. Paranoid as I was, though, I took a circuitous route back to the Lucky Deal, shimmying down every side road that presented itself. I arrived back at the casino five minutes before I was due to check in with Danny.

A small crowd was standing outside the closed doors, mentally scratching their heads as they stared at a sign proclaiming the casino closed for repairs. In all my time in Lost Angeles, the Lucky Deal had never shut up shop save for the hours of torment. Such an unprecedented move would bring unwelcome attention.

I hammered on the door and was rewarded with Sid's muffled voice. "Can't any of you clowns read? The sign says you should fuck off. So fuck off already."

"Where'd you learn your customer relations, Alcatraz?" I shouted. "It's Kat. Flo is expecting me."

Sid hauled one of the doors open and let me in, slamming it shut in the faces of the itchy-fingered gamblers who surged in pursuit. Danny had obviously told his crew that I held the keys to his slice of the city. Now I saw why the casino was out of action. Brown suits packed the gambling floor—sliding rounds into the chambers of their stubby submachine guns, checking their sights, strapping on knuckle-dusters, and practicing their battle faces. The room buzzed with excited chatter. It had been a while since they'd seen action on this scale.

"Getting ready to go to war?" I asked Sid.

"Yup," he said. "Gonna kick some ass."

From the look of enthusiasm on his face, Danny hadn't informed them of the nature of the lumpy hippo ass he wanted them to kick. Lucky for them I'd turned up. "Where's Flo?"

He pointed over my shoulder. Danny strode toward me from the side of the room, cradling a stubby shotgun like a baby. He dropped the gun, threw his arms around me, and pulled me into a fierce embrace. Over his shoulder, I saw every face turn toward us in slack-jawed astonishment.

"Sorry, folks. The war's canceled," Danny shouted. "Everybody back to their posts and open up."

A groan rippled through the casino as if he'd told a bunch of kids that the trip to the zoo they'd been promised as a treat for being good had been called off.

"I told you not to come after me," I said as his private army shuffled off in dejection.

"And I put my fingers in my ears and said, 'La-la-la.' As you would have done. How'd it go?"

"Let's go upstairs and I'll tell you."

As we trooped up to the apartment, I drew filthy looks from the would-be warriors who'd put two and two together and realized I was the reason for the cancellation of the night's merriment. Once we were installed in his apartment, I laid out the events of the evening and Laureen's side of the story, playing down my head-to-mouth with the Ammit. I didn't want Danny to get freaked out at how close I'd come to spending the rest of eternity lodging in people's underwear and gritting up their sandwiches.

"A tall tale," he said.

"Maybe. But if anybody had told us about this place while we were still alive, we'd have called the cops and had them whisked into a straitjacket. If I've learned one thing from Lost Angeles, it's that anything's possible—even Franklin's undercover angel schtick."

"I suppose her version does explain a lot."

"Yeah, but it doesn't get us any closer to knowing who to trust."

"So what's next?"

I'd stopped short of revealing the new plan. It had been far too long since I'd had the chance to show off to Danny, and I wanted to milk the moment. "What's the best way of knowing if somebody means to kill you?"

He groaned. "Here we go. The great Kat Murphy gets all cryptic. Save it for somebody who doesn't already know what a brainbox you are."

I put my hands behind my head and pouted. "Can't you allow a girl a bit of drama as she reveals her masterful plan?"

"Fine, I'll play. Seduce their lover and find out through pillow talk?"

"That's how you get them to want to kill you in the first place. Try again."

"Bribe their barman. Give them a picture of your face and see if they throw knives at it. Actually, scratch that one. Everybody would do that with you. Honestly, I'm too frazzled for this bullshit. I was starting to think you might be a goner. Just tell me what you're thinking."

"You put a gun in their hand and stand out in the open, waving your hands and shouting, 'Shoot me!' I'm going to give Franklin what he wants."

He crinkled his eyes. "That's your big plan? Give him the box? You've had some bad ideas in your time, but this one blows whale dick. If he isn't on the level, it's curtains for the world."

"Give me some credit. I didn't say the gun had to be loaded."

I waved a hand at my backpack, which I'd dumped on the bedroom floor. It was bulkier than it had been when I'd climbed up into Avici Rise. Danny unzipped it and frowned when he saw what was inside.

"There's another one?"

"It's a replica," I said. "After the real one went AWOL, Laureen had it made in the hope she could fool her boss."

Danny pulled out the fake, turning it over without any ill effects. "It'll never work," he said. "But for the sake of argument, say Franklin buys it. What do you expect him to do?"

"I expect him to give something away about his true intentions."

"I'm not convinced. The moment he touches it, he'll know you're diddling him."

"I need to make sure he doesn't touch it then, don't I?" I said, trying not to sound as sulky as I felt. Danny wasn't anywhere near as impressed as I'd hoped he would be. "Give me the bag you keep the real one in. That should make it more convincing. He gave the bag to Sebastian himself, so when he lays his peepers on it, he'll know I have access to the real box. He'll have no reason to suspect I've pulled a switcheroo. I'll show the box to him and see if it pushes any buttons."

"If he isn't legit, he's going to be pissed you've slipped him a cheap knock-off. In fact, he'll be pissed even if he is what he says he is."

"If he's legit, I'll tell him I was testing him and bring him here."

"And if he isn't?"

"I'll deliver the box to Laureen."

"Either way, you'll need some backup. I'll tag along."

"No. If we're both there and it goes south, who's going to do the needful with the box? I have to go. That leaves you holding the baby. If it'll make you feel better, give me a handful of your best homicidal maniacs." He frowned but said nothing. It made sense for him to stay in custody of the real deal, and he knew it. "If I don't come back with Franklin, get the box to Laureen. See if you can get my payment for yourself and get on with your life."

"You'll come back," he said, his eyes looking watery. "If you don't, I'll raze this city to the ground to find you."

"Then at least your little helpers will have their fun. Well, there's no point in hanging around. Let's roll the dice and hope we come up sixes."

I rang Franklin, who answered so quickly that I suspected he'd been hovering by the phone waiting for my call.

"I've got the box," I said.

"I never doubted you would. What do you intend to do?"

"Make sure it doesn't fall into the wrong hands. Meet me tonight, at four AM, at Enitan's. I'll have it with me."

He fell silent for a while, but his breathing changed—coming faster and shallower. "You've made the right decision," he said finally.

"Why Enitan's?" Danny asked when I hung up.

"We can't do it here. That would be a giveaway. We can't do my apartment, thanks to all the watchers outside. Plus Enitan's is familiar territory. Franklin spent a lot of time there the last few days. He'll feel comfortable."

I could have met him at Benny's, but the bar was too close to the casino. If things went wrong, I didn't want Danny within earshot. He would come barging in to save me and screw what happened to the box. I made two more phone calls—a retroactive check that Enitan was fine with me using his shop for the meet and a request for a favor from Benny—then flopped onto the bed. Danny snuggled up beside me, his hand resting lightly on my chest.

A silence fell: one of those moments creaking with the weight of words unsaid and about to be said. I didn't want to go there. If we got all heavy and started professing undying love for each other, we'd be saying our good-byes and acknowledging that the plan could misfire. I wanted to go in with the confidence—no matter how faked—that everything would work out fine. Anyway, that wasn't who we'd been, who we still could be despite Bruno and Lost Angeles doing their worst to us. I'd moped around long enough. Our relationship had been about laughter and competition, about who could get in the last barb. Life—and death—was serious enough without giving it any more encouragement. If I was going to end up a dust devil, I wanted the memory of the crackle and spark of our interplay to try to cling to—along with the added bonus of a recent memory of how it felt to be a hot-blooded human.

"How long does a girl need to lie here looking all rumpled and sexy before she gets some action?" I said.

"When somebody rumpled and sexy comes in, I'll let you know. Until that happy day, I guess you're going to have to do," Danny said.

28

Enitan and I sat side by side, sipping on coffees so thick, you could slice them with a knife, as we waited for Franklin. I didn't want Enitan there, but he'd refused to make himself scarce. He said he wouldn't miss the reveal for the world; I suspected he really wanted to help if the play went sour. I'd never seen anything to suggest he could be useful in times of trouble, but I supposed I could hide under his robe if push came to shove. Anyway, Danny's hard nuts were around the corner, ready to burst in blasting if they heard any commotion. I also had insurance tucked away in Enitan's reading room: Benny, armed with his shotgun. He had so few customers, he wouldn't miss a few hours behind the bar and had been happy to come along in exchange for a hundred bucks. The lead-lined bag sat on the countertop behind us, undone so the top of the globe stuck out. I wanted Franklin to get a good look at it as he came in, when he was too far away to touch it and realize I was stiffing him.

"Do you really believe this is going to work?" Enitan asked. "Even if he has dark motives, he may be too smart to reveal them."

"Why does everybody want to pick holes in my plan? I never know if anything's going to work, but that's no reason not to try. If I don't get any signals, I'll toss a coin and hope God's guiding my hand."

"If God was so worried about this contraption, I do not believe he would leave its retrieval to the likes of Franklin or us. He would come down here himself."

"And get all Old Testament on their asses?"

"Why not?"

"I don't think that's his style. If the Bible's anything to go by, he's like a don: never do the dirty work yourself when you have minions to do it for you."

"I still believe Franklin is lying."

We turned our heads to the window in concert as a car pulled up outside and a door slammed. "Looks like we're about to find out if you're right."

The bell tinkled, and Franklin entered, wearing the same plaid shirt as the first day I met him. He looked as dangerous as a stuffed panda and just as likely to be planning to end the world. He raised his hand in greeting. It stayed up, frozen in place, when his gaze fell on the box.

"You do have it," he said. "I knew I was right to trust you."

He walked toward us but stopped when I held up my hand. I couldn't let him get within touching distance yet. "That's far enough. To tell you the truth, I still don't know if I can trust you. I'm going to destroy it myself. You're going to tell me how."

Franklin licked his lips, his gaze flitting to the box again. "We can't take the risk. Trying to destroy it might set whatever's inside loose. Give it to me, and I promise they'll never find it. You've done enough already. You've saved the world."

"Hurrah for me," I said. "I'm sure they'll build a statue of me in Heaven for the doves to crap on. That'll be a real comfort while I'm rotting down here."

"I'll put in a good word for you with God," he said. "Maybe he'll get you out."

233

Enitan shot me a glance and shook his head almost imperceptibly. He was getting the same vibe as me. Franklin was shaking, naked longing painted on his face as he stared at the box. He looked like a nymphomaniac who'd spotted a sign for an all-you-can-fuck deal at a brothel. His wasn't the face of a man confronted by something he feared, something he wanted to put out of commission. He didn't want the box. He craved it. Now, in such close proximity to his object of his lust, he could barely contain himself.

I patted Enitan's knee, signaling him to rise. We got up, moving to the side of the aisle to clear a path for Franklin. "You're right, we've done enough. I just want to get this out of my hair. It's all yours."

Franklin strode past us, his hands reaching for the box as if it were a long-lost lover. I pulled out my gun and backed toward the door. He paused at the counter, running his hands through his hair to compose himself, and grasped the box. He stood there for a few moments, shoulders hunched and head bowed. Enitan and I were at the door now. I fumbled for the handle behind my back, keeping the gun aimed squarely between Franklin's shoulder blades. If he came at us, I'd empty the chamber into him.

Franklin made a low keening noise, which grew in volume. His shoulders shook, and the muscles in his neck tensed. The keen turned into a roar, and he hurled the box across the room. It bounced off an old grandfather clock, sending springs pinging through the air. Both box and shattered clock clattered to the floor. When he turned around, his eyes were bugging out of his head, and his cheeks were rippling. It looked like his face was trying to change, as if whatever raging beast lurked within him was about to burst out. Suddenly he didn't look so harmless.

"You lied," he said.

Finally, I had my answer. Franklin was a psycho. All I needed to do now was fetch the real box and hand it over to Laureen—negotiating Danny's release from the Torments before giving it up, of course. But now wasn't the time for triumph. I'd celebrate once it was all over.

"It's like I told you: the first rule is to assume everybody's lying. Anyway, you can talk. You were full of shit when you told me you were an angel. Did you prepare your cover story in advance or make it up on the spot? I have to give it to you, it was damn convincing."

He didn't seem to hear a word I said, still spinning in the maelstrom of emotion prompted by having his prize snatched from beneath his nose.

"You poisonous, deceitful cunt," he said, his voice a grating snarl.

"Now, now. That's not very angelic."

"I do believe he is mad," Enitan said.

Franklin breathed deeply, holding the air in his lungs until his body stopped trembling and his face settled down. When he spoke again, his voice was calmer. "Oh, I'm quite rational. It's humanity that's mad: with rage, with lust, with hate. The human world is a festering sore on this beautiful universe, and God's too blinded by love to see it. Do you have any idea how long I've been down here, watching you wallow in your own filth, seeing how few of you deserve the chances God has given you, how few of you are capable of change? Humanity deserves to die. Once the world is destroyed, Lost Angeles will be all that remains. Soon you'll all go to the Ammit, and this foul place will be torn down. We can start again. God will thank me."

"After you've wiped out his experiment? I doubt that. We're leaving. I'm giving the box to Laureen. And you, my friend, are screwed. Maybe Franklin isn't your real name, but I'll point you out on that picture on her fridge. I wonder how the Ammit likes the taste of Administrators."

A nasty grin warped his face. "Think you have it all worked out, don't you? You're not going anywhere."

"I beg to differ. I'm the one holding the gun."

I hauled the door open and backed out alongside Enitan, which was a squeeze given his girth. Franklin stayed where he was, grin widening in a way I didn't like one bit. The back of my neck prickled, warning me somebody was standing behind me. Before I could turn, however, cold metal pressed against the base of my skull.

"Surprise again, fucko," said Jake.

He pulled the trigger. When I resurrected, cursing and spluttering, I was back in the chair. Blood coated the back of my shirt and wetted my wrists, which were tied to the frame of the chair. I looked at Enitan, who was in a similar state of captivity. Franklin and Jake loomed before me. I glanced at the window, hoping to spot the cavalry running to the rescue. All I saw was a junkie tottering past the streetlights.

"Looking for your backup?" said Jake. "They took a dip in the river to cool off. I expect it'll take them a while to climb out."

I cursed under my breath. I'd believed Danny's boys were too good for anybody to blindside them. Wrong again. "I thought you were busy getting acquainted with Yama's dungeons."

"Yama likes money more than he likes inflicting pain," Franklin said. "I felt the investment was worth it. I thought you might have something up your sleeve. You're not very trusting, which brings me back to your earlier question. I guessed you'd work out I wasn't a bumpkin lost in big bad Lost Angeles. Layers within layers, Kat. I let you peel away the first to make you feel good about yourself for exposing me. I had the whole angel story lined up from the start. It didn't work as well as I'd hoped, but it was good enough to bring us here. My acting must be getting rusty. I worked with Shakespeare, you know."

At least that explained why he'd been able to fool me at the start. But he wasn't the only one who could act. I twisted as though trying to fight against my bonds. Really I was looking at the door to the library. It was still closed, and there hadn't been enough time for Jake's pals to tie us up and go inside to find Benny—which begged the question of what the hell he was doing. The gunfire should have alerted him to our predicament.

"I suppose you're going to try to torture me into telling you where the real box is. Well, you can forget it," I said. "I'm not telling you a thing."

"Jake is going to torture you, but just for fun. I don't need to ask where the box is. You see, I heard some interesting tales over the last few hours. About how you and Flo are suddenly all cozy. Did you think that would go unnoticed? I can hazard a good guess where I should look."

"You're wrong," I said, putting every fiber of my being into the lie. "He simply succumbed to my plentiful charms. Hrag has it."

"Don't insult my intelligence. I thought I'd give you the chance to hand it over, but you were too stupid. Now I'm going there to get it."

"You'll never make it," I said, giving up the pretense. "He's got hundreds of men with guns coming out of every orifice."

"I've got something better. Now that I'm so close, there's no more need for subterfuge. I'm going up to fetch the Ammit. Guns won't make any difference to it. Once I've got the box, I'll take it upstairs and open it. And it's all thanks to you, Kat."

"As much as I hate to be a party pooper, there's an obvious flaw in your plan."

"Which is?"

"When I was a kid, a friend of mind lit a cherry bomb. Fuse was shorter than he thought. Blew his hand clean off."

"And the point of that childhood reminiscence is?"

"Seeing as how you're going to open the box that will swallow the world, don't you think you might end up a touch obliterated too?"

"God will protect me," he said serenely. "I'm doing this for him."

"Enitan was right. You're nuttier than a squirrel's larder. Open the box, and you're done."

Franklin shrugged. "You say potato. Anyway, I don't have time for this. I have work to do. One more thing before I go. I want you to know that I'm going to let the Ammit eat your new boyfriend."

My body grew cold, and I pulled hard on my bonds. The blood-slicked rope gave a little but not enough for me to free my hands. "Jake, you clown," I said urgently, "he's going to destroy the world."

"No skin off my nose," Jake said. "It's not like I'm ever going back there."

I hopped forward on the chair, hoping to get close enough to bite the gorilla in the nuts. Jake sidestepped and clubbed his huge fist into my temple. I slumped in the chair, head reeling.

"I had a couple real shitty days thanks to you. On the bright side, I learned a few new tricks," Jake said. "Since I'm such a generous guy, I'm going to share them with you."

Franklin left without a backward glance. I imagined him driving back up to Avici Rise, where nobody knew what he really was. I saw him follow the Ammit into the casino, walking calmly behind as it chomped through Danny's defenses. Then I saw it enter the bedroom and suck him out of my life forever. I yelled at the top of my lungs, through fear and frustration and as an attempt to let Benny know that now would be the ideal moment to spring into the room and spray some bullets around. Nothing happened.

Jake slipped a knife from his waistband and, eyes glinting, advanced.

"I'm going to enjoy this," he said.

29

Jake started off slow and intimate, like a skilled lothario easing his partner into the more intense dance to come. Clearly he'd learned something from Yama's dungeons. Any torturer worth his salt, like any accomplished lover or musician, knew how to build up: if you went hard and fast from the start, you had nowhere left to go but down. There needed to be a progression, a promise of more to come, an intensification that stressed the mind as much as the body.

He placed the tip of the knife on my cheekbone, applied enough pressure to break the skin, and drew it to the edge of my mouth. The cut stung, but the pain wasn't much worse than a paper cut. What really ripped at me was the feeling of helplessness. I should have given the box back to Laureen and hoped she wouldn't open it. Danny would have been safe; instead, he was about to meet the Ammit. I'd killed him once before. Now I'd done it again, only this time for keeps. The pain I could bear; that thought I could not.

"I've got a dilemma," Jake said. "See, I have the big finish in mind. I'm going to pluck out your eyes, then slice off your nipples and jam them into the empty sockets. Maybe I'll paint some pupils on them for laughs. Then, when you die in screaming agony, I'll do it all again. And again. When I get tired, I'll hand you over to my pals and sit back to watch."

"What's your dilemma? Sounds like you've got it all planned out," I said, far louder than necessary. Benny was still in the library, and I had a sneaking suspicion I knew why he hadn't reacted. I'd forgotten to frisk him for the hip flask he habitually carried. He'd probably gotten bored—he wasn't the reading sort—and drunk himself into a deep slumber. I needed to keep Jake talking and hope Benny was sober enough to point the shotgun in the general direction of the goons when he finally staggered out.

"I don't know where to start," Jake said. "You're usually full of good ideas. What do you think?"

"I really hate being tickled."

"Oh, I'm going to tickle you all right," he said, holding the knife aloft.

I knew Jake's sort. They got off on the reaction of the victim. Screams and pleas for mercy validated the power they wielded. If I bore the torture in silence, he'd get to the nasty parts faster. Plus I needed to make an unholy racket to cut through Benny's drunken stupor.

"Please," I shouted, making my voice as shrill as possible as he snicked off the top button of my blouse. "I've got a stash of cash back in the apartment. I can give it to you."

Jake grinned. "You already pulled that trick. Won't do you any good this time. Your backup's in the river, remember?"

I turned my head and met Enitan's gaze. When I flicked my gaze toward the library door, he got the message.

"Please do not torture me!" he bellowed in his deep baritone, so loud that half the assorted crap in his shop jangled in response. "I am innocent!"

"Not you too," Jake said. "Clam up. I haven't even threatened you."

He sliced off another button, making sure to jam the point into the top of my left breast and flick out a chunk of flesh at

240

the same time. I shrieked like a B-movie actress confronted by an extra in a latex monster suit, thrashing around so the chair legs thumped on the floor.

"For Christ's sake, can you two keep it down a bit?" Jake said. "You're going to burst my eardrums, and we haven't even started yet."

Enitan and I ignored him, bawling entreaties, kicking our legs, and leaping around on the seats like Mexican jumping beans. Still Benny didn't emerge. I was beginning to panic for real, which helped add convincing gusto to my pantomime of fear. Franklin would be halfway to Avici Rise by now. Soon enough he would be on his way back to the casino, Ammit in tow. I needed to find a way out of this mess, and fast.

Jake held the knife in his left hand and, despite his claims of having learned a few new tricks, began ramming his fist into my face. My nose cracked, and fragments of broken teeth swilled around my mouth in a puddle of blood. The fluid backed up into my throat, forcing me to stop yelling to swallow it. It was too early to feel real pain, the blunt-force trauma shocking my nerve endings into numbness, but they would wake up. If Benny didn't come out soon, that would be the least of my worries.

Jake stopped, blew on his bloodied knuckles, and transferred the knife to his business hand.

"I've had a bright idea," he said. "The first time we met, you shot me. I think it's fair if I take your trigger finger."

He walked behind me, grabbing my hair and yanking my head as he went. Strong fingers encircled my wrist. I braced myself for what was to come. When the knife bit home, I shrieked in earnest for the first time. He sawed and jabbed and hacked, knife grating against bone. I fought my body's instinctive response to black out, instead embracing the pain and using it tether me to the here and now. When he was done, he stood in front of me again and held the severed digit in front of my face.

"What did you say again? You hated being tickled—that was it."

He skipped past my flailing legs and, with his back to me, grabbed hold of my right calf. I stopped fighting, conserving my energy for the appropriate moment. I was already faint, and it felt like somebody had inserted a red-hot poker through the hole where my finger had been and run it all the way up inside my arm. He pulled off my right shoe and sock and, smirking over his shoulder, tickled the sole of my foot with my finger. Somehow I didn't feel like laughing.

I spat blood and teeth all over his face. "You're a sick bastard."

Jake wiped off the gore and growled deep in his throat. "You shouldn't have done that."

He turned around and ripped my blouse fully open, clearly planning on going straight to the nipple removal phase. I kicked at him again, but he was too close for me to get a good shot in. I racked my brain for a way to reach through the fog and spur Benny into action. As Jake sliced through my bra strap, I hit upon the one thing Benny really cared about.

"Benny!" I shouted. "Somebody's trying to leave the bar without paying!"

Jake paused, frowning down at me. I could almost see his slow brain chuntering along, trying to figure out what I was up to. Yes, he was smart enough to have worked out that I was looking to call in assistance with my screaming but not smart enough to have checked the premises for further surprises. He must have dismissed my words as delirium, for he dropped his head again and yanked off my bra. I stopped breathing, stopped thinking, stopped registering anything but the feel of the cold steel on my right nipple.

The cut never came. The library door burst open, followed by the deafening blast of a shotgun. As one of the goons fell against my back, another shot boomed out. The second guy toppled past, his back a bloody mess, and cannoned off Jake. Jake reeled backward, dropping the knife. His mouth, open in comical surprise, was now the right distance for me to pull my leg back and put the boot into it with all the force I could muster. He went all the way down, sprawled on his back. I stood up, bent double with the chair glued to my ass. It was neither easy nor elegant, but I bunny-hopped over and leaped onto his head. On the second jump, he managed to grab my ankle. I lost my balance and landed heavily on my side. The knife lay within reach, but my hands were still bound. Jake's weren't. He grabbed it and thrust it deep into my chest. I didn't even have the breath to shout as the blade found my heart, stilling its beat. The last thing I saw as my vision dimmed was a shotgun butt slamming down on the back of Jake's neck.

Resurrected for the second time in the space of half an hour, I opened my eyes to see Benny weaving back and forth, trying to put new cartridges into the shotgun. He finally succeeded, snapped the gun shut, and pointed it at the head of the insensible Jake. I flexed my hands, which were now fully digited again, and ran my tongue over my reinstated teeth. Jake had done me a good turn by killing me. I didn't intend to return the favor.

"No!" I shouted.

Benny turned his bloodshot eyes on me. "Why not?"

"If you kill him, he'll be up again in a few minutes. Better to have him unconscious. Get the knife and cut me loose."

Benny complied, giving me a few accidental nicks on the wrist for my trouble, and turned his attention to Enitan's bonds. I rose shakily to my feet. The other two goons were also still alive and crawling toward the door. From the two thick trails of blood left in their wake, they weren't going to be alive much longer. That presented a problem.

"Give me a hand," I said.

I grabbed one of them by the legs and dragged him into the library, the task made easier by the slippery blood trail. Benny and Enitan took care of the other two. Once they were inside, I closed the door.

"Lock it," I told Enitan. "And pile some furniture up against it to be sure."

While they shored up the prison, I grabbed the phone. More than enough time had passed for Franklin to reach Avici Rise, fetch the Ammit, and start heading into town. Danny's crew couldn't stop the monster, and nor could I, but I knew a woman who could. I'd told Laureen to stay put in case I needed to get in touch, but her phone rang and rang. As I was about to dash the whole apparatus against the wall, her voice came on the line.

"Laureen," she said.

"I don't have much time, so listen carefully," I said, forcing myself to speak slowly so my vital message wouldn't be garbled. "Your Administrator pal calls himself Franklin, but I don't think that's his real name. He was the one standing behind you in the picture on your fridge—the young, sensitive type."

"The little shit," Laureen said. "I know exactly who you mean."

"He's a total loon and wants to end the world. Check the Ammit kennel. He was going to take it and come for the box. He probably went out through the side gate. The box is in Flo's private apartment at the Lucky Deal. Franklin's going to use the Ammit to force his way in. I'm heading there to see if I can hold him up. But if he's already got the Ammit, I need you to get down there as well, and pronto. You're the one person who can bring the thing under control. Understand?"

"I'm on my way," she said.

244

She dropped the phone instead of hanging up. Her running footsteps faded into the distance. I slung the phone back on the hook, fighting the drone of panic that threatened to drown out my thoughts.

"You, wino," I said to Benny, "stay here with Enitan to make sure those clowns don't get out."

"I'm coming," Enitan said.

"Can you shoot? Run fast? Dodge bullets?" His lips parted as if he wanted to confirm he could do all those things and more, but he shook his head. "Then you're staying. Don't worry, I'll write you a book when it's all over."

I gathered up my gun and the weapons Jake and his cohorts had dropped and sprinted out the door. I jumped into the car and accelerated away from the shop, not even trying to avoid the startled junkie who sprang out of a pile of garbage bags and into the road. He sailed over the bonnet and spun out of sight. I didn't even look back. I wasn't thinking about saving the world. I was thinking about saving Danny. To do that, I'd run over anybody who got in my way.

30

pushed my jalopy to its limits, trying to ram the accelerator through the floor. The engine shrieked and shuddered, begging for respite from the relentless punishment I was forcing it to endure. I sympathized. Traffic was light; everybody ensconced in the den of iniquity of their choice, so there was nothing to impede me as I tore down Route 666. Unfortunately, Franklin would have made good time too. I'd seen how fast the Ammit could move, and I doubted it would slow him down even if it were lolloping along behind his car, scaring twelve bells of shit out of the other motorists.

My fears were confirmed when I saw the panicked crowds streaming out of the Lucky Deal, shedding chips like confetti. Gunfire crackled as I screeched to a halt fifty feet away, unable to force my way through the fleeing mob. I jumped out without turning off the engine and pushed my way toward the entrance, gun in hand. At the top of the steps, I heard a voice shout my name above the hubbub. I looked up the street and saw Yolanda running toward me at the head of the pack that had been staking out my house. Either they'd heard the shooting and decided to investigate or, like Franklin, they'd heard the tales about my relationship with Flo and had been watching his place to see what I was up to.

I was about to ignore them and plunge inside when it occurred to me that they could be useful. I could see through the doors from where I stood. The Ammit was bounding around the room, trying to clear a path for Franklin, whom I couldn't spot amidst the chaos of running bodies. Bullets fizzed through the air, some of them thudding into the beast with no visible effect, most of them missing the moving target and shredding the tables, chandeliers, and unfortunate gamblers who hadn't made good their escape. Franklin couldn't have reached the stairs yet, packed as they were with a phalanx of brown suits unloading their weapons. They couldn't hold off the Ammit forever. I needed as much bedlam as possible, more firepower to delay the thing until Laureen arrived.

"If it isn't the invisible woman," Yolanda said, stopping beside me. "How'd you pull the disappearing act?"

A stray bullet chipped plaster off a column. I ducked. Yolanda didn't even twitch.

"There's no time for that now," I said as the stragglers arrived and crowded around her. "You know the item your boss wants so badly? It's in the casino, and somebody's trying to steal it."

"Something, you mean."

So they'd been watching the casino and had seen the Ammit. That would make them more reticent to enter the battle. "Doesn't matter. In a few minutes, the item's going to be out of your boss's hands for good. I doubt he's going to be pleased about that."

I didn't wait for her reaction. I ran into the casino and, bent double, made for the cover of a row of fruit machines, still blinking their merry lights and promising jackpots to the unresponsive bodies sprawled on the floor. I peeked around the corner and saw the Ammit, crouched atop a blackjack table amid scattered cards, slurp up one of Flo's crew like a strand of spaghetti. It jumped off the table, disregarding the bullets disappearing into its body like rocks into quicksand. It looked like it was going to munch through every single person in the room until it opened up a route for Franklin. It padded forward, targeting another brown suit. He was on his haunches, shuffling away and pulling the trigger of his obviously empty gun. As the Ammit lowered its thick neck toward him, a bullet aimed at his attacker hammered into the top of his skull. He flopped dead to the ground. The Ammit stopped, peering from side to side in a myopic manner, and stepped over the body to fasten its maw on the head of a blue-haired old lady in fake pearls quivering under the next table.

Franklin had to be out there somewhere, probably working his way forward behind the rows of gaming tables. I was about to do the same thing when fresh tracers streaked across the room, this time emanating from the front door. The other crews had joined the fray, the fear of their employers' wrath overcoming their reticence to venture into the charnel house. They concentrated fire on the Ammit at first, with as little success as the others. When some of the brown suits turned their guns on the intruders, no doubt thinking they were part of the assault, it became a deafening free-for-all. Bodies hit the ground faster, and fragments of wood, plaster, concrete, and flesh dappled the air. Above and behind the Ammit, fresh dust devils coalesced, drawing together the detritus in their attempts to find form.

I dropped to my stomach and crawled up the side aisle until I was within ten feet of the stairs. The Ammit's mismatched feet were visible beneath the tables, plodding ever closer to the last barricade to Danny's sanctuary. I prayed to the God who had forsaken me for Laureen to get here soon. In a matter of seconds, the beast would be among the group on the stairs, which the bullets of Yolanda and the others had thinned out considerably. Neither God nor Laureen were anywhere to be seen as the Ammit leaped out of sight. I stuck my head up in time to see a pair of shiny loafers disappear into its mouth. Some of the defenders ran up the stairs; others dove over the banister to get away from the creature. The Ammit stood on the bodies of those who'd recently died, seemingly unaware that they were prey, and stood stock still in a momentary lapse of fire.

I kept my eyes peeled for Franklin, ready to put a bullet in him the moment he dashed for the breach his monster had created. He was directing the Ammit, so I figured if I put him out of commission for a few minutes, it would return to the casino floor to feast rather than take the stairs. Sure enough, Franklin popped up from behind a roulette wheel and streaked for the Ammit. I raised my gun, but as I pulled the trigger, a bullet punched me in the calf. My shot went high and wide. Franklin burrowed underneath the Ammit. Up the stairs it stalked, body low to the ground to provide maximum cover for its master.

I tried to rise, to get close enough for an accurate shot, but my leg gave way beneath me. From the grating, bone-deep pain, I could tell the bullet had shattered my shin. It would take me ten minutes to haul my body up the steps after Franklin, bleeding and growing fainter all the way. My one option was to reset and hope the two minutes or so I would be out didn't cost Danny his life. I put the gun in mouth, feeling an awful sense of déjà vu, and squeezed the trigger to send my mind dark.

When I sat up, blood was lapping at my feet—my own mingled with the gallons spilled in the battle. Gunfire continued as the dead resurrected and restarted the futile process of blowing holes in each other. Nobody was guarding the stairs now; they were all farther forward, firing in the direction of the entrance. I duck walked to the edge of the table and, without further ado, burst into the open. I'd almost made the top of the first flight when a bullet splintered the handrail. The next one entered my back. Blood sprayed from my chest as it exited.

"This is getting ridiculous!" I shouted, pitching forward into death for what felt like the millionth time that day.

I was already running before I was fully alert again, almost crying with frustration and fear. Franklin was at least five minutes ahead of me; he had to be in the apartment by now. My only hope lay in the fact that he couldn't kill Danny straightaway. He had to extract the exact location of the box from him. Danny wasn't stupid—he would give it up under the threat of the Ammit, but he would take his time leading Franklin through and opening the safe. There was still a chance I could save him.

This time I made it out of the firing line from the floor below. I ran with my gun before me, in case I met some of Danny's trigger-happy crew who mistook me for an attacker. There was nothing on the way up, not even a single body. The door had yet to be replaced, so I hauled ass up the hallway. Outside the bedroom, I forced myself to stop. I couldn't afford to burst in and lose the element of surprise. My best bet was to creep in and put a bullet into Franklin before he realized what was happening. I had no plan for dealing with the Ammit afterward. I was hoping inspiration would strike.

The door was ajar, although I couldn't see much of the dimly lit room through the crack. I inserted the gun barrel and eased it open. The Ammit was squatting by the walk-in closet, its back to me. Voices drifted through from the control room. My heart soared despite the Ammit's malevolent influence. Danny was still intact. I crouched and pointed the gun toward the closet. Franklin would have to come out, which meant I would have a clear shot at him. Once he was down, I could only hope it would confuse the beast long enough for Danny and me to get a head start.

The voices grew louder, and clothes rustled. They were coming out of the chamber. The Ammit half rose, jaws parting as it saw another meal coming. Danny appeared first, bleeding from a cut above his eye and darting glances at the Ammit. I chanced putting my hand through the crack in the door and waggling my fingers. He saw me and froze. I held up the gun, jerked it as if firing, then walked my fingers in the air to mime running. He blinked long and slow to indicate he'd understood. All I needed now was for Franklin to show his face so I could splatter it.

"I know I promised I would let you go if you gave me the box," Franklin said from inside the closet, "but I already promised your girlfriend I'd let the Ammit have you. One of those promises has to be broken, I'm afraid, and since I made hers first . . ."

At an unspoken command, the Ammit opened its mouth. Danny tried to back into the closet, but Franklin's hand appeared and shoved him in the small of the back. I caught a glimpse of Danny's eyes, wide and filled with sorrow, before the beast's snout obscured his face. I was about to dash into the room to throw myself on its back when I remembered what I'd seen on the casino floor, how the Ammit had passed over the dead in favor of squirming prey. I knew what I had to do. Our lives had come full circle back to a moment where I pointed a gun at Danny and shot him dead. Only this time it would save him. The beast's mouth was closing as I took careful aim at Danny's heart and, filled with the awful memory of the Nimrod Motel, pulled the trigger. The bullet hit him full in the chest. He dropped on the spot, blood spurting from the wound. I cried out, fighting against the images of him dying in my arms. The Ammit reared back and turned its soulless eyes toward me. I had a few bullets left, but they would be useless against the beast. Instead, I pumped them into the wall, hoping they would pass through and find Franklin.

"Close, but no cigar!" Franklin shouted. "I'm guessing that's you, Kat. Nice idea, shooting your man, if a little callous. Shame it isn't going to save either of you."

The Ammit slinked around like a dog trying to find a comfortable spot. I kicked the door fully open, threw my empty gun at its head, and let it catch a good sight of my juicy soul. I needed it to pursue me. As long as I reached the casino floor, Danny would have a chance. Franklin had his box, which was all that really mattered to him. With luck, he wouldn't waste time hanging around to make sure the Ammit got Danny too. What was one more life when he was about to claim billions? The moment the beast launched itself into the air, I took flight. It slammed into the doorframe, shaking the walls. Then heavy paws were thudding behind me. I made it as far as the shattered door before claws slashed at my back. I lost my balance and tumbled down the stairs, somehow managing to land on my feet. The Ammit was coming down, sliding sideways as its cumbersome hippo feet scrabbled for purchase.

I ran again, pushing my body the way I'd pushed my car. I'd forgotten all about Laureen in the frenzied moments when I'd believed Danny was a goner, but now I remembered. She had to be in the casino by now, although she could be trapped in the crossfire. If I reached her, I might still have a chance. The Ammit made the corridor and began to gain again, but I reached the next set of stairs and recovered some distance as it struggled downward. At the top of the stairs leading down to the casino floor, I looked over the tables. Fighting was still going on—some of it now hand-to-hand as ammunition diminished. Yolanda stood at the heart of the maelstrom, cracking heads with fists and feet. I scanned the bodies struggling for supremacy beneath a whirling cloud of dust devils. At last I saw Laureen, working her way down the same route I'd taken.

"Up here!" I yelled, not caring if I drew fire. At least if I got killed, the Ammit would be temporarily confused. If I'd still had my gun, I would have shot myself again.

I didn't get an opportunity to see if Laureen had spotted me, for the Ammit barreled into me from behind and knocked me clean off my feet. I landed on my stomach, all the wind knocked out of me. Lion paws landed on either side of my head, and I felt the weight of the creature above me. I would have prayed, but God didn't care about the plight of one lost soul. Either Laureen would save me or she wouldn't. I closed my eyes and held my breath, vowing I wouldn't scream when it took me and hoping that somehow Danny would escape the same fate. When my lungs began straining, I realized I'd been holding my breath for a long time. I opened one tentative eye and saw Laureen's head appear at the top of the stairs. The Ammit, now placid, stepped away from my prone form as she grabbed my hand and helped me to my feet.

"Where is he?" she said.

"Still upstairs."

I led the way, this time comforted rather than petrified by the pound of the Ammit's feet behind me. The missile now had another target. We burst into Danny's bedroom to find him sitting up, rubbing not his chest but the flabby gut that had reappeared when he resurrected. He gave me a filthy look.

"You shot me again," he said. He patted his stomach. "Do you know how long it took me to get rid of this?"

"It was the only way to save you."

"You deserve a lot more than being shot," Laureen said. "You tried to blackmail me."

"Technically, it was ransom," Danny said. "And bite me."

"You can sort your issues out later," I said. "Where's Franklin?"

I followed the line of Danny's pointing finger to the far side of the room. Franklin stood motionless in the shadows, stroking the carved globe.

"Yes," he said. "Yes. I'll open you. Soon."

"You're in deep shit," I said.

My guttural voice tore him away from the box.

"Isn't it divine?" he said, his voice dreamy.

"Yes," Laureen said, "and it's up to the divine to open it, not the likes of you, Ignatius." So that was his real name. No wonder he'd gone for Franklin.

"Oh, hello, Laureen," he said, emerging further from his trance. "I suppose this means I'm out of a job?"

"You're out of your bloody mind is what you are. Seriously, think about what you're doing."

"I've thought about nothing else for decades. How many sinners have paraded their depravity through Hell down the centuries? Tens of millions? Hundreds? It never ends, this parade of wickedness. It will never end. Unless somebody does something."

"Do you think you know better than God? He still has plans for humanity."

Bitterness sucked at Franklin's cheeks, accentuating the shadows around his face and making him look like a talking skull. "It's easy for him, up there in his throne room, all big picture and strategic thinking. We're in the trenches with the blood and guts. I can't take it anymore."

"Then I'll get you a transfer," Laureen said in a soothing voice. "Give me the box."

Franklin—I couldn't think of him any other way—shook his head, backing farther into the room. "It's too late."

Before any of us could react, he spun on his heels, took three fast strides, and hurled himself headfirst through the open window. I grabbed Laureen's shoulders and shouted into her face, venting my frustration at the insane shithead's escape. "You didn't tell me you people could fly! Get after him!"

"We can't fly," Laureen said.

"Oh," I said and hustled over to the window, Danny at my side.

Franklin lay on his back in the alley, a dark pool of liquid spreading underneath him. The box was still in his arms.

"He'll be up in a minute," Danny said. "Send the Ammit after him."

"It won't fit through the window," Laureen said. "We need to go through the casino. If we get separated, head for the Black Tower. He needs to go up to Earth to open it, to Megiddo to be precise. It's a fail-safe to stop the box from being opened by mistake."

"There's an elevator in the tower?" Danny said.

"Metaphorically speaking," Laureen called over her shoulder as she dashed out the door, the Ammit hot on her heels. "Now stop talking and follow me."

I stayed put, contemplating the long drop. "They're never going to make it down in time. They have to get through the madness downstairs and around the side of the building. He'll be gone by then. I doubt the Ammit's fast enough to catch him if he's in a car."

"What do you suggest?" Danny said. "Jump out after him?"

"Now that, my love, is a great idea."

I grabbed his face and gave him a swift, deep kiss. Before I could change my mind, I ran for the window and executed a picture-perfect dive. I wanted to make sure my head hit the ground first. I didn't want to survive somehow and lie there bleeding and broken while Franklin skipped off to destroy the world. My stomach dropped into my groin, and wind roared in my ears as I plummeted. I had just enough time to think this wasn't such a good idea after all before my skull popped like a watermelon.

31

I cranked open my eyelids to a closeup view of a rat's pointed face, its little tongue flickering at the blood my abrupt communion with the ground had splattered everywhere. A near-human look of disappointment crossed its features when I batted it away. I unpeeled my sticky face from the concrete and looked up the alleyway to see if I could spy the bigger rat I was after. He'd already made himself scarce. As I rose to my feet, a hand grasped my shin. I looked down and wasn't terribly surprised to see Danny lying in the middle of his own splat mark. Blood slicked his face and clothes, but his eyes were bright and alert.

"Did you think I'd let you have all the fun?" he said.

"Call that fun? Let's get after him."

He bombed ahead of me—skipping over a festering mound of trash piled up outside the side door. I blundered through it, scattering more rodents. He made Providence first and stopped to look up and down the street. I joined him, already panting. Hundreds of people had gathered in the middle of the road at a respectable distance from the entrance to the casino—caught between prurient interest in the bloodshed and the desire to avoid being munched up.

"There he is," Danny said, pointing past the casino to where, through a gap in the mob of rubberneckers, I saw our quarry climb into a worryingly rapid-looking fire-red Cadillac. The throaty roar of the engine was audible above the hubbub of the crowd as he powered away.

We dove into the crowd, shouldering people out of the way and ignoring their halfhearted curses and threats. The Penitents were out in force, waving their placards and working themselves up into a righteous lather. As we passed the entrance to the Lucky Deal, a fresh burst of gunfire broke out inside. A stray round blew a fine mist of blood from the head of one of the Penitents who'd climbed the stairs to achieve a better oratory platform. Laureen and the Ammit must have made the floor, drawing the few bullets that remained, but we couldn't waste any time waiting for them to force their way out. Franklin was accelerating down Providence toward Route 666. From there, he had a straight shoot up to Arcadia Road, through Eleutherios, and past Desert Heights to the tower, where he would climb up and away in Laureen's metaphorical elevator. Luckily, my car was still idling in the middle of the road, looking too crappy to steal. We leaped in.

"There are guns in the glove box," I said. "I'll get on his tail."

Franklin was already at the end of Providence. I could tell that, even with its souped-up engine, my car was no match for the raw speed of his. I was going to have to take a lot of risks to catch him. I stomped on the accelerator and roared through the underpass. I pulled the parking brake and spun the wheel to slide on to the on-ramp, the tires screeching like scalded cats. In my eagerness to catch up, I'd taken the corner too fast. The car tipped onto two wheels, heading inexorably toward the tipping point. For a moment, it looked like the pursuit was over before it even began. Panic froze my muscles. A delivery van chugging up the ramp saved me. I scraped along its side as I overtook, shearing off my wing mirror; the rebound set me back on all four wheels.

"I see your driving hasn't improved," Danny said as I inhaled a deep breath through my nostrils to recover my composure.

"I meant to do that," I replied as the car hit the end of the on-ramp. It rode the air for a split second before thumping back onto the asphalt and rear-ending a motorcyclist. His bike spun away. He wasn't so lucky, disappearing under my front wheels. Danny clutched the dashboard as the car lurched.

"And that?"

"He'll get over it," I said, peering forward to seek out the tail-lights of the Cadillac. The car was a good hundred feet ahead, too far for a clear shot. Danny leaned out of the window anyway and held the gun he'd fished from the glove compartment as steady as he could, waiting for an opportunity.

"Get closer," he shouted, squinting into the wind.

"I'm trying," I said, swerving into the inside lane to undertake a truck, forcing Danny to duck back in briefly.

He leaned across and planted a sloppy kiss on the side of my lips. "You do realize this is the first time we've worked a case together? We should totally do it again."

"If we get the chance."

He leaned back out the window, closed his eyes, and let loose a loud whoop.

"Are you enjoying this?" I said.

"Hell, yes!" he shouted back. "Do you have any idea how long it's been since I was in a car chase?"

Momentarily distracted, I cannoned into the side of a bulky Pontiac I hadn't noticed cut in from the fast lane. For a moment, we were locked together, the drag of the other vehicle losing me precious seconds. I wrenched the wheel back to the right to free my car. The Pontiac veered off the other way. I winced as metal crunched but didn't look back. Whatever destruction I left in my wake would be nothing compared to what Franklin had in mind.

I concentrated on the road ahead, tracking Franklin through the traffic. While he had a fast car, he wasn't the most skilled driver. I had the feeling he'd never had cause to drive so urgently before. Every time he came up against a knot of traffic, he weaved uncertainly before choosing which way to pass. He also made the mistake of tapping on the brakes when rounding a bend, increasing his chances of going into a skid. I was hoping that somewhere along the line, his inexperience would send him into a tailspin, but every time it looked like he was about to wobble out of control, he managed to recover. I didn't take my foot off the accelerator, bullying other cars out of the way and sliding through every gap that presented itself at full speed. The problem was that when Franklin hit a stretch of empty road, his superior speed allowed him to open up the distance again. I looked back to see if there was any sign of Laureen and the Ammit. I saw nothing. They could have taken another route. Maybe they'd summoned a few Torments to airlift them. Either way, I didn't see how they could arrive in time to head Franklin off. Danny and I would stop him or nobody would.

A good few hundred feet ahead now, Franklin zoomed down the off-ramp to Arcadia Road. I followed, turning hard into the corner. A concrete pillar under the freeway claimed my other wing mirror. The wind had picked up, blowing clouds of sand across the road from the open desert on our right-hand side. Distorted faces welled up in the murk, disintegrating on impact with the windshield. Danny withdrew into the car, spitting out dust.

"Can't see a damn thing," he said.

I had the same problem. It was almost as if the dust devils were trying to shield Franklin from view, hoping that the oblivion he promised would somehow also free them from the last vestiges of their miserable existence. If so, they were out of luck. I had no intention of letting the insane little turd escape. I gritted my teeth, straddled the center line, and drove full tilt, flashing my lights to force oncoming traffic off the road. We left a trail of blaring horns, and at least one car folded into a lamppost, in our wake.

The dust cloud dissipated as we entered the more built-up area of Eleutherios, and I caught sight of Franklin up ahead. We were gaining on him. I just wasn't sure we were gaining fast enough. The tower was growing ever closer and broader, jutting above the skyline. Still it gave up no features—it was an absence rather than a presence, a malign column of blackness that gouged a strip out of the sky, now a deep blue as dawn approached.

Franklin swerved around a queue of traffic and mounted the sidewalk without slowing. Tables, chairs, and a few people went flying as he ploughed through the crowds sitting outside to enjoy the relative cool of the early hours. I followed suit, speeding along the path he'd cleared, until the cause of the stationary traffic became clear. Two cars were snarled up in a fender bender, the drivers resolving the disagreement over who was to blame by punching lumps out of each other in the middle of the road. Sparks showered from Franklin's bodywork as he shaved the rear bumper of one of the cars. He wobbled, losing more speed.

"Hold it steady," Danny said.

He took a deep breath and pulled the trigger three times in quick succession as the Caddy swerved back onto the road. One bullet knocked out one of his taillights, and another cracked through the rear window, but his car didn't falter.

"I see your shooting hasn't improved," I said.

Franklin belted past the first dilapidated buildings of Desert Heights, curving around the district toward the tower approach road. He was going to be a good minute ahead of us by the time we got there. We didn't talk as the rotting tenements whizzed past. There wasn't much to say. If we failed, the world we'd known would soon be gone. We would be trapped in Lost Angeles with our Torments—there could be no reincarnation if there was nowhere to go—until our final appointment with the Ammit. And it would all be my fault. If I'd been smart enough to figure Franklin out sooner, this could have been avoided. Some detective I was. The body count on my tab was about to go from two to seven billion and two.

When we finally turned onto the short approach road, the red Caddy was parked sideways by the wall surrounding the moat, the door thrown open. Franklin stood beside the vehicle, one hand aloft like an Old Testament preacher. A section of the wall was sliding into the ground in apparent response. A glistening bridge rose from the moat. He glanced over his shoulder and leaped down before the bridge had fully reached his level.

Danny made to loose off a shot at Franklin's head, the only part of him visible. I grabbed his arm. "Save your bullets until you get a clear shot."

The bridge continued to ascend, bringing ever more of Franklin's running form into view. He was well on his way to the tower, the box tucked under his arm. We wouldn't catch him on foot, which left one option. The bridge clunked into place as I whizzed past Franklin's car. We made it through the freshly opened passage with inches to spare, but the second my tires hit the bridge, I found out why Franklin had chosen to finish the journey at a run. Dank river water slicked the surface, and the car began to aquaplane. Either side of the road, which had no guardrail or barrier, was a twenty-foot drop into the waters of the Styx. If we slid too far, we would sink without trace, much like the world above. Danny barely seemed to notice our peril. He focused on our target, breathing loud and slow as he sought to steady his hand. I eased off on the gas, kept the tires pointed straight ahead, and hoped for the best.

Franklin had attained the base of the tower, a speck of an ant at the foot of a giant trouser leg. We were closing rapidly, but a queasy slide to the left accompanied our forward momentum. It was only a matter of whether we would reach the tower, where Franklin was pressing his hand to the wall, before the lateral motion took the car over the side. If God really did care, this would have been an ideal moment to intervene, but no divine hand split the skies to set us on a true course.

We were twenty feet away now, the front driver's side tire kissing the edge of the bridge. The Black Tower filled the entire windscreen, making it feel like we were rushing into the void Franklin planned to unleash. Danny fired off two rounds as a door slid upward, revealing more blackness beyond. One shot pinged off the tower above Franklin's head; the other caught him in the arm. He jerked but stayed on his feet. I could feel the vehicle begin to cant and knew we were seconds away from tipping over the edge. Franklin was still outside, the rising door as high as his waist now, his head half-turned toward the radiator grille bearing down on him. He ducked, aiming to roll under the gap.

I took one last gamble. I hauled the wheel to the left, trying to keep more tire on the road and buy us a few more seconds. The rear end of the car reacted to the sharp movement, slithering forward until we were sliding side-on, still moving at forty miles an hour. Danny grabbed the dashboard a split second before we hit with a bone-shuddering impact. I was vaguely aware of the bodywork thumping into Franklin's body before we hit the rising door. With a sickening screech of warping metal, we came to an abrupt halt. I lurched to the right, Danny's body absorbing the impact. Danny had nothing to cushion the blow. His body kept moving—at least until his head flew out the window and met the door pressed up against the side of the car. He rebounded and slumped forward, eyes rolling back into his head.

The engine ticked, smoke streaming from the hood, as I shakily patted myself down. I'd emerged unharmed, if jarred. Danny was out cold but still breathing. I had no choice but to leave him there and trust that the car would stay in place; the hood hung over the water, but the buckled tower door had firmly wedged into the trunk, providing an anchor point. I opened the door and scurried around the back of the vehicle, holding the second gun from the glove compartment. From inside the tower came a low, pain-filled groan.

I ducked under the door into darkness so complete, I couldn't see my hand in front of my face. Then there was light: white fluorescents embedded in the walls flickered to life to reveal a circular space hundreds of feet wide. The light quickly petered out into blackness above me. In its sphere of influence, I saw thousands of chambers carved into the walls, each one containing a Torment curled up like a diseased embryo. A million wings twitched in response to the stimulus, their whispers echoing and magnifying until it seemed like a single papery voice was emanating from the tower's dark throat. Beyond the light, I sensed millions of blank faces swiveling to regard me with unseen eyes. A sense of immensity, of the interior rising into the inky blackness forever, assailed me. For a moment, it I felt as if I were looking down into a bottomless pit. I went down on one knee, slapping my palm on the ground to reassure myself that gravity was keeping me moored to it rather than sending me falling up.

When I felt secure enough to stand, I turned my attention to Franklin. He was dragging himself across the stone floor with one hand in the direction of an elevator door in the dead center of the tower, the other hand still clinging to the box. The steel doors sat in a low block of concrete, a call button affixed to one side. There was no shaft, no visible means of carrying passengers upward. I walked parallel to the trail of blood until I caught up with Franklin. One leg jutted out at an unnatural angle, dragging uselessly behind him. Bone stuck out of his left forearm, muscles bunching around the white protuberance as he tried to find enough purchase to drag his broken body closer to his distant goal. Thick blood oozed from his mouth, and his breath came in ragged whoops. He kept going, like a flattened cat looking for a quiet bush to die in. The man was determined, I had to give him that.

I kicked the box from his hand. He moaned and rolled onto his back. His plaid shirt clung wetly to a nasty indent in his chest. One eye was a blood-red globe; the other bulged and flickered as it tried to focus on my face.

"Why are you stopping me?" he said, every word choked with effort and accompanied by bloody spit bubbles. "You see humanity. The sin, the despair, the horror. Help me. We can make it stop."

The madness came off him in waves now, as palpable as the stink of his broken insides. I was amazed that he'd been able to hide it so long. Now, with his goal so tantalizingly close, the bottle had come uncorked, and the rancid contents of his mind were foaming over. I felt a stab of pity for him and fought to suppress it. I'd come close to going nutty several times in Lost Angeles, but he was wrong about the world, wrong about people. Laureen had been spot-on: I'd spent so long making my living from strife, lying in the gutter and looking up into the city's dark underbelly, that I'd forgotten there could still be good.

I thought of Danny, insensible in the car. Yes, he'd killed a man. Yes, he'd tortured Bruno. But there was love in him as well. Love for me. He'd punished himself for years, locked away in his chamber of solitude, as he tried to atone for his sin. He'd put his existence on the line to save billions of people he'd never met and would never meet. Enitan had done the same without question, regardless of the risk involved. There were bound to be others like them, others not beyond saving. Hell, maybe even I wasn't as big an asshole as I'd thought. And we were the worst of the worst, the excrement of humanity. Yes, there was brutality and grief upstairs, and I'd seen more than my fair share while still alive. But there was also more beauty than one human could perceive in a thousand lifetimes. That far outweighed the evil people could do. It had to.

"You've got me all wrong," I said. "Underneath this cynical exterior, I'm a big softy. At least, that's what everybody keeps telling me. I think they're giving me too much credit. But here's the thing: there's being world-weary, and there's being a homicidal maniac. You're sick of existence, I get it. But you don't get to take everybody else with you."

His chest heaved as though he were about to scream at me. Instead, he hacked up a thick clot of blood. The Torments rustled again in response. Franklin's good eye snapped into focus, some of the intelligence returning. His gaze roved over my shoulder. I turned, half-expecting to see Jake thundering in through the door. The tower remained empty, yet Franklin smiled through scarlet teeth.

"Silly me," he said. "I forgot. I don't need your help."

He screwed his eyes shut and arched his back. I thought he was about to expire, and I moved closer to make sure he couldn't make a dash for the elevator when he resurrected. I'd shoot him as many times as I had to until Laureen and the Ammit arrived. Above me, something stirred—not a restless shift this time but the firm beat of wings on air. Too late I remembered that the Administrators could control the Torments too. He wasn't dying at all. He was calling for help. My finger was tightening on the trigger to put a bullet in his skull when a dark blur thudded into my chest. I too became airborne, although briefly and without any aerodynamic grace. I landed on my back ten feet away, the impact reverberating along my spine. The gun fell from my hand and skittered away. As the Torment that had ambushed me hopped over to Franklin,

I wheezed in a trickle of oxygen, rolled onto my belly, and began crawling the way I thought the gun had gone.

The Torment dug its talons deep into Franklin's shoulders. He screamed as it lifted him. He was too heavy for the creature to bear him fully into the air—one foot dragged along the ground, the other flopped at the end of the shattered bone—but still they crept toward the elevator. Franklin wailed on, but it was a weird sound: rising and falling, shuddering and breaking. He was laughing at the same time, the crazy bastard. I scrambled faster, but I couldn't see the gun. As I jerked my head around—looking for the weapon but too frantic to focus properly—another Torment swooped down and closed the claws on its feet around the globe. It hovered, as though listening to further instructions, and then flew toward the elevator. It dropped the box by the doors and began to circle overhead.

Franklin was now only ten feet from the elevator. I needed to put him down so the Torments would stop doing his bidding, but the gun was still nowhere to be seen, and I hadn't recovered enough air to get to my feet and finish the job with my hands. It would have been nearly impossible anyway. I was at the dead center of the overhead Torment's flight arc. I had no doubt it would come for me if I got too close to Franklin or the box. Franklin fell silent, and for a moment, I hoped he'd died of his injuries. But the Torment kept dragging him, its beating wings now so close that they brushed against the doors.

"My name will go down in heavenly history," Franklin said, his voice weak but more even than it had been. "Yours too. I'll make sure every soul in every remaining realm knows Kat Murphy was the one who made it possible to exterminate the human scourge. You should be proud."

I now had enough breath to speak, but I said nothing. He truly believed he was doing the right thing. Words would be wasted on

266

him. They always were on fanatics. Instead, I concentrated on gathering my strength. He still had to get the doors open and maneuver his broken body and the box inside the elevator. As he tried to do so, I hoped he might be distracted enough to lose his hold on the Torments. Maybe I would have a chance to snatch the box and make a break for it. I tensed my legs, one eye on the dark shape gliding above, and prepared to run. It was a futile course of action, but I had to try.

Franklin twisted, reaching behind him with his good arm. As his finger settled on the button, I burst into life. My lungs rebelled, but I pushed past the dizziness and the searing pain in my chest to close the distance. Out of the corner of my eye, I saw the winged shadow plummet to intercept me. I braced myself for impact, wildly imagining that I could punch the Torment out of the air and keep going but knowing I was fooling myself. The world was screwed, and it was all my fault.

A single shot cracked, repeating up and up into infinity. I skidded to a halt. Franklin hung slack in the claws of the Torment, blood pumping from a hole in the center of his forehead. The Torment overhead swept past and arced back up into the darkness. The other one released its hold on Franklin. His lifeless body crumpled to the ground as, with no one to pull its strings, the second Torment followed its friend back to roost.

"Lucky shot," a sluggish voice said.

I turned to see Danny swaying in the doorway. He took three steps forward and collapsed. I hurried over to the box and, kicking it before me like a football so it wouldn't try to convince me that helping Franklin would be an excellent idea, ran back to him. We needed to be out of there before Franklin came back. If I'd counted right, that was Danny's last bullet, and I didn't have time to ferret around for my lost gun. When Franklin woke up, fully in control again, he could send dozens of Torments against us.

The only option was to kick the box into the moat, where it would sink to the dark depths, and flee. I reached Danny and saw he was unconscious again. I slipped my arm under his body, ready to drag him out and gain as much distance as possible before the Torments came.

Before I could heave him forward, the door shook. I looked up to see the Ammit squeezing through the opening, its broad back pushing the door upward. With the gap now bigger, there was nothing to hold my Chevy. The trunk tipped up and, with a squeal of undercarriage on the road, the car slid out of sight. A loud splash told me I would never see it again. Even though I'd lost my pride and joy, my legs were weak with relief. I sat down hard on the floor, keeping my arm around Danny. It was over.

Once the Ammit was free, it stood tall and shook off its flanks. Laureen came through next, moving so fast that she almost tripped over my outstretched legs.

"You took your time," I said.

She surveyed the scene—Franklin still dead by the elevator door, the box lying by my side. She let out a long, hissing breath and ran her fingers through her messy hair.

"Traffic was murder," she said, to her credit doing a good impression of nonchalance. "Anyway, looks like you had it under control."

"Something like that. Don't worry, I left you something to do."

I nodded at Franklin just as I blinked hard. He sat up gasping, hands slapping the ground around him.

"Looking for this?" I shouted, pointing at the box.

He didn't even glance in my direction. He now had eyes only for the Ammit, which was stalking toward him with Laureen in his wake. Franklin screwed his eyes shut. No Torments swooped to the rescue. The Ammit kept on coming.

"Won't work," Laureen said. "I outrank you. Hierarchy's a bitch, isn't it?"

Franklin let out a piteous mew. Again, I had to dampen a wave of pity. I was scared enough looking at the creature, feeling its aura cloak me in dread, and it wasn't coming for me.

"Don't take me—take her, take them!" Franklin yelled. "They're evil!"

"There's no such thing as evil," Laureen said softly. "There are only broken souls. And yours is broken beyond repair."

Franklin jumped to his feet and lunged for the elevator button, but the Ammit was already streaking across the floor. It butted him in the back with its skull, knocking him to the ground. Franklin screamed and thrashed, but the Ammit swatted aside the feeble blows with a powerful paw and, almost tenderly, closed its jaws over his head. Franklin's last screams echoed as his body slid down the creature's throat like a coffin trundling into a crematorium furnace. When he was gone, silence filled the tower. There was no dust, nothing for the remnants of his soul to snatch around itself. There was only the empty air. Laureen's shoulders sagged. When she turned around to walk back to me, I thought I saw sadness flicker across her features. As much as Franklin had been an insane, homicidal prick, I hoped she was correct in her assumption that the dust devils didn't really feel anything.

I prodded the box toward her with my toe. "As promised."

She blinked and bent over to touch it with one finger. She snatched her hand away instantly. "Not exactly low-key, though, was it?"

"You can't make an omelet without breaking a few eggs."

"You didn't break a few eggs. You drove a tractor through the whole chicken farm."

I shrugged. "I got the job done, didn't I?"

"Yes, I suppose you did, even though you had a few wobbles along the way. Unfortunately, I'll have to tell Mr. Stanton about this mess. Half the bloody city saw the Ammit chowing down. Plus we're an Administrator light now. Still, at least I got it back."

"At least *I* got it back, you mean."

"True. Which means I owe you one Torment-free existence."

I licked my lips. I hadn't had time to bargain, and now the box was as good as back in her hands. All I could do was appeal to her better nature, which despite my initial impressions, she did appear to have. "About that. I think I, we, deserve a bonus. How about two?"

Laureen raised an eyebrow and glanced at Danny. "For him? I don't think so. He's the one who stole the box in the first place. I'm not sure we can even do business any longer. It may be time for him to stand down."

"He didn't steal the box. He diverted it. And he didn't do it for himself. He did it for me, to make amends."

"Amends for what?"

That surprised me. I'd assumed that Laureen knew what I'd done. "You don't have files on us?"

"There's too many of you to keep records. The system sorts all that side of things out. We keep the wheels turning, give you what you need to be naughty. That's why we're called Administrators."

"Well, we've got history. Look, when he found out what it really was, what Franklin wanted, he did the right thing, didn't he? He was the one who stopped him in the end. Shot him as he was about to get in the elevator. That has to count."

Laureen massaged her temples. "Fine. He can stay in his job. Mainly because I'm too exhausted after this debacle to deal with any more upheaval. But our deal stands. One free pass."

My gaze flickered to the elevator. If the Ammit hadn't been there, maybe I could have overpowered Laureen and dragged Danny behind me, hoping to carry us both to freedom. I looked up at the endless chambers. In one of those cubby holes, Danny's

Torment was slumbering. Later it would stretch out its wings and take flight across the city to claim him. The punishment would be worse this time. I'd given him hope of a better life, and I hadn't delivered. I couldn't let that stand.

"Then I want you to give it to him."

"No."

"You were giving it to me."

"You're different. I've never seen much contrition from him. He's been keeping a man in a jar for years, for Christ's sake."

"He let him go."

"Very forgiving of him. Let me guess—you asked him to do it, right?"

"Does it matter? He did it."

"The why matters, Kat. I've already told you that. The deal was for you only. Do you want it or not?"

I looked down at Danny and stroked his cheek. I could take my payment. But what then? I couldn't bear the thought of lying beside Danny as he suffered, watching him retch and tremble when he came out of it. And he might grow bitter at my enjoyment of the freedom I'd been unable to secure for him. I didn't want that between us. We had enough to deal with already. Besides, even though Bruno had set us up, in the end my sin had brought us here. It was like Laureen said: actions had consequences. My action, the pulling of the trigger, and so my consequence. I'd been kidding myself to think I could escape so easily. "No, I don't want it."

Laureen raised her eyebrows, but I thought I detected the faintest hint of a smile on her lips. "Your choice. Aren't you disappointed, coming away from this job empty-handed?"

"I got him back," I said, drawing Danny closer. "That's far more than you were offering."

This time, there was no mistaking Laureen's smile. "Then take care, Kat. I hope you find what you're looking for."

She patted the Ammit on the backside. It scooped the box up in its jaws. Together, they walked through the door into the rising sun.

32

Once they were long gone, I dragged Danny from the tower. The movement roused him, and he peered up with a look of stupefaction on his face. Lucky shot, indeed. There was no way he could have aimed accurately. Maybe God had our backs after all. When he saw me, his pupils struggled to dilate, but he shook off enough of the fog to ask, "What happened?"

"You stopped him. The Ammit took him. Laureen got her doohickey back."

He was too befuddled to ask about the payment, and I didn't have the heart to tell him we weren't free. When I leaned in for a kiss, he puked over my chin, a sure sign of concussion. I wet my hand on the slick surface of the bridge, wiped off as much of the vomit as possible, and got him to his feet. We staggered to where Franklin's Cadillac was waiting, the keys still in the ignition. He wasn't going to need it any longer, and I figured that since my car was gone, I might as well appropriate his. I would sell it as soon as possible and buy something less likely to be stolen.

When I pulled up outside the casino, the streets were quiet save for one lone figure: Yolanda, sitting on the stairs, nearly every inch of her body caked in drying blood.

"I thought you'd be back," she said as I climbed out. "You're like a shit that can't be flushed."

"I'll take that as a compliment. Before you ask, I don't have the item."

"Not smart. You promised it to Yama."

"You did see the scary monster cavorting around in there eating people, right? Tell Yama to take matters up with it and the Administrators. They've got the item back now."

"Too bad. You gave your word. Yama holds people to their word. And when I tell him what I saw here, how much your little item matters to them, he's going to want it even more."

"You can't always get what you want."

"Yama can," she said, her voice matter-of-fact. "I'll be seeing you."

"Not if I see you first," I said as she sauntered off down the road, picking lumps of gore out of her hair.

I hauled Danny out of the car and supported him up the stairs. Inside, the uneaten portion of his crew was righting tables, sweeping up debris, and sponging the blood-soaked carpet. They stopped working as I walked across the casino floor, Danny mumbling nonsense and dragging his feet. Sid hustled up, concern all over his hard face.

"Is he okay?" he said.

"Just a bang on the head. He'll be fine tomorrow. If he isn't, I guess we'll just have to shoot him. How'd it wrap up here?"

"Everybody left. We all ran out of ammo. Even Yolanda gets tired of breaking necks after a while."

"I'm not so sure about that. I think she has a few more on her to-break list. I'd advise you to pop out to the gun shops and buy some more bullets. There's going to be blowback."

He darted glances left and right and leaned in to speak quietly. "Will that thing come back too?"

"No. You're safe." I didn't add, *for the moment.*

On the ride through the lightening streets, I'd mulled over whether to spread the word about what I'd uncovered. The city would be rife with speculation about this previously unseen beast and what it meant. I'd decided I would tell as many people as possible that they could escape from Lost Angeles and start again with a clean slate if they behaved themselves. Laureen was wrong not to have done so. But when I saw how scared even Sid was at the thought of the Ammit's return, I realized I didn't want them to know what would happen if they didn't behave. The carrot would hopefully be enough. People had enough to worry about already, and, like I'd told Sid, there would be fallout from my heat-of-the-moment ploy to draw more guns into the action. I would have to go back to Laureen and ask her to tell the Trustees—Yama in particular—that they shouldn't mess with Danny and me. But at that moment, with my adrenaline supplies depleted, I was too exhausted to do anything. I helped Danny up the stairs and into his room, where he collapsed fully clothed on the bed. I showered, threw on one of his T-shirts, and lay down beside him.

When I woke up, the sun was almost down. Danny was still out for the count. I turned on the lamp and rolled his eyelids back to check that his pupils responded to the light. I cuddled in to his warm body, drinking in the last few moments before the Torments came for us. Part of me hoped the coming nightmare wouldn't hold the same power, but my body's response—the lump in my throat, the weakness in my limbs—betrayed that as wishful thinking. It already had me in its grip. You never remembered who you were once the Torment took you; all my travails and triumphs of recent weeks, the knowledge that I had Danny back, would mean nothing in that motel room. The feelings of shame and hollowness would still follow me out into the real world.

I heard the beat of wings off in the distance and squeezed Danny harder. Over the last days, I'd grown accustomed to thinking of the Torments as a natural phenomenon—bats streaming from their cave at dusk or swallows flocking in preparation for migration, something of no threat to me. Now they felt like carrion birds, great black vultures spiraling over a battlefield. And once more, I was one of the corpses to be pecked apart. I stared at Danny and tried to burn his living face into my mind so I could carry it down into the nightmare and dilute the horror.

A loud thump announced the arrival of the Torments, and I had to look. My own face stared back at me from one of the black mirrors. I had a second to wonder why it looked so peaceful in comparison to the haunted look on Danny's beast, before the creature hurled itself into me. It took me not to the Nimrod but back to the tower.

I stood in front of the elevator, dizzy from the seemingly instantaneous and unexpected transition. The doors lay open, revealing padded velvet walls lit by a warm-yellow bulb. For a moment, I thought this was a new nightmare—that I'd somehow sinned by helping Laureen take Franklin and was now being punished for it. That theory didn't make sense. The elevator hadn't been open, and there was no sign of Franklin. I remembered exactly who and where I was and all that had happened. And I didn't regret the role I'd played in Franklin's fate. He was the sole author of his own misfortune. I was just his publisher. The final clue to the reality of the moment was my Torment, which crouched at my feet, putting the finishing touches on its reassembly after oozing out of my orifices. It took to the air, spiraling up into the tower until it was gone. The other nooks and crannies sat empty, which meant its pals were still at large. The Torment must have sleepwalked me through the streets to this place.

"Hello, Kat," somebody said, so close behind me that breath tickled my neck.

I started like a skittish racehorse jumping the gun. I turned to face Laureen. "Why did you bring me here?"

"I didn't bring you. Your Torment did."

"I don't get you."

"I told you: they're largely mirrors. They look into your soul and reflect your sins. They serve another function, though. While they're rummaging around your dirty laundry, they also notice other things. Like how well your sins have been washed. They decide if a soul is ready or beyond saving."

A freezing lump of fear coalesced in my gullet. My time had come, as I'd known it would. I just hadn't expected it to be today, not when I'd saved the damn world. I didn't know why the Torment had brought me here instead of the clearing, but I knew the Ammit would be lurking in the shadows. I wanted to rail and roar against the injustice of it all, but I knew there was no point.

"Tell Flo what happened," I said. "Tell him I love him. And make it quick."

Laureen looked puzzled for a second and then, astonishingly, laughed. "You think you're being fed to the Ammit? It's the other way around. You've been redeemed, Kat. All sins forgiven."

I goggled at her, unable to believe what I'd heard. "What? Why?"

"Oh, I don't know. Putting another's happiness before your own? Putting the fate of the world before your own selfish needs? Either way, it boils down to doing the right thing in the face of temptation." Her index finger clicked shut my hanging jaw, and she waved a hand toward the elevator. "All you need to do is step in. Then it's back to Earth, in a fresh body in a cozy little womb."

"You have an elevator straight up into somebody's womb? That's got to sting."

"It's not really an elevator. We find that the concept of 'up' helps ease the transition. I won't go into the metaphysics, but essentially it's a portal between planes."

The elevator called to me the way the box had. The light from within was soothing, almost hypnotic. It radiated tranquility, offering the promise of facing the world as an innocent once more and carving out a different, better path. I'd longed for such an escape from the moment I entered Lost Angeles. Pretty much every single person in the city would have ripped my arm off and beaten me to death with it for the chance to be standing there—although such a violent approach would have disqualified them. And yet I hesitated.

"Will I remember anything?"

"No. You might have the odd strange dream, get déjà vu from time to time. But your soul will remember. Not the details but the lessons you learned down here. It'll guide you through life. Hopefully you won't end up back down here on the next cycle."

"What about Flo?"

"He stays here."

"But he's the one who stopped Franklin."

"Please. He showed up at the last minute and claimed all the credit, like a typical man. This is your doing, not his. Now in you pop."

My legs began moving toward the elevator, but I forced them to stop. Giving in to the alluring promise of a new life would mean leaving Danny alone to cope with my absence and the mess I'd left behind. He'd worked all those years to get me back; I'd spent the same amount of time wishing for nothing more than the chance to be together again. If I chose to leave, I would be okay. I wouldn't remember anything. All those years of suffering would be erased. I would have no regrets, no longing for the man I'd left behind. I'd be abdicating my responsibilities, taking the easy option. You didn't do that when you loved somebody; you signed on for all weather, and when the storm came, it was your job to hold the umbrella over your partner's head. Laureen was right: Danny had issues to work through. He'd murdered a man, and his vengeance on Bruno had hardened him further. If I left, that hardening process would accelerate. To leave would be to condemn him to a final appointment with the Ammit. And in the end, it no longer mattered that Lost Angeles was a stinking pit, because it was the stinking pit where Danny lived. It was my home.

"No," I said.

I expected Laureen to insist, perhaps to call in reinforcements to drag me kicking and screaming into the lift. To my surprise, she didn't look at all vexed. In fact, she looked pleased. "I was hoping you'd say that. There's another option, offered to a select few."

"Which is?"

"I must confess to an ulterior motive. I didn't only hire you because you're a good detective. You had a reputation for honesty, for being a good person. I already had my eye on you. Why do you think I let you bop around the city, finding out all our secrets? I had a feeling you were almost baked. We could use a woman with your talents around the place. Join us. Stay here and serve God."

"You're joking."

"Not at all. I told you there were no angels or demons. I didn't tell you I was like you once. All the Administrators were. We're not some separate species crafted by God from different clay. We were all human once, imperfect and steeped in sin. We served our time, like you, and proved our worth. I guess you could say we got promoted. Now it's your turn."

"And that's the only way I can stay? Become one of the people responsible for this madness?"

"It isn't madness. Like I told you, it's part of God's greater design. And there are perks. A nice house up on Avici Rise—one's just freed up, incidentally. Four weeks' holiday per year and the chance to travel and meet interesting people."

"Like Satan?"

"Yes, but please don't call him that to his face. Like I said, it's an unofficial job title. His official title is executive director of Hell. He prefers ED for short. So, are you in?"

"Can I still see Flo?"

"You can see whomever you like. We've all had our little flings. But understand this: the day might come when the Ammit takes him. When that happens, there's nothing you can do to stop it."

I glanced at the elevator doors one last time. Up there, I'd be lost in the wash of humanity with no greater purpose. Down here, I could do some good. With time, I could even change the system to something less hideous. I wouldn't have to leave Danny. And, of course, I could satisfy my curiosity. There was still so much to puzzle out about Lost Angeles, Hell, and the whole bizarre system God had built. As an Administrator, I'd get the chance to do just that. As choices went, it was a no-brainer. "Then I need to help him so that day never comes. I'm in."

Laureen clapped her hands and shot me a toothy grin. "Excellent. All kinds of bullshit you don't know about goes on, here and in the other cities. Having a detective on the payroll would be a big help."

"Hell's detective?" I said. "Now that does have a nice ring to it."

Acknowledgments

Thanks to Kat Urbaniak for wielding the Bechdel test and prompting this novel's gender-reassignment surgery.

Thanks to Nats for her encouragement, constant feedback, and penmanship.

Thanks to Rebecca, Scott, Andy, and Tom for reading early drafts and their suggestions.

Thanks to Renee for taking this project on and finding a home for it.

And thanks to Faith at Crooked Lane Books for taking a chance on something a little different.